Amethyst, The Shallows

Amethyst, The Shallows

BOOK TWO OF THE YELLOW COTTAGE STORIES

KELLYE ABERNATHY

atmosphere press

Published by Atmosphere Press

Cover design by Kevin Stone

Atmospherepress.com

With love to Ian, Brendan, Mackenzie,
Melissa, Dagny and Brady

Read. Dream. Imagine.

AUTUMN EQUINOX

It is the magical hour before dawn. An old woman strides purposefully across the sand, balancing a large, woven basket on her shoulder, moonlight sparkling on the braid of pewter hair coiled upon her head. Ribbons of mist twist off the waves, unfurling over the indigo-black waters of a sleeping sea. The air is thick and laced with night dew, sand slaked with foam and moon shadow.

At the waterline, she bends gracefully, setting the basket down. Squatting, she uses her hands to dig deep into a cluster of air bubbles, unearthing a bounty of clams. Incoming waves crash over her, drenching her old, bleached dress, tugging at the net tied loosely around her waist. She doesn't mind. Cold cannot touch her. Her steady old heart beats to the cadence of the tides—for more moons than most can remember.

The water peels back. Quickly, she fills the basket to the brim. Standing erect, hands on hips, she sniffs the air, searching for that certain curl of cool, signaling the change of seasons. The autumn equinox is almost here, an unpredictable time when a quirk of the moon presses the tide to run wild.

Placing the basket above the waterline, she hurries to the long, layered slab of granite rock known as Craggy Point.

Climbing with speed and deftness, she ascends to the high shelf, the one overlooking the sea. A smattering of starlight dapples the rock and the wind tugs gently at her dress. Carefully, she steps to the edge of the shelf. Anchoring her feet, she breathes in, tightening her gaze. Breathing out, she scans the sea. *No time to waste.* She has many mouths to feed. It will be impossible to keep the secret much longer.

Cr—ack!

The jolt rumbles through the rock, almost knocking her off her feet. Crouching, she grabs the ledge, waiting for the shaking to cease. She is unafraid, as she well understands the ways of the ocean. The great underwater volcano, a few miles offshore, is tuning to the equinox, resetting the ocean currents. The small quake is a warning. The weather may hold for several days, but a significant storm is on the way.

Rising, she steps to the lip of the ledge and surveys the dark water. The bioluminescent bands spin, a galaxy of sea enzymes, twinkling, dancing lights. Beneath the waves, in the heart of the vortex, a ripening sea harvest awaits. Fat grapes of sapphire kelp, heavy with nectar, and clusters of plump sea strawberries are being released from the deep caverns. During the change of seasons, summer to autumn, these mighty ocean plants are faithful, producing the best medicines the sea can yield.

Untying the net looped around her waist, she breathes deeply, face to the moon. Rising high on her toes, she lifts her arms, braid falling loose, spilling silver down her back. Making an arcing dive through curls of mist, she pierces the heart of the light bands, disappearing into the sea.

It will be a long while before she surfaces. An expert free diver, the old woman can hold her breath underwater for extended minutes. Suspended in the deep, she will gather the precious plants, moving like a meditation. When she emerges from the waves, the net will be full. Dawn will be breaking, sprinkling rose and gold light on her brine-crusted hair, glazing the harvested sea plants with shine.

No one knows how she does it. How can one so old dive so far and so deep? The truth is: no one knows. To the town, she is simply Triponica, leader of the Beachlings, the tribe of mysterious old women who have lived in Dipitous Beach for as long as anyone can remember.

On the high terrace of the yellow cottage overlooking the cove, Grand Ella stretches her arms to the sky, basking in the salt-laced air of early morning. Today, the sea is gentle, ripples of teal and amethyst ruffling the shore with foam. Gazing out at the horizon line, she sets the rhythm of her breath, matching it to the ebb and flow of the sea. Thankfully, her body feels stronger today, though there's no doubt her recent battle with the Sickness has taken quite a toll.

Inside the cottage, her beloved granddaughter, Condi, remains asleep in the loft. Twisting the silver chain of her infinity necklace, Grand Ella wonders what the day will bring. The long, isolating months of lockdown have left a cruel mark on her granddaughter's spirits. For too many days, when the weather was fine, Grand Ella watched Condi climb the stone stairs to the top of Windy Hollow, a tall tower of rock on the loneliest tip of the cove. There, tucked between two half-moon rocks, Condi sat cross-legged on the old upside-down orange-red rescue kayak, staring out to sea. Grand Ella didn't ask why Condi spent hours alone on the top of the Hollow. She knew. Without the company of friends, hours weigh heavily on a young soul. When a mercurial surfer boy named Trustin Davis left town last year, a part of Condi's heart went with him. The top of the Hollow had been their special place.

One by one, the lights in the town of Dipitous Beach blink awake, the homes of the inner cove twinkling into the promise of a new day. The lights blaze in the kitchen of the Arondale's Bed and Breakfast on the top of the hill. Grand Ella wonders how bookish Casey Arondale is faring. An only child, Casey lives with his parents in the charming B&B, closed for almost a year, like the other beach hotels. On the top of Upper Main, a bright light flickers on in the casement window of the gloomy Hardy mansion. The head of a dark-haired girl appears, silhouetted against the light. Grand Ella smiles. Seventeen-year-old Kait Dooley, taking some air—much needed, no doubt. Newly arrived from Ireland before the Sickness struck, Kait is stuck inside the dark walls of the rambling mansion caring for querulous old Mary Hardy.

On the far southern shore, the night lights on the long dock of the Craggy Point Marine Sanctuary click off, signaling sunrise. A gust of wind spins across the deck of the terrace. Petals from the sea lily on the trellis scatter, releasing the spicy scents of fading summer.

Placing her hands over her heart, Grand Ella bows her head. Though the contagion is passing, many have died. The Sickness devastated the fragile bonds of community in her beloved beach town.

A brilliant glowing orb, the sun rises.

Determined, Grand Ella lifts her chin.

Time to reset.

Things will get better...
...well, because they must.

#

Andy Marshall wakes up in the surfboard storage room of the Billabong surf shop. Rolling off his cot, he pulls his unruly mane of white hair into a ponytail and gazes in satisfaction at the jade-green longboard suspended by cables over his bed. The room is filled with racks of glittering jewel-toned surfboards, casting early morning sun sparkles. The Billabong is Andy's home and workplace on the beach, housing his prized collection of rare vintage surfboards, collected over the many years of his long life, beginning in the sixties, when he was out there every day, riding the big ones.

Shuffling over to the open garage-style window, the old surf master leans out, stretches his aching back, and sniffs appreciatively at the clean salt breeze lifting off the waves.

At last.

The beach is opening today.

The past months of the Sickness have been long and lonely. The world went crazy, especially in the beginning. First reports claimed the mysterious illness was caused by toxic fumes wafting off the sea. Though the idea was insane, and later proved to be false, the damage was done. People were terrified. All the beaches were closed.

In the kitchen, Andy puts on a kettle of Grand Ella's special brew, anise euphoria tea with a sprig of peppermint. When the old pot sings, he pours a mug, breathing in the soft aroma of sweet licorice. Leaning against the doorframe leading out to the porch, he lifts his mug and toasts the heavy Pacific Islander board standing sentry by the front door, granting safe passage to those who cross the threshold. The board is one of his favorites, a Tongan masterpiece, made of wili wili wood and balsa. Thoughtfully, Andy rubs a finger across the distinctive shaper's mark, carved on the nose by the surfboard's maker. The mark, a majestic feather, is a sign of adaptability. His finger tingles. He smiles, recognizing the familiar buzz of remnant energy left by the artful magic of the ancient craftsman. Mystical stories are contained in the shaper's marks of precious old surfboards...courageous stories of times gone by, great tales of wind and weather. The stories wait, ready to be told—but only when the time is right.

Yes.

Adaptability.

Before the Sickness, Andy was in perpetual motion, spending his days teaching surfing at his wildly popular Gregarious Grommets Junior Surfing School. At night, he repaired surfboards. As the leading restorer of vintage surfboards in the world, Andy received shipments of damaged boards from around the globe. When the Sickness locked down the town, surfboard shipments stopped. The surfing school closed.

One day, simply to pass the time, Andy huffed and puffed his way up the beach stairs to the high parking lot overlooking the cove. Prem Lindgren's old food truck, *Sweets and Sippers*, was parked under the eucalyptus trees, rusting away in the salt air. That very afternoon, Andy called Prem and asked to buy the truck.

"Sure thing, Andy," Prem had said. "Engine's a mess, though the gourmet oven is a gem. Bakes light and airy, makes the best muffins and scones around."

"Sold," Andy declared. "I'm a whiz with engines—and I might as well learn to bake. Throw in your recipe for peppercorn scones?"

"That's Grand Ella's recipe," Prem had laughed. "Be warned—those scones are no joke. They'll wake you right up in the morning!"

Andy was an expert fixer upper. Restoring the old food truck turned out to be a breeze. Soon the rusted body was painted bright ocean blue, the pop-up window oiled to glide like a feather. Prem was right—the specialty oven worked great. Soon Andy was baking up a storm, trying out Grand Ella's favorite recipes—cardamon muffins, peppercorn scones, honey-drizzled ginger buns, midnight chocolate cookies.

At first, Andy's plan was to drive around town delivering bakery treats to isolated children stuck at home. He missed being around kids and hated that they couldn't play on the beach or swim and surf in the sea.

One morning, everything changed. Andy discovered Lorelei Finch had left a book about sea creatures in one of the lockers at the surf shop. Before lockdown, Lorelei faithfully attended Andy's junior surfing class. Every Saturday morning, she arrived at the surf school with her purple board, the one she called Amethyst, eager to hang out with Casey Arondale and Condi Bloom, both serious surfers. But Lorelei's heart wasn't in learning to surf. She preferred floating around on her purple board, exploring sea caves off Craggy Point, searching for sea creatures.

That's why Andy knew Lorelei was sorely missing her oceanography book. He didn't waste a minute. Jumping into the food truck, he drove to the Finches' house on the far side of the hill, put the book on the front porch, got back in the truck, and tooted the horn.

Lorelei rushed outside. "Thanks, Mr. Marshall," she yelled, clutching the book to her chest.

That's when Andy got his big idea, though he was uncertain if it would work. After all, before the Sickness, he'd hardly been a reader himself, only poring over instruction manuals and labels on surfboard wax. But the long nights in lockdown taught Andy how much cozy comfort there is to be found between the pages of a good book.

Adaptability.

That very evening, Andy got on it, building floor-to-ceiling shelves out of reclaimed beach wood, installing them beside the gourmet oven, converting the food truck into a mobile library. Soon he was making rounds in the truck, visiting the children of the town, dropping off books, collecting new donations, handing out freshly baked treats. Stopped in front of a home, he'd stand behind the pop-up window. Patiently, he'd hold up titles, keeping a safe distance, waiting for kids to choose. He didn't care how long it took. Andy had all the time in the world.

Soon the old food truck was overflowing with books and displaying a newly painted sign: "***Sweets and Stories***."

Oh, Andy was adaptable all right.

The old food truck made kids' lives bearable.

If you have a book—you're never alone.

Chapter One

THE COVE

LORELEI

The little beach town is waking up, the air properly balmy, the breeze sweet and warm and slow. Rolling to one side in a tangle of covers, Lorelei Finch eases awake. The open window of her room looks out into a thick grove of catalpa and eucalyptus trees. Though her house is too far from the cove to glimpse the sea, it is near enough to hear the wildest of the waves when the wind is right. Today the morning tide is tattooing an exuberant beat off the peninsula of rock called Craggy Point on the other side of the hill.

Gathering her energy, she slides to the edge of the bed, and takes her time sitting up. The room whirls. Grasping the bed frame, she takes deep careful breaths, waiting for the dizziness to subside. Coming to her feet slowly, she gropes her way over to the dresser and looks into the starfish mirror. Her bluebell eyes stare back, way too big for her hollow-cheeked face, sunken in a tangle of butterscotch hair. The wan person in the mirror is not the girl she knows.

On the dresser, her phone vibrates.

Tidepool? 9am?

Casey.

A small surge of energy lights her up inside. It's hard to believe that she gets to see him later today. For this whole long year, she's looked forward to their daily ZoomIn calls. Despite the isolation, they've gotten closer. They think alike, in every important way. Science is their thing, and they both want to be oceanographers. Casey's her rock, her best friend (and, of course, something more). Until she got sick, they were talking every day.

Yes!

Slowly and methodically, she pulls on her clothes, ignoring the fact that her breath is coming faster, her heart pounding way too fast. With shaking hands, she pulls her hair into a messy knot on the top of her head, trying to ignore how thin it's become.

When she reaches for her tide pool notebook, her heart rate soars, flip-flopping wildly as the room spins. Clutching at the bedpost, she closes her eyes and counts backward from one hundred until her pulse slows. Cautiously, she slides the notebook into her backpack and slips it over her shoulder.

Just. Get. Through. Breakfast.

No matter what, she can't alarm Papa. She's determined to slip out of the house and get to the cove. Traversing the hill and crossing the high dunes to reach the hidden tide pool won't be easy. But she's going to do it.

After six long months—the beach is open.

At last, she gets to see Casey again.

TAD

Tad Finch pushes the scrambled eggs around on his plate. Eggs are gross. No way is he opening his mouth. Not for one instant.

Papa's cell phone buzzes. Distracted, he taps the screen, pushes away from the table, and leaves the room. Tad seizes the moment and slides the eggs into the napkin on his lap.

Cara snickers. "I'll tell."

"Let it go," Lorelei hisses.

Tad is glad Lorelei is sticking up for him (though Papa knows Tad doesn't eat squishy or crusty things). He smiles at Lorelei. Calm and logical, she is his favorite sister. He frowns at Cara. She is not his favorite. He searches for the right words for her in his brain. *Drama. Queen.* Yes, those are the right words.

Lorelei is too skinny. Her collarbones are poking out. It worries Tad. Watching her throat, he counts how many times she chews her food. She is breathing funny, not filling her lungs all the way up. This is not good. She isn't well yet.

"Are you okay, Lori?" he whispers.

"Of course." She smiles sweetly, but her eyes look worried, too.

Tad doesn't understand why Lorelei is acting like she is fine. Or why Papa isn't noticing. Maybe he is too worried about Mama.

When Papa gets off the phone and returns to the table, he says, "I have bad news, kids."

Cara and Lorelei stop eating. Tad freezes, studying Papa's face. It is serious and sad.

"That was Dr. Everett," Papa says quietly. "If Mama

isn't better soon, she'll have to go to the hospital."

Lorelei and Cara are quiet. Hospitals are not a good place to be these days.

"Mama will get better, Papa..." Lorelei's voice trails off. She reaches over to pat Papa's hand.

"Sure, she will." Papa tries hard to smile, but his real smile isn't there.

The silence at the breakfast table is terrible. Tad knows they are all thinking about Mama.

Cara breaks the mood. Flipping her hair, she pushes back her chair and jumps up from the table. "I'm going to get changed. The beach is open."

"Fine." Papa rubs his temples like he has a headache. "Keep a safe distance from other kids. We can't risk bringing home more illness." He looks at Lorelei. "I know you want to go, too," he says. "Are you feeling okay?"

Nodding, Lorelei glances away, biting down hard on her lower lip. Tad knows why she's lying. She wants to go to the beach to meet Casey Arondale. Casey is her boyfriend.

"Run along then," Papa tells her. "Tad and I will take Care Watch."

Lorelei's face breaks into a huge smile. "Thanks, Papa." She winks at Tad. "And you, too, Tad."

Tad doesn't know why she is thanking him. "I don't want to go to the beach," he says. "I like Care Watch."

Papa lays a hand on Tad's shoulder. Pride washes over him. He knows he is helping. Tad likes being with Mama, sitting quietly beside her bed. Except for Mama and Lorelei getting sick, Tad hasn't minded lockdown one bit. He is sorry it is over.

CASEY

Casey Arondale slouches on the stool at the kitchen counter. Staring down at his phone, he scrolls through online posts about sea creatures, determined to find something awesome to share with Lorelei today. At the gourmet stove, his dad flips saffron and honey pancakes on the cast iron griddle, while his mom sets white mugs beside the milk-frothing machine. It will be another minute before the brass and chrome specialty machine ceases chugging and gurgling. Meanwhile, it spouts a delicious cloud of cinnamon-scented steam into the room.

Casey's mouth waters as his dad hands him a plate of fluffy pancakes. Craning his neck, his father tries to peek at Casey's phone.

"Dad." Scowling, Casey shields the screen with his hand.

"David," Casey's mom says reprovingly. "Remember what we discussed? Casey is growing up. He needs space."

"MOM." Casey shoots his mom a look. Both of his parents are annoying, his mom overprotective, his dad always trying to be cool. Casey can't wait to get out of the house today. He's going crazy here. There haven't been guests at the B&B for ages. He's been stuck practicing piano for hours and doing unnecessary chores his parents make up to kill time. It's been awful. Being in lockdown with your parents is no joke—and being an only child sucks.

As he scrolls through ocean posts, he wipes his sweaty palms on his shorts. He's super nervous about meeting Lorelei. It's been a long time. What if she doesn't like him like she did before the Sickness blew up their lives?

His mother hands him a mug of froth-topped cocoa. "What are your plans today?"

"Hanging out with Lorelei," he mumbles.

His mother raises a brow. "What about the marine sanctuary? Aren't you needed there?"

"Nope," Casey says emphatically. "Mr. Huddleston doesn't need me for a few days. He's picking up his son today."

There's a long, awkward silence. Casey's dad goes to the window and stares gloomily out at the beach.

"Poor kid," his dad says, shaking his head.

"So many losses," his mom murmurs. Joining her husband, she slips an arm around his waist and kisses him on the cheek.

Yuk.

Casey goes back to scrolling. He doesn't want to talk about it. The arrival of Mr. Huddleston's son is going to change things. Casey hopes it doesn't affect his job. Getting to work at the Craggy Point Marine Sanctuary is the best thing that's happened to him during the Sickness. When the sanctuary closed to the public, Mr. Huddleston—the lead oceanographer and marine biologist—stayed on. Desperate for help, he offered Casey a part-time job cleaning tanks and feeding turtles. Surprisingly, Casey's parents agreed. Working at the Sanctuary is a solitary job, with no exposure to people.

"Have fun at the beach today," his mother says lightly, trying to lift the mood. At the sink, she fills a metal pitcher with water. "When you see Lorelei today, tell her we're praying for Gabby."

Casey's throat tightens. "I will." Gabby is Lorelei's mom. Mrs. Finch has been sick for a long time. Lorelei's stopped talking about her on their ZoomIn calls. He's not sure what that means.

The pitcher overflows. His mom startles, pouring off

the excess water. Smiling brightly, she says, "Off to water the flowers on the patio. A special guest is coming this afternoon." Shooting him a wink, she leans against the swinging doors and leaves the kitchen.

"Guest? Since when?" He looks at his dad. Though the beach is open, tourism still isn't allowed. Pushing away from the counter, he goes to the dishwasher and noisily loads his mug and plate.

His dad shrugs. "Some high-profile biologist from the Center for Disease Control has a special clearance to come to Dipitous. He's staying at the B&B and working at the marine sanctuary. Word is that he's researching medicinal properties of sea creatures, trying to find a cure for the Sickness."

"Cool," Casey says flatly. Dodging his dad's quizzical look, he heads up to his room to change clothes. He's got to get to the beach. Lorelei will be waiting.

At the top of the stairs, he does a fist pump. A dude from the CDC is coming to do marine biomedical research at Craggy Point.

Wait until he tells Lorelei.

KAIT

Kait Dooley throws open the casement window of the high turret of the mansion at the top of Upper Main, taking in gulping breaths of sea air to escape the cringy smell. The cloying reek of bleach and disinfectant is everywhere in this awful old house, clinging like a nasty second skin.

Gloomily, she shakes her head. How is it possible she's been in America for almost a year—and not a wee bit closer to her goal than when she first arrived?

Stop your maudlin, Kait.

After all, the whole wide ocean is out there beyond the window and things are looking up. The Sickness is ending. She isn't going to be stuck in this horrid old place forever, caring for a fretful old woman.

"*Awk!*"

Turning away from the window, she grins at the parrot perched on the low rung of the wrought-iron cage in the corner of Mr. Hardy's library. Turquoise and silver with a flaming red throat, the parrot cocks its head and pecks at the latch on the cage door.

"Don't scold. I'm no good at this." Kait sighs. "If only Gabby was here. She'd know what to do. It's terrible, me not knowing a thing about birds."

The parrot pecks at the latch again, watching her with bottle-green eyes.

"Poor thing," she whispers. "You miss Mr. Hardy."

On impulse, she flips open the door of the cage, jarring the feeding tray. Birdseed sprays over the wooden floor, scattering and bouncing into every corner.

"Holy Mother of Careless Messes." Groaning, she bewails her clumsiness. No matter how hard she tries, she bungles things. Taking a job as a maid was her worst idea yet.

The parrot soars out of the cage and climbs high above Kait's head, settling on the rafters. For a moment, it puffs out its chest feathers. Then, without warning, the bird dives out the open window, flying up and over the trees in an arc of turquoise and silver.

Stunned, Kait stares at the empty cage. "Sure, and I'm hoping you'll be returning—or I'll be in a whole heap of trouble with that old witch downstairs."

Swearing softly, she cleans the parrot's cage and takes the bag of birdseed out from under Mr. Hardy's desk. Carefully, she refills the feeding tray, breathing in the scent of pipe smoke lingering among the rich leather smell of books. How she misses the kind old man. When he was alive, the library felt safe, comforting as a hug—now it only feels sad.

She almost can't bear to clean his favorite room. Stacks of research papers remain scattered over his desk, just as they were before the Sickness. Sun glints on the photo of the Craggy Point Marine Sanctuary hanging on the wall. Mr. Hardy founded the marine sanctuary. In the photo, he is smiling broadly, like people do when they've achieved a dream. Mr. Hardy's passion was protecting sea turtles. Kait shakes her head. Mr. Hardy was her protector, too. Now she's lost him—along with Gabby Finch.

Sweet Gabby. Kait closes her eyes. Spread over a worktable by the window are her notes. She was Mr. Hardy's research assistant. The two spent hours in this library, poring over oceanic discoveries and planning explorations in *Limelight*, the small research submersible tethered to the dock at Craggy Point. When Kait arrived in America, Gabby became her second mother. Now Gabby has the Sickness, too. The pain of missing her is almost worse than the loss of Mr. Hardy. Mam was right. Kait should have never left Ireland. Things went awry the minute she set foot on this strange faraway shore.

What a fool she was to run away—to follow someone else's dream.

ISAAC

Isaac Huddleston isn't sure he's alive. A crushing weight sits on his chest, pressing hard, leaving no room for his heart to beat. He thought the pain couldn't get worse. The red eye from New York to LA was a nightmare, but the despair that nearly choked him struck when he saw his father waiting outside the baggage claim. The tall, burly man with the mop of black curls is a stranger.

On the way from the airport to his dad's house, in some pitiful beach town on the Cali coast, Isaac contemplates leaping from the van as it speeds down the highway. After he refused to sit in the front seat, his dad got all nervous and started talking nonstop, glancing at him in the rear-view window every few miles. The ride's been one run-on sentence about how kids in Dipitous Beach are great, the weather amazing, the surfing incredible.

Defiantly, Isaac puts in his ear pods and raises his eyes to the rearview mirror. When his father glances back, the hopeful look in his eyes is infuriating. Isaac smirks, raises his middle finger, and double taps the left ear pod. Hope fades in his dad's eyes. He stops talking and stares back at the highway.

Message received.

Satisfied, Isaac leans back in the seat, closing his eyes. As the acoustic guitar kicks in, the metallic colors in his head fire—pounding, brutal, hard—like his whole messed-up life.

Surf?

His father's delusional.

Isaac doesn't even know how to swim.

CONDI

This morning, after waving goodbye to Grand Ella at the yellow cottage, Condi Bloom makes her way through a ripple of waves to climb the stairs up to the top of Windy Hollow, as she has every good weather day since the Sickness began.

Despite everything, the Hollow is still Condi's favorite place in the world. Rising out of the sea on the far north shore of the cove, the tall tower of rock is safe to climb only at low tide, when waves aren't churning around the jagged stand of rocks and the stone steps aren't slick with spray and surf.

On the top of the Hollow, she breathes deeply, gazing out at the teal-blue waters of the cove. Pushing curly, dark hair out of her eyes, she shifts her weight on the shell of the sunbaked orange-red kayak, adjusting her body to face the wind. The ancient craft, turned upside down and tucked between the two half-moon rocks, groans under her weight, mournfully synchronizing with her mood.

Does it ever stop?

Constant heart pain washes over her like a wave.

Two years ago, it was Mama and Papa. Lost at sea. Then, last year, at this very time, the autumn equinox, her best friends left town. A month later, the Sickness struck. Isolation sliced through Dipitous Beach like a knife. The spirit of community created after the town's recovery from last year's destructive hurricane was lost. People shrank into their homes, afraid of neighbors and friends.

Taking a deep breath, she closes her eyes, vowing to release the pain. After all, she is lucky to have Grand Ella, her wise and loving grandmother. Together, they live in the cozy yellow cottage high on a cliff, with a splendid view of Windy Hollow and the cove.

The wind swirls, tousling her hair, playfully tossing up a wing of spray.

Without warning, the memory comes out of nowhere—

Staring eagerly out at the horizon line, she sees him, just as he was the day they met. Surfing on his molten black board, backlit in wings of spray, skimming across shining water...laughter in his turquoise eyes, sparkles in his onyx hair.

She blinks.

The memory fades away.

If only...

Disappointed, she wipes away the sting of salt from her eyes.

No matter how hard she tries, being grateful doesn't help.

She can't get over missing him.

Chapter Two

THE SHALLOWS

Weighted down by her backpack and the purple surfboard she calls Amethyst, Lorelei makes the winding climb over the hill separating her house from the cove. The trek is long and challenging. Everything feels heavier than usual. When she crests the steep hill, she drops the board in the grass, stopping to wipe sweat from her forehead. Panting heavily, she takes a moment to drink in the view she's longed to see for months.

At last.

There it is...the slender curve of the cove...hugging a shining aquamarine sea.

Ignoring the tightness in her chest, she picks up her board and plods down the hill. Reaching the high beach road, she follows it until she arrives at Craggy Point, the grand slab of layered granite stretching out into the sea. An ideal launching pad for surfers, the Point is the natural boundary between the sweeping sand of the populated inner cove and the secluded habitat of the Craggy Point

Marine Sanctuary, with its rocky shore, deep tide pools, and spooky underwater caves.

Holding Amethyst, she slips and slides down the scrubby pitch of dunes flanking the marine sanctuary side of the Point. Here the shoreline is rough and ragged, tufted with tall seagrass surrounding hidden pockets of water, natural collecting pools for sea creatures stranded by the tide. Struggling to keep her breathing even, she moves slowly; the footing here is precarious, clotted with hard-packed sand and broken shells, tangles of sea oats and prickly thistle. Below the crusted dune is the narrow ribbon of shore leading to the marine sanctuary, a sprawl of buildings on a steep slope overlooking an L-shaped metal dock.

At a familiar thicket of tall grass, she eagerly pushes her way toward the sound of gurgling water. Fed by fissures in the rock layers of Craggy Point, every beat of the waves pumps fresh seawater into a large, oval basin of ink-black rock, filling at high tide, draining to empty at lowest ebb.

With great care, Lorelei lays Amethyst on a bed of sea oats, entranced for an instant by the sparkling shaper's mark on the nose of the board, glinting in the sun. The mark is unusual, rather like the kind and quirky girl who gave Lorelei the surfboard last year before her family moved away. Marissa Davis was a true original, Lorelei reflects sadly. And her brother, Trustin, was one of the nicest boys around. If only the Davis twins hadn't left town after the hurricane.

When her vision wavers, she realizes how tired she is. Her breath is shallow and fast. Sitting on a sun-warmed rock, she closes her eyes and takes several slow breaths.

Soon the tide works its magic, calming her racing heart, tuning it to the familiar glug-glug of water pulsing in the pool. Though everything else has changed, at least the tide pool is the same...water flowing in, water flowing out...

Feeling better, she slides her tide pool notebook out of her backpack and leans over the water, scanning the bumps and ridges of the dark lava rock basin.

Look for something new.

Mama's gentle voice.

A flash of crimson peeks out of a hidey-hole. Eagerly, she pokes at it with a sliver of driftwood. Irritated, a plump sea urchin rolls away, exposing a nest of tiny, rosebud-pink anemones. Disappointed, she sits back on her heels, flicking away the stick. Hardly something new.

Record everything you see. Scientific observations are never wasted.

An expert researcher, Mama taught her the importance of collecting data. Carefully, Lorelei catalogs the contents of the tide pool in the notebook. The red sea urchin and rosebud anemones are entry 432. After the date and time, she records species type, color, size, estimated temperature of the water. Every bit of data is essential to the scientific method.

Sadly, she notices that entry 431 was many months ago.

Before Mama got sick...

...before everything changed.

Willing away the dark thoughts, Lorelei snaps the notebook shut. A wave flushes the tide pool, sucking the sea creatures into a fissure. When the water clears, the pool is empty...glistening in the sun.

The nose of a hunter-green surfboard parts the tall grass. Casey steps through the thicket, casting a long, lanky shadow over the pool.

"Hey."

Lorelei's breath catches. From the opposite side of the pool, she shoots him a radiant smile, tucking a stray strand of wispy hair behind her ear. How she wishes she could hug him. Of course—he's cuter than ever.

Dropping his board in the grass, he moves uncertainly toward her.

"No," she says, putting up a hand to stop him.

He stares, not understanding. The hidden tide pool has always been their special make-out spot.

"We can't," she says, hating the yearning in his hazel eyes.

This is so wrong.

They had it all planned.

Kissing. Holding hands. Getting back to the way things were.

"I don't get it," he says, throwing his lanky body down beside his board.

"It's Mama. She isn't better. All of us kids must be extra careful." Longingly, she looks at him across the black basin of rock, willing him to sense how bad she feels. It isn't fair. They've waited so long to be together again.

Staring at her lips, he looks dazed.

She knows that look. He's not listening. All he really wants is to kiss her. Moving up higher on the rock, she pulls her knees up to her chin and wraps her arms around them, pulling into herself like a snail into a shell.

"No new germs," she tells him.

"Not even a hug?" he asks hopefully.

Her temper flares. Suddenly she's furious. The sweet, clueless look on his face makes her crazy. Of course, he doesn't get it. An only child, Casey spent lockdown living in his mom and dad's cushy coastal hotel. No one in his family got sick. His life is pretty much the way it was before. He even got a fun job working at the marine sanctuary.

She glares at him.

His face flushes. "I'm sorry."

Her lower lip wobbles. She knows he really means it. The worst of the anger ebbs away. It's not his fault. Of course, he doesn't get it.

"Thanks," she answers, trying to smile. "Go on. Surf. Have fun. I can't hang out with the other kids."

"No way." He looks confused. "I'll stay here with you."

"Casey." Letting her eyes catch and hold on to his, she lets him see her yearning, hardly able to bear the look on his cute, sweet face. He's making a big sacrifice for her. He loves surfing. How she wishes she could snuggle up in his arms and kiss him.

His face lights up.

He leans forward.

No.

In a split second, she knows that if he stays, she won't be able to resist him.

Stumbling to her feet, she sways on the rock. Sparks fly across her vision.

Casey leaps to his feet and grabs for her arm. "You don't look right."

"I'm fine," she tells him, regaining her balance and backing away. "I need you to go. I want to be alone."

The hurt on his face is awful. Lying to him is the hardest thing she's ever done. He's the cutest and nicest boy she's ever known. But it doesn't matter. Mama isn't getting better. Casey can't understand how hard it's been. It's not his fault, but his family doesn't struggle. He can't know what it's like to live in a cramped inland cottage, sitting by your mother's bedside, watching her fight for every breath.

"I need to be alone," she repeats. "I'm going down to the shore. I'll put on my wetsuit and float around on Amethyst, checking out sea caves."

Helpless, he stands on the other side of the pool. "Are you mad at me?" he asks, shoving a lock of the russet hair she loves so much out of his eyes.

Shaking her head, she manages her best smile. "Text me tonight, okay? We can talk on ZoomIn like usual." Picking up her board, she pulls her wetsuit out of her backpack and steps through the seagrass. Glancing over her shoulder, she blows him a kiss.

She knows she's hurt him badly.

But they can't be together, at least not right now.

She's got to protect Mama.

Isaac Huddleston grits his teeth as his dad's van rattles through the security gate of the Craggy Point Marine Sanctuary. The long ride from the airport sucked, but now he's really and truly trapped. In a godforsaken beach town.

Slowly, the van rolls to a stop beside a quaint house with a wide front porch. His father gets out of the van. Isaac stays in the back seat, staring straight ahead and eyeing the keys in the ignition, wishing he could drive. The minute he gets out of this van, his life is over.

Cautiously, his dad taps on the rear window. "Come inside."

No way. Isaac flings open the door, jumps out of the

van, and starts running. He doesn't know where he's going, and he doesn't care. Bolting past the house, he heads down the slope toward shore, his black leather rocker boots slipping and sliding on crushed shells and gravel.

"Hey," his father calls. "Wait up."

Isaac runs faster, taking a flight of stone stairs leading down to a long metal dock two at a time. At the ramp to the dock, he pauses. In front of him the metal dock glints—a long, stiff arm extending out into a blinding blue sea.

Panting, his father comes up alongside him. Cautiously, he puts a hand on Isaac's shoulder, and points to the small lime-green dome bouncing on the waves next to the dock.

"Like it?" he asks proudly. "It's a submersible. State of the art. For underwater exploration and research."

Isaac yanks his shoulder away. Stuffing his hands into his pockets, he paces to the end of the dock, staring at the blank eye of the sea. *End of the road. Nowhere else to run.* For an instant, he contemplates hurling himself into the water. In his black leather jacket and boots, he'd sink like a stone.

"Alright then." His dad calls. "You win. I'll go unpack the van."

Isaac hears weary receding footsteps. Sinking to his knees, he cradles his head in his hands. How did he end up here, living with a parent he's never known? God, he misses his mom. She was the best. Beautiful and brave, filled with light and music. How can someone like that just die?

Thwack. Glug, glug.

Glancing over, he glares at the sub. Bobbing next to him, bumping against the dock, the lime-green bubble hatch ogles him like an eye. Anchored with thick twisted cables, it makes sucking noises, squeaking across the rubber bumpers of the dock like an alien in a bad movie.

Popping in his ear pods, he lies down on his stomach on the warm dock, fixing his eyes on the hypnotic wavering of the ocean floor. Tapping his left pod, he turns up the volume. An electric guitar screeches orange, screaming red...erupting into full-blown rage.

Ironically, it numbs the pain. Getting lost in ragged sound and jagged color is all he knows to do. Like his wildly talented mother, he has perfect pitch, hearing musical frequencies and seeing notes in color.

It's not fair.

She almost got her moment under the big lights.

After working so hard, taking classes, playing for years in seedy bars and lounges, his mom finally got a break. Discovered by a teacher, she was invited to audition at Carnegie Hall.

Then the Sickness happened.

Ripping off his pods, he jams them into the pocket of his black leather jacket. He's not sure he can stand it—the pain, the heat, this town.

The sun burns through his jacket. Despite a cool breeze spinning off the water, he's sweating fiercely. He considers taking the jacket off. But the jacket is the last thing she gave him, to celebrate her big break. He can't risk it blowing into the water.

Squinting through the rocking ripples of the tide, he examines the shallow waters under the dock, searching frantically for a sharp fragment of shell within reach, something pointed and thin.

Stupid airline took away his knife.

#

Lorelei struggles into her wetsuit and carries Amethyst down the precariously steep dune until she reaches the rocky shore of the marine sanctuary. This side of Craggy Point is solitary, pock-marked with sea caves and a natural habitat for sea creatures. While surfing is strictly forbidden here, it's easy to explore the caverns of the Point while floating on her board.

Stashing her backpack above the tideline, she wades into the waters of a rising tide, holding Amethyst like a blade. Icy water splashes and slaps her tired body, drenching her wetsuit. For a moment she wonders if she's too winded to go out. Then she talks herself out of the thought. After all, the sun is energizing, and salt water is healing. Bellyflopping on her board, she determinedly paddles out, dodging the telltale ripples of the strong riptide lurking off the tip of the Point.

Once she moves past the breakers, the water calms. Dragging one arm through the water, she lets herself float, laying her cheek on the board and savoring the rock of the tide. Exhaustion takes over...she falls asleep.

Casey has spent the last hour surfing, cutting through frothing high rollers, tube riding, pushing his skills to the max. The minute he hits shore, he flips the hunter-green board and paddles out for another run, stroking toward the furthest line of high waves. Nothing gets you out of your head like cold water and time on a board.

Relaxed, he paddles out again, realizing that he took Lorelei's rejection way too personally. After all, her mom is sick.

And Lorelei's been sick, too—

Like a rogue wave, guilt socks him in the gut. How could he have missed it? In the pain of her rejection, he missed the obvious. The dizzy spell, the awful way she struggled to catch her breath. She's not well yet. How could he have let her go to the other side of the Point alone?

Blowing his breath out hard, he digs into the waves, paddling out toward the far line of high rollers. If he wants to crest the Point, going out past the riptide is the only way. Using all his strength, he forces his board seaward. When he hits the breakers, the tide takes it from there, directing his board toward the shore lined with sea caves.

At the mouth of a yawning sea cave, a huge, slapping wave crashes into Amethyst, yanking Lorelei awake, tumbling her into the heart of a vicious rolling undertow. The board is sucked from beneath her. A hidden vortex of water pulls her, dragging her face down over rocks. Pain shoots through her cheek. Flailing and kicking, grasping for a handhold of kelp, she desperately fights to stop the relentless pull of the sea.

It's no use.

Her lungs scream.

The current tugs her down and back, away from shore.

Squeak!

Lurching to his feet, Isaac angrily kicks the bouncing sub away from the dock with the toe of his boot. The annoying squeak of the hull on the rubberized bumpers is the last thing he needs right now.

A rivulet of sweat runs down his cheek. Wiping off his brow, he looks out to sea.

The water is a blinding blue. Inside the swells off the Point is a girl, floating on a purple surfboard close to a giant sea cave. Lying on her stomach, golden hair covering her face and one arm trailing languidly through the water, she appears to be asleep.

With the sun directly overhead, he shields his eyes. A few high waves slap the dock, shoving the sub into the rubber bumpers again. He grits his teeth, eyeing the girl on the board. What a dumb chick. There's no surfing this side of the Point. Signs are everywhere.

A high roller breaks over the girl on the board, sweeping her into the water. Shaking his head, Isaac doesn't wait for her to surface. Turning around, he heads toward shore. He's burning up in his leather jacket. Time to go up to the house. He doesn't want to be hanging out on the dock when she swims in.

At the base of the stairs, his neck hairs prickle. Something's off. Nervously, he glances back over his shoulder and surveys the waves.

The purple surfboard is floating on an empty sea.

No sign of the girl.

Heart thudding in his chest, he races up the stairs to the house, yelling for his dad.

The sand settles, the water clears. Dreamily, Lorelei floats above the sea floor, staring up at a canopy of rippling waves, a watery lens to a brilliant blue sky.

Strange—she isn't scared.

It's peaceful here.

Vaguely, she wonders if she is dead. A flicker catches the corner of her eye. In astonishment, she watches as a luminous octopus floats into view. The body shimmers, eight glistening arms unfurling in waves. The creature gazes soulfully at her, an orb of white light glowing behind wise, kind eyes. Lights at the top of each arm sparkle, hypnotic and mesmerizing, each a different color—red, blue, orange, golden-yellow, green, purple, pink, and aquamarine.

Her scientific mind thrills. Curious, she leans in. The twinkling golden-yellow arm wafts toward her like an outstretched palm, reaching to touch her face.

Flooded with a deep sense of contentment and understanding, she smiles and extends her hand. The creature's arms lift and shimmer, sparkling in pinprick lights of every color. Gently, she is comforted by many arms and pulled close ...rocking rhythmically in the tide.

Splat!

Everything goes black.

After what may be the hardest paddle of his life, Casey skirts the rip current. On the far side of the Point, the long metal dock of the marine sanctuary glints in the sun, where Mr. Huddleston and a skinny kid dressed in black are pulling a limp form from the water. Abandoning his board, Casey swims with fury, stroking toward the dock. When he reaches it, he stretches out one long arm and lunges for the metal ladder, hurling himself up and out of the water.

"How long was she under?" he shouts.

Startled, Mr. Huddleston turns around. "Good grief, Casey. How'd you get here?"

"How *long* was she under?" Casey repeats.

"She's going to be okay," the oceanographer answers. "Settle down. We got to her in time."

On the dock, Lorelei's breath is coming in short, staccato gasps. Looking bored, a boy in a black leather jacket leans against a piling. Kneeling, Mr. Huddleston wraps Lorelei in a towel, vigorously massaging her arms and legs.

"Are you okay?" Casey asks, grabbing for her hand.

Dazed, she pulls her hand away and looks at him with puzzled eyes.

"She's coming out of shock, Casey," Mr. Huddleston tells him gently. "Give her space." Raising a brow, he adds, "You made quite a swim."

Sagging against the dock railing, Casey anxiously watches Lorelei's chest rise and fall. At last, the confusion clears from her eyes and her breath slows.

"Your cheek," Casey says, leaning forward. "That's a bad scratch. It's bleeding."

Grabbing the towel from Mr. Huddleston's hand, she dabs at her cheek with it, examines the blood smear, then shrugs. "No big deal. I'm fine." Clutching the dock rail, she stands up.

"Whoa there," Mr. Huddleston says. "Take your time."

Casey lunges for her. She waves him off. The boy in the leather jacket snickers.

"Isaac." Mr. Huddleston shoots the kid a warning glance. Turning to Lorelei, he says, "Do you think you can make it up the stairs? I've called your dad. He's on the way."

"Sure." Swathed in a thick towel, Lorelei cracks a smile at Casey and nods her head toward the purple surfboard rocking next to the submersible. "Rescue my board, will you, Case?"

Head held high, she walks down the long dock toward shore. Casey grabs Amethyst and his own board from the shallows, then falls into step beside her. Side by side, they walk to the base of the long flight of stone steps leading up to the parking lot where her dad is pulling in.

"I can't wait to tell you what happened," Lorelei whispers excitedly, looking over at him. "I was terrified. My lungs were exploding. I thought I was drowning. Then—"

"Stop," he interrupts. "You almost died." The thought terrifies him. It takes all his strength not to wrap an arm around her waist, pull her close and bury his face in the scent of her salt-washed hair.

Annoyed, she snaps her fingers in front of his nose. "You're not listening. I'm trying to tell you something important, Casey."

"Sorry." Pulling himself together, he tries to focus on what she's saying, but the faraway look on her face is scaring him.

"An octopus floated out of the kelp." Her bluebell eyes are alight with a strange fire, and her voice is unusually excited. "Oh, Casey, it was beautiful, translucent, sparkling with light, every arm a different color. It reached for me—"

"Lorelei," he interrupts. "You hit your head. Your cheek is scraped. Seeing lights means you have a concussion."

"No." The faraway look on her face fades. "You're wrong."

"You have a concussion," he repeats stubbornly. If he could just hold her close...

"Stop acting like you know everything." She shoots him an angry glare. "My dad's here." Running up the stairs to the parking lot, she dashes over to her father, who swallows her up in his arms.

Behind Casey, the kid in the black jacket calls out, "Way to go, dude."

Gritting his teeth, Casey makes his way over to Mr. Finch's car and straps Amethyst to the luggage rack. Already, he hates Isaac Huddleston. Who wears a black leather jacket to the beach anyway?

Thoughtfully, Isaac watches the girl hug her dad. Gesturing with her hands, she eagerly tells him a wild story about how she saw an octopus with colored arm lights when she went under. The more she talks, the louder her voice gets and the more far out her story sounds. "Casey doesn't believe me," she says emphatically, glaring at the boy awkwardly holding a hunter green surfboard.

Over her head, Isaac watches her father exchange a worried glance with his dad, who says solemnly, "The unconscious mind plays tricks—especially when deprived of oxygen."

Lorelei's eyes blaze. For one short, happy instant Isaac thinks she's going to square off with his dad.

"Honey." Pulling her under his arm, her father kisses the top of her head. "Listen to reason. You passed out. That's a whopper of a scratch on your cheek."

"Lore, you almost drowned!"

Isaac snorts. He can't believe it. The panicked dude who must be her boyfriend won't shut up.

Lorelei whirls around. "I know what I saw, Casey Arondale."

Isaac steps forward. "I believe you."

His bold words surprise him almost as much as they do the girl. Giving her a shy grin, he puts on his innocent face, the one reserved for teachers and busybody adults like social workers. Her story is crazy, but she's cute.

"Thank you," she answers with a dignified sniff.

"Lorelei," her boyfriend says morosely. "Can I call you later?"

"I'm going home now." Flinging open the car door, she slides into the front seat.

"C'mon, son." Isaac's dad puts a hand on her boyfriend's shoulder. "Let her go. She needs rest. I'll take you back to the B&B."

Son.

Isaac's heart twists like a knife in his chest. His father called the stupid dude *son.* Head down, he takes off for the house. Slamming through the screen door, he paces around the unfamiliar house until he finds his room—the one where his suitcase and backpack are stacked on the bed, next to his guitar case.

Sweeping everything onto the floor, he locks the door and flops down on the bed, shuddering with the awful truth—this is his new life.

I hate this place.

Clasping a pillow to his chest, he sucks in his breath, desperate to stop the pain. With a shaking finger, he taps his pods, hoping to find a frenzied mean guitar solo that sounds the way he feels—like raging and tearing up the room.

But the first song that plays is not any of that. Instead, the track is a classical piece his musician mother loved to play at the end of the night for lonely hearts in the late crowd. Honey to amber, willow green to smoke, the colors in her fingers played the haunting melody in waves. The crowd felt young again, though most of them were older than the hills.

She was everything.

Beautiful and talented and exciting.

Now he's lost her forever.

Chapter Three

SURPRISES

On the terrace of the yellow cottage, Grand Ella draws strength from the early morning sea, twisting her silver infinity necklace around her little finger. She must go today. The road barricades are down, the main highway on the coast open again. No time to lose.

Returning to the kitchen, she resolutely packs a braided seagrass basket with freshly baked treats. After grabbing keys from the hook beside the front door, she closes the door to the yellow cottage softly, hoping that starting up the old gray van won't wake Condi, though she suspects it will. The old van is reliable, but it never fails to start with a bang and a whistle.

A crystal rose dawn is breaking over the high beach road, paving the way with morning light as Grand Ella pulls away from the cottage. Adjusting her posture, she lifts her chin and lowers her shoulders, relaxing into the worn driver's seat. *My, it feels good to be out and about again.* Humming softly, she makes the hairpin turn off the high beach road onto Coastal Pass and accelerates. The miles fly by. Soon, she noses the van off the highway and chugs up the peaked hill, navigating the winding turns of Spindle Mountain.

The cell phone on the seat next to her buzzes. Sitting up a little bit straighter, she ignores it and presses her foot to the pedal to give the van more gas. The phone on the seat stops buzzing. She exhales in relief. Then the phone shudders, emitting the sound of a winding clock, switching from text to phone call. Sighing, she glances down at the screen.

The caller is who she thinks it is.

Sheriff Clive Coodle, her good friend—and maybe something more.

Calmly, she clicks the phone to silent. Clive can't know where she is. For one thing, after being sick for months, she technically shouldn't be driving yet, though she knows she's fine. After her morning cup of Three Herbs energy tea with a shot of cayenne, she's invigorated and infused with strength.

Besides, she's got to show up. They'll be wondering where she's been. Smiling, she smooths back a lock of silver-streaked hair. A powdery sweet smell wafts up from the braided grass basket covered with a worn cotton towel in the back seat. Freshly baked goodies are in the basket, all her best concoctions; peppercorn scones, coconut papaya tarts, midnight chocolate cookies, popovers with poppyseed and orange. And, of course, everyone's favorite—lavender honey muffins.

With a deep inhale, she settles her mind as the van nears the top of the mountain. All of them will have changed, of course—after all, it's been a long time. Shaking her head, she gives into an uncharacteristic moment of irritation. First, there was all that nonsense about toxic fumes off the ocean causing the Sickness. Then, the authorities blocked access from beach towns to the main roads, making it impossible to travel, though she's certain there were ways. If she'd been well, she would have found a way to return months before this.

The phone lights up.

Clive.

Sighing, she turns it off. How she hates deceiving him. While she tends to break rules, Clive Coodle is obligated to enforce them. As the sheriff of Dipitous Beach, he works tirelessly for the town. Most of the time she respects his badge. But it's complicated. Like now, when she's traveling up Spindle Mountain on an unauthorized secret mission. Beach residents are not allowed to use the main highways for at least another week. If Clive knew, he'd stop her.

As she nears the top of the mountain, a large, weathered sign stares out of a forest of gnarled oaks.

"OVERLOOK HOME"

Indeed. She checks her temper. *Overlooked* is more like it, the dilapidated old place is hardly a home at all! Firmly, she presses down on the gas pedal. The van lurches up the last incline, making the final winding turn. Through a veil of moss-covered trees, the house appears, stern and gloomy as ever.

When she pulls into the gravel parking lot, she hits the brake, bringing the van to an abrupt stop, staring in shock. The front walk is overgrown, the once-vibrant roses drooping and tangled, the windows shuttered and dark.

Where in the world are they?

#

Jolted awake when the old van starts up with a bang and a whistle and chugs away from the yellow cottage, Condi wonders where Grand Ella is going so early in the morning. Last night her grandmother was in one of her powdered sugar flurries, baking tasty treats for a mysterious errand she didn't want to talk about.

Leaning out of the window of her bedroom loft, Condi drinks in the breathy cool of clean sea air. On the trellis outside the window is a bursting cascade of elegant white sea lilies and smiling pink hibiscus spilling over the sill, drenching the room in last-of-summer fragrance.

After pulling on her faded yellow swimsuit, she climbs down the ladder from her loft bedroom and goes into the kitchen to grab a berry-nut popover. Stepping outside on the high terrace, she looks to the horizon, where the rising sun is flushing ballet-pink, dancing gold across the water.

Her gratitude prayer comes easier than it has in months. After all, the popover is delicious, warm from the oven, Grand Ella is well enough to drive, and best of all, the beach is open, and she can go to the inner cove and surf. For the first time in a long time, it's going to be a good day. Tugging on her wetsuit, she pulls Aquamarine out from under the trellis, where it's been stored these long past months. Carrying her precious surfboard, glittering blue and green and sparkling silver, she runs down the zigzag stairs to the beach.

On the slender sliver of shore below the yellow cottage, she pauses, gazing to the north, toward the rugged, rough side of the cove where the tall tower of Windy Hollow rises out of the sea, morning light glinting off the wet hull of the orange-red kayak between the two half-moon rocks. A nostalgic wave rolls over her, as it always does. The top of the tower was their place.

Shaking back her hair, she turns toward the cove and sets her mind on surfing. Walking along the curve of shore to the Billabong, she revels in the icy wash of the sea on her feet. Though the walk is quite a distance, she'll never whine about it again. For too long, she thought she might never get the chance to return to town.

At last, she reaches the beach below Andy Marshall's Billabong, wisely re-built higher on the shore after last year's catastrophic storm. How good it feels to be back, though there aren't many people out. Three small children chase sea birds on the shore while their mothers keep a polite distance from one another, too-pale faces raised to the sun. A lone surfer kid, skinny and desperate-looking, staggers down the beach stairs with his board, heading for Craggy Point.

"Condi!" Andy, perched on a ladder, is rolling out a new awning over the front porch of the surf shop. Swaying precariously, he points at the Surf School sign on the porch of the Billabong. "Surfing classes start soon. You in?" he yells.

"You bet!" she yells back. Last year some of the best moments of her life were spent teaching at the surf school.

"Good girl!" Throwing up an arm, he waves, waggling his hand, thumb and pinkie extended. *Hang loose.*

Grinning, she shoots the familiar surfing sign back. At least the surfing master hasn't changed. A free spirit, he's always up for a chuckle and a story, especially ones about his surfing glory days. It will be fun to help him teach grommets—newbie surfers of all ages—again.

Finding a soft spot in the sand, she lays her board down and spreads out her beach towel. Right now, the tide is low, but soon it will turn, waves spinning off the Point, high and shiny, big and grand and wide. Ideal for surfing. Sitting down on the towel, she stretches her arms above her head, surveying the beach. Cradling the cove on the south side is Craggy Point, where a flight of wooden stairs leads up to the high deck supporting Grand Ella's open-air yoga pavilion and the Beachlings' bunkrooms, built after the ravages of last year's storm. Lushly overhung with beach roses, the pavilion and bunkrooms have a spectacular ocean view.

When a tall old woman with loose braids of pewter hair emerges from one of the bunkrooms, she spies Condi right away. Waving a sun-bleached scarf, she regally descends the stairs from the high deck and hurries across the sand.

"Trippy!" Jumping to her feet, Condi rushes to meet her.

"Condi, my dear, is it really you?" The woman envelops her in a hug and smiles, her weathered face cracking into a mosaic of glorious lifelines.

Condi nods, brushing away a happy tear. "Oh, I've missed you so much, Trippy!"

"And I you, my dear," the old lady replies.

"How are the other Beachlings?" Condi asks.

Triponica slips a muscular arm around Condi's shoulders. "Some are well, some are not," she answers quietly.

Condi's chest tightens. Quickly, she glances up at the bunkrooms, scanning the deck. "Oh, no, where's Francie? Why isn't she out sunning in her wheelchair?"

"Asleep, my dear. Too weak to leave her bed." Triponica sighs. "Francie's lost strength since you last saw her."

"Is it the Sickness?" Condi asks slowly, afraid to hear the answer.

Trippy shakes her head. "Not everything is about the

Sickness, though our focus on it makes it seem so." Her eyes fade far away, looking to the horizon. "Francie is dying, my dear."

"Oh, no!" Condi whispers. "How awful!" She thought today might be a better day, but clearly it is not.

"Come now." Triponica sweeps back a lock of Condi's dark hair. "Francie's passing is not to be feared. It is a natural and lovely thing." Stepping back, she grasps Condi's hands and studies her face thoughtfully. "You are filled with a deep sadness, my dear. It is not only the news about Francie. Are you well?"

Condi shrugs. "I'm not sick."

A crease appears in the old woman's brow. "I'm certain your physical health is fine—but that is not what I mean." Her eyes catch and hold Condi's, glinting amber and gold.

Condi cannot look away. She takes a deep breath. It's impossible to deceive Triponica, who seems to know everything, all the time. "It's hard, Trippy. I feel so alone. No one else knows what I know."

"No one?" The old woman's eyes soften, crinkling at the edges into shooting stars.

"No other kids," Condi amends.

Trippy clucks her tongue. "Now, now, do not be impatient. Everything is revealed in time. You must wait."

"I hate waiting," Condi blurts. "It's awful to know—and not be able to help people. Like Lorelei. She's my best friend and her mom might be dy—"

"Hush, my child," Triponica interrupts, laying a single knotted finger on Condi's arm. "Listen to me. Lorelei will find her way. It is not for you to reveal what you know."

Chastened, Condi bites down hard on her bottom lip. "I know, Trippy." She grimaces. "Lorelei would never believe me anyway. She wants to be a scientist. She only believes in things that are logical and proven."

Triponica chuckles. "Lorelei certainly has a lot to learn."

Condi flushes.

"Oh, my dear, I'm sorry," Triponica says quickly. "I don't mean to make light of your concerns. Come, let us go for a walk on the beach." Taking Condi's hand, she leads her toward shore.

Condi feels better at once. The day is crisp and clear, and lines of surfing waves are rising off the Point. It's a challenge to keep pace with Trippy's surprisingly sure, quick steps. Not for the first time, Condi wonders what it is that keeps the old woman vibrant, considering her great age. Is it the daily swim in the icy waters off the Point? Or the elixirs she makes from exotic ocean plants gathered in diving expeditions to the sea caves?

At the waterline, Trippy gestures at the high shore where a few more brave people are staking umbrellas and laying out towels. Opening her arms to the sky, she sighs in satisfaction. "Things are getting back to normal. The fear is easing. It's been too long since people have been together without feeling afraid."

"Forever—" Condi answers, "or at least it seems that way. I hate how the Sickness has changed everything."

The old woman puts a firm hand on Condi's shoulder. "Not everything, my dear. The most important things are the same."

"I hope you're right," Condi mumbles.

"Keep your mind fixed on good," Triponica tells her firmly.

"I'll try," Condi answers. "At least Grand Ella is well again. She's going to start teaching sunrise yoga again next week." Gratefully, she looks at Trippy. "I don't know what I would have done if you and the other Beachlings hadn't left food and medicines on the terrace when she was sick. We were running out of everything. I don't know how you knew to come...but thank you."

"Hush, child." Triponica brings a finger to her lips. "No need for thanks. Your grandmother is one of us. We love her—as we love you."

"I was so alone," Condi says, shaking her head. "She was so sick. I didn't know what to do."

"Ah, Condi," Triponica says softly. "Of course, you knew what to do. You poured out your energy—loving her—in all the ways you could."

"I guess so," Condi mumbles. As usual, the Beachlings make things sound way too simple. Everything comes back to love.

Beckoning, Triponica takes a step toward the waterline. "Follow me. I wish to show you something." Wading into the tide, she splashes out to the tip of the Point, where the slab is slick and algae covered. Stooping low, she ducks under a jutting lip of rock into a shadow, vanishing from sight.

Nervously, Condi wades through the swirling eddies of foam toward the shadow. The tide is rising. This part of the Point will soon be underwater. When she reaches the lip of rock, the shadow dissolves, revealing a crack with a wide opening at the bottom. Crouching low, she crawls inside and looks around in wonder. The fissure is a well-disguised entrance—to a spacious tidal cave.

"Come in, my dear. We won't be here long." Trippy's reassuring voice echoes through the cavern, tall enough for the old woman to stand upright. Light and airy, the sea cave is lit with shafts of sunlight. The walls glisten with a rippling crystal sheen, curtains of salt left behind by outgoing tides. Tiny diamonds of water drip from the ceiling like tears, spinning circles into the shallow pool at Triponica's feet.

The old woman stoops to dip her fingers in the pool. Extracting a white shell with pale translucent whirls, tightly spun, ethereal as air, she hands it to Condi.

"Remember, my child. You have learned lessons that cannot be forgotten."

Obediently, Condi clasps the shell.

"Breathe in."

The command releases Condi's shoulders. She inhales deeply. A rush of bright energy flows into her lungs.

"Breathe out."

Condi exhales, letting go.

"People never really leave us, Condi." Gently, Triponica takes the shell from Condi's hand and drops it back into the pool. "All you have to do is remember."

Condi sinks to her knees, gazing into the pool. The delicate shell shimmers among the water diamonds falling from the ceiling of the cavern. Widening into slender, broadening bands, the circles of water slow and spin... until at last they disappear.

As she starts to get to her feet, a wavering face emerges in the surface of the water, reflected, as if from a mirror. The face is blurred, shadowed in dark and light.

Startled, Condi turns. Looking up, she scans the ledge above the pool, searching for the source of the image. A shaft of sun shudders, casting the ledge in darkness. The cave rocks, violently splashing water out of the pool as a powerful wave spins backwash into the cavern, throwing up ragged ribbons of foam.

"Clear the cave!" Trippy cries, grabbing Condi's hand and tugging her toward the entrance.

Whoosh!

As suddenly as it arose, the great wave recedes. Condi and Triponica slip outside through the crack in the rock and run through the quickly rising tide to the safe sand of shore.

"Is someone in the cave?" Condi asks. "I saw—"

The old woman's eyes are dark and unreadable. "Not now, child."

"But—"

Triponica shakes her head in warning. "Say no more."

Condi nods and bites her tongue. She knows better than to push. Triponica is a mystery, elusive as her elixirs, formidable as her midnight swims beneath the moon. Whatever the proud leader of the Beachlings knows, she will not share it until she is ready.

Lorelei feels wonderful. After yesterday's excitement, she slept long and hard, waking up energized and happy. The exhaustion of the past few months is gone. Best of all, she's hungry for the first time in weeks.

Taking a swipe at her hair with her fingers, she shakes out the tangles and peers into the starfish mirror over her dresser. To her relief, the mirror reveals a healthy girl, backlit with sun sparkles and the heart-shaped leaves of the catalpa tree outside her window. No doubt about it—she's well.

On the dresser, her phone vibrates.

Casey.

Again.

Wearily, she taps the screen. “Hello?”

“Lore—”

“I’m fine. *Perfectly* fine.”

“How’s your head?” he asks anxiously. “Yesterday you were confused.”

“You’re the one who’s confused,” she says, speaking firmly. “I know what I saw, and I don’t want to talk to you about it. You already said you don’t believe me.”

“Lorelei.” His voice breaks.

The break softens her heart.

“Sorry I scared you,” she murmurs.

“Do you have a headache?”

“CASEY.”

“If you have a headache, you have a con—”

“Hanging up now.” Clicking the phone off, she snaps it to silent and slides it into her pocket.

Sadly, she looks in the mirror. The happy dancing lights in her eyes are gone.

Casey is her person.

At least he used to be.

Juggling a plate of strawberry mango pancakes and a pot of hot coffee, Casey leans his back against the door to the terrace of the B&B. He’s in a horrible mood. Lorelei is mad at him—and he hates it.

Outside, the terrace is dappled with morning sun. Gentle gusts of a balmy breeze ruffle the cheerful raspberry-red tablecloths on the wrought-iron tables. The tables are empty, except for one at the far end of the terrace, occupied by the Arondales' new guest, Dr. Heath, the visiting medical biologist sent by the CDC to do research at the marine sanctuary.

Carefully, Casey carries the tray to the far end of the terrace and sets it down on a nearby table. "Hello, sir," he says politely.

The man at the table doesn't look up. Impeccably dressed in a long white lab coat, his polished black shoes glint in the sun, matching the unnatural sheen of his carefully styled hair.

Casey hesitates, not sure whether the doctor heard him. Engrossed in his laptop, the doctor is typing furiously. Piles of notecards are stacked on the table, lined up in meticulous rows, weighted down by glasses, mugs, and silverware.

"Sir?" Casey says again, clearing his throat.

The doctor looks up, glaring, eyebrows knitting together over arctic blue eyes.

"Er...where should I place your breakfast, sir?"

Closing his laptop, the man grunts and sweeps the notecards closer together, clearing a small space. With a manicured finger, he impatiently taps the table.

Casey sets the plate down and steps back.

"Anything else, sir?"

Eyeing the notecards anchored against the sea breeze with forks and knives, the doctor barks, "More silverware."

"Of course," Casey replies tersely, and heads back toward the kitchen.

Outside the kitchen door, he pauses, listening as his dad slams pots and pans around inside, a sure sign he's annoyed.

"I'm telling you, Amber, Abe Huddleston's in for it with this one." His dad, usually the calm one in the family, is definitely out of sorts.

"Dr. Heath was exhausted last night, honey," Casey's mom says soothingly. "His plane was late. You know how long and tiring coast-to-coast flights are."

"No," his dad says stubbornly. "It's more than that. He's rude. Blew me off when I told him we'd saved him a hot plate. Demanded to be shown straight to his room. Guy's going to be a real pain. Watch and see."

The instant Casey swings through the door to the kitchen, his parents break apart and stop talking. Shooting him an awkward smile, his mom returns to washing dishes over the sink and his father goes to stand at the stove, pretending to concentrate on diligently flipping pancakes.

"He's a real pain all right," Casey tells them pointedly. Grabbing several rolls of silverware, he heads back to the terrace. Almost fifteen, and his parents still insist on protecting him like he's a little kid.

At the doctor's table, Casey sets down the rolls of silverware.

"Anything else?" he asks coldly, omitting the "sir."

Without looking up, the doctor snorts and picks up his knife and fork, making a flurry of surgically precise cuts into the pancakes.

The movement is fast and disturbing. At first it unsettles Casey, then it infuriates him. Why is everything so screwed up? First, he messed up with Lorelei, now he's got to deal with a creepy doctor with slasher habits and zero manners.

"More coffee?" Casey says innocently, holding the steaming pot of coffee directly over the doctor's lap.

The doctor puts down his knife and fork. The red tablecloth shivers. His knee is shaking under the iron table. Eying Casey with disdain, he pushes his chair back from the table, staring at the coffee pot.

Casey takes a deep breath. He's got to check himself. These past months have been a nightmare. The Sickness has hurt the beach hotel business. His parents work hard to make the B&B a pleasant, hospitable place. Losing his temper won't help anything.

Out of the corner of his eye, Casey sees his mother's head pop out of the pass-through kitchen window overlooking the terrace. Her pointed gaze drills right through him. Stepping back, he swallows the hot words that almost poured out. What is he thinking? The doctor is a guest.

The door to the terrace flings wide. Breezing outside, carrying a white watering can, his mom hurries their way.

"Good morning, Dr. Heath!" she sings out. Gaily moving around the terrace like a butterfly, she casually waters the pots of fresh peonies perched on the railing. "Casey, go inside. Let the doctor eat in peace."

Casey sets the hot coffee pot back on the tray and takes off for the kitchen, where his dad is calmly polishing the silver. Everything in the kitchen gleams. It should. His dad's been cleaning the same things over and over for months.

"Mom told me to come inside," Casey says morosely.

Slinging a dish towel over his shoulder, Casey's dad chuckles. "You were ready to pour scalding coffee all over our guest. What's gotten into you?"

"Sorry," Casey mumbles. No matter what, guests are always right.

His dad breaks out a grin. "Hey, don't tell your mom,

but I don't blame you. Our distinguished guest is difficult." He sighs. "Thing is, we've got to treat the guy with kid gloves. He's on a special project. The government is paying top dollar for him to conduct research at the marine lab. Whatever he wants, he gets."

Casey lets out his breath.

Welcome to being treated like dogmeat.

"Hey, don't look so glum. I've got good news. Abe Huddleston called. He wants you to work in the aquarium on Saturday mornings, in addition to your weekday hours. He says he'll need more help. Heath is going to be gathering a lot of live specimen samples in the submersible."

Live specimen samples? Casey scowls. He doesn't like the sound of that. The marine sanctuary is into saving sea creatures, not collecting them for experiments.

"Case?" His dad eyes him with concern. "Not the reaction I was expecting."

"Sure. It's great." Shrugging, he gives his dad a half-hearted smile.

"I'll never understand you." His dad returns to polishing silverware. "I thought you liked working for Abe."

"Huddleston's fine, but his son's a pain," Casey mutters.

"Casey." His dad puts down the polishing rag and spears him with a serious look. "Isaac Huddleston just lost his mom. He could use a friend."

Dropping his eyes, Casey sighs. "Right, Dad. I get it."

"Kaitlin Rose!" Despite the mansion's thick walls, Mrs. Hardy's demanding voice vibrates through the kitchen.

Filling a pot to the brim with water, Kait sets a pan of eggs on the stove to boil. "Why can't she call me Kait?" she mutters, wiping her hands on her frilly white apron. The ridiculous uniform is part of Mrs. Hardy's fantasy of a lady's maid, designed in the old French style. It doesn't suit Kait. She's hardly a petite French girl; rather a tall, tomboyish Irish one.

Pulling her black curls into a high pony, Kait puts on a silly lace face mask, picks up a heavy silver tray, and makes her way to the end of the long hall. Juggling the breakfast tray on her arm, she pulls a disinfectant wipe out of the canister that sits on a table outside Mrs. Hardy's bedroom. After covering the curved gold handle with the wipe, she pops open the door.

"Morning, ma'am," she says politely. Chin high, she breezes into the room and moves to the old woman's bed-side.

"Stop," Mrs. Hardy commands. Her palm snaps upward like a stop sign. Dramatically, she covers her face and nose with her bed jacket.

Kait tries not to roll her eyes. When will the old woman stop being fearful? The two of them have been alone in the household for months now. Kait is forbidden to go out-side the mansion gates. No one is allowed in. Everything is delivered. Despite the extreme isolation and excessive cleaning, the old lady's germaphobia is worse than ever.

Cautiously, Kait sets down the tray and lifts the lid on a plate of toast. Pouring coffee from a silver urn, she acci-dentally dribbles a few drops over the side of the delicate cup.

"Clumsy girl!"

Dabbing up the spill, Kait flushes. Despite her best inten-tions, the graceful ways of a lady's maid persist in eluding her. Why oh why did she ever take this job?

"What is wrong with you? Return that toast. Brown it properly."

Kait nods. Stepping forward, she reaches for the plate.

"Never mind. Leave it," the old lady snaps, shooing Kait away from the bedside. Flopping back onto the pillows, she puts a hand to her forehead. "Get my pills. I feel a headache coming on."

Thankful for the mask, Kait sets her lips in a grim line. Turning her back on Mrs. Hardy, she goes into the ornate bathroom and retrieves a vial of pills from an overflowing medicine cabinet. After filling a small crystal cup with water, she steps outside the bathroom door, watching in disbelief as Mrs. Hardy covertly devours the offensive piece of toast.

"Don't just stand there. Bring me those pills."

Kait hurries to the old woman's bedside. Holding her newspaper like a fan, Mrs. Hardy shields her mouth and nose, peering over the top. Kait shakes two pills into the old woman's palm and hands her the glass of water.

"Have you cleaned the library?" Mrs. Hardy asks, wiping her mouth primly with a napkin.

Kait's temper rises. Of course, she hasn't cleaned the library yet. The old woman has had her on the run since daybreak.

"No, ma'am," Kait answers. "I'll do it directly."

"You must feed the parrot."

"Yes, ma'am."

"If only Gabby was here. She'd know how to get my Frank's bird to talk." The old lady's lower lip wobbles, as it always does when she mentions her late husband.

"Sure, and I wish it, too," Kait agrees. Closing her eyes,

she prays for patience. Mrs. Hardy's obsession is maddening. Mary Hardy adored her husband. Ever since he died, she's been fixated on getting his exotic parrot to speak again. Since Mr. Hardy was with the parrot when he died, his widow is certain the bird will someday repeat her husband's final words.

Due to his wife's fears, Mr. Hardy died alone in the library, coughing out his life among his beloved books. The thought incenses Kait. Over the annoying lace of the mask, she looks at Mrs. Hardy with cold eyes. "Will you be needing anything else, ma'am?"

"That is all," Mrs. Hardy replies with a sniff.

Relieved to be dismissed, Kait moves quickly to the bedroom door. After shutting it with a loud click, she sprints up the stairs to the library.

The cage remains empty. *Oh, no, please come home.* Mr. Hardy's parrot has been gone over a day. Leaning out the open casement window, she frantically searches the treetops. Whatever possessed her to let it fly free? The answer comes with perfect clarity. She felt sorry for the creature. She knows well what it is like to be locked in a cage. Held like a hostage behind the big iron gates of the mansion high on the hill, Kait's not been off the Hardy property for months, not since the lockdown to halt the spread of the Sickness began. Now that things are better, she supposes she could just leave, abandoning the old woman downstairs. But she promised Mr. Hardy she'd care for his wife—and she plans to keep her promise—at least until Gabby Finch returns to work.

Her cheeks relish the cool of the sea breeze and her eyes drop down to the shore, drinking in the splendid view of the glistening silver gray rocks of Craggy Point. Leaning her elbows on the windowsill, she supports her chin with her hands. With all its changing moods, the sea never fails to calm her. Today the restless waters are covered in ivory-tipped waves. Beyond the Point, a lone surfer kid glides in and out of a spinning wheel of water, cutting a furrowed line through pearly celestine waves.

She should be out there surfing, too.

But then—nothing's ever the way we dream it.

Child, child, you're a fool...all because of love.

Mam's chiding voice cuts into Kait's thoughts. She cringes. The last quarrel at home with her mother was a terrible thing.

Calamity awaits, when you do not stop to think.

Dropping her head, she lets homesickness wash over her. Mam was right. Seventeen's young to leave home. Running off to America was a cruel and foolish act.

Lifting her chin, she shakes away regret. With the Sickness passing, there is hope. The beach is open again. She can finally do what she came for.

All she needs is time.

Time—

Her eyes fly wide.

Tearing out of the library, she runs down the stairs and races for the kitchen. How could she have forgotten? She left the pot on high boil. Water is frothing over the top, cascading onto the floor. Grabbing a towel, she rushes to turn off the heat. Skating through water, she loses her balance on the slippery tile, crashing into the stove.

The pot tips.

A rain of scalding water pours over her thigh.

Chapter Four

COLORS

Lorelei is on Care Watch, determined to bring nothing but positive vibes to Mama. Creeping into her parents' bedroom, she slips into the old rocker by the open window across from the bed, hoping her mother can smell the sweet scent of beach roses and sage drifting in from the garden.

"Hello, Mama," she says softly.

Mama doesn't stir.

A light breeze spins into the room, ruffling Lorelei's tide pool photos and Cara's high fashion drawings, taped to the walls from floor to ceiling. The bed is crowded with Tad's precious stuffed marine animals, overflowing onto a table piled high with Mama's favorite marine biology books, and poetry, which Papa loves to read aloud. They want Mama to be reminded of how much she's loved.

Talk to her, even when she's sleeping.

Tell her about the things that make you happy—

Lorelei leans in close to the bed. "Mama, guess what? I

think I discovered a new kind of octopus."

Mama's mouth softens into almost a smile.

Lorelei waits, counting the minutes and hoping her mother will open her eyes. But nothing happens. Mama shifts in the bed and groans. Disappointed, Lorelei slumps back in the rocker.

Take a deep breath.

Energy is shared–

Lorelei recalls Grand Ella's yoga classes. *Change defeated postures. Let go of negative thinking.* Shifting anxiety to enthusiasm, Lorelei sits up straight and eagerly tells Mama what happened under the sea, leaving out the part where she foolishly fell asleep and rolled off Amethyst. Mama is a stickler for water safety. That part will only worry her.

"A translucent octopus came floating through a curtain of algae fronds. You wouldn't believe how amazing it was, Mama." Lorelei's voice catches. Suddenly she doubts herself, reluctant to mention the inexplicable sparkling, colored arm lights. Maybe Casey is right after all. It hits her in a rush. She *did* scrape her cheek and bang her head... maybe the lights weren't real after all. Overwhelmed with uncertainty, she finishes lamely, "The next thing I knew, I was safe on the dock of the marine sanctuary."

Discouraged, she sits back in the rocker.

Mama lets out a long sigh.

Trust your intuition. Lorelei.

Startled, Lorelei stares at Mama. Her eyes are closed, but there's a twitch around her lips. That small twitch is all Lorelei needs. Suddenly, she knows with a fierce faith that her mother *would* believe her. Good scientists are intuitive, and they're open to improbable occurrences. Fresh anger at Casey flares. For a moment she was second-guessing herself–all because of him.

#

Tad's anxiety is ramping up. He feels prickly and red. A lot of things are going wrong. First, Papa yelled at him for talking so much, then Cara hid his favorite video game.

Going into the bathroom, he washes his hands for five minutes, counting to himself. The warm water and the counting are soothing. The red feeling fades into the calm of blue. After drying his hands, he drops the white towel in the laundry basket and sneaks down the hall to Lori's room.

Even though he shouldn't go in without permission, he doesn't think she'll be mad. He likes his big sister's room, small and cozy, with a window opening to the shady backyard garden with the catalpa tree. He likes how the catalpa bends in the breeze, nodding its big heart-shaped leaves.

Tiptoeing over to the dresser, he looks into the starfish mirror hanging above it. The mirror is extra sparkly today, tossing glints of rainbow light around the room. Gazing into the glass, he studies the ring of multi-colored lights reflected in his eyes, liking how the lights dance and play in the shifts of the sun.

A flash of color streaks across the glass of the window opening into the garden. The top of the catalpa tree is shaking. At the top of the tree, a turquoise and silver parrot with a scarlet breast fluffs its wings. A heart-shaped leaf floats down to the windowsill. Tad smiles. Mama says the leaves of the catalpa are messages of love.

The parrot is sending him love.

The tree stops shaking. Reverently, Tad picks up the heart-shaped leaf and puts it in his pocket. When the parrot flies away, he retrieves Lori's laptop from her bookcase and sits on her bed, careful not to muss up the covers. She doesn't mind if he uses her computer, though he is supposed to ask first.

As the computer boots up, Tad thinks about how glad he is that his big sister lets him look at her tide pool files. Going through the files relaxes him, taking his mind off worries. Like how Papa is always jumping up to check on Mama, forgetting to cook dinner, and letting Cara do whatever she wants. The last thing is the worst. Big trouble is coming, Tad is sure of it. Cara's been sneaking out to meet boys—and Papa hasn't noticed.

Tad opens the tide pool files. He knows the contents by heart. When he opens each file, he says the scientific name of the sea creature out loud, liking how the words roll off his tongue. Mud Bottom Sea Worm. Sunburst Anemone. Baby Sea Dragon.

Methodically, he clicks through the tide pool files. Three are his favorites. Rare finds—a Devil's Fork Stingray with a neon orange tail, a brutal-looking Lionfish (scarily poisonous), and a Puss Mouth Moray Eel, hardly ever found on the coast.

After reviewing the files, he sits with the computer in his lap, feeling the warmth, reluctant to leave. Lori's room is peaceful and quiet. When he's in his own room, Cara's music thumps through the walls. She plays music way too loud.

"Caught you."

Tad pulls his eyes from the screen. Cara stands in the doorway, smirking.

"Taddy." Coming closer, she keeps her voice low.

His eyes narrow. Cara only uses his baby name when she wants something.

"Whatever you want, I want my video game back," he tells her.

"Fine," she says, rolling her eyes. "If you take my Care Watch."

Tad's mind races. Cara has an angle (that's what Lori calls it when Cara tricks people). Cara is tricking him into taking her Care Watch again. "It's your turn," he answers.

"Papa doesn't care." Tossing her long brown curls over her shoulders, she opens her eyes wide and flutters her lashes.

Tad studies her. People say Cara is very pretty. But right now, she is trying to trick him, and he does not think she is pretty.

"You are going out to meet boys," he says, crossing his arms across his chest. A warning of pink annoyance makes him flush. Tad knows Cara has not asked Papa if it's okay to trade Care Watch. Her eyes are open way too wide.

"*One* boy, Tad," she answers carelessly. "If you trade Care Watch, you'll get your video game back, and I'll take your turn this afternoon."

"Fine," he says flatly, not wanting to admit he is glad to take her Care Watch. And he knows she won't be home in time to take his turn. He doesn't care. He likes to be with Mama as much as he can.

"Your video game is in the bottom of the laundry basket," she says victoriously.

Without a backward glance, she flounces out of the room.

Lorelei studies Papa as they finish washing up lunch dishes. The crease in his brow is deeper than ever. Cara has sneaked out to go to the beach again, and Tad is with Mama, though it's Cara's turn for Care Watch.

Every day Papa is more exhausted and forgetful. Each evening he is with Mama, waking her up to feed her small spoonfuls of broth. Late into the night he reads her poetry and then works on his laptop, trying to keep his small online chef's business going. Before the Sickness closed the businesses in town, Papa was a chef at a big hotel.

"Want me to stay home from the beach?" Lorelei asks softly.

"No, hija." Absentmindedly, he pats her arm. "Go hang out with Condi." Pouring a mug of coffee, he sags against the kitchen counter, looking at her with sad, lost eyes. "But please, no more accidents. You were lucky you didn't drown."

Lorelei drops her eyes. "Don't worry. I'm not going in the water today. Just to the surf shop, then Condi and I are getting gelato at Maretti's Food Truck."

Her father cracks a wan smile. "Tell Condi hi for me."

After giving her father a hug, she slips out the front door. With her tide pool notebook tucked in her backpack—just in case—she's set for the long hike over the hill to the cove. The day is pristine, clouds floating like laundry-white fluff in a denim-blue sky.

When she crests the hill and sees the sea, she stops to inhale with delight. Atop the hill, the entire cove is in view, the ocean shining, whipped with froths of foam, filling the long, sweeping curve extending from Craggy Point to Windy Hollow. Leaning over a low fence overhung with beach roses, she delights in the stunning beauty of the beach below, loving how great she feels. The tightness in her chest is gone, her appetite is back, energy flowing like it used to.

"Dom!" A high-pitched giggle rings out of the grove of olive trees at the base of the hill.

Lorelei winces. Cara's pink beach towel is flung carelessly on a patch of grass.

Storming down the hill, Lorelei hurries into the grove. Under a silver-trunked tree are two figures. One of them is Dom Jacobs, three grades too old for her little sister. Cara, in a skimpy pink bikini, pulls away from Dom and leans against a tree.

Snatching the pink towel up off the grass, Lorelei flings it at her little sister.

Casually, Dom stretches out a brawny arm and snags the towel. With a mock bow, he hands it to Cara.

"What is your problem, Lorelei?" Cara hisses.

"MY problem?"

Dom backs away. "Later, Cara," he says quickly and jogs off toward the beach.

"Thanks a lot," Cara says bitterly, knotting the pink towel at her waist.

"Are you kidding me?" Lorelei retorts. "Making out with Dom Jacobs? How could you?" She shakes her head. "You know you can't bring germs home to Mama."

To Lorelei's surprise, Cara's face crumples and her eyes fill with tears. "I know," she sniffles. "I'm the worst."

"Dom's too old for you," Lorelei says firmly.

"I know, but I've liked him for so long. Before the Sickness, he never even looked at me."

"You can't trust a boy like that," Lorelei reminds her. "Dom's into lots of girls."

With a sudden shift in mood, Cara lifts her chin. "What do you know, Lorelei? You can't understand." She glares at her sister. "You *already* have a boyfriend."

Lorelei lets out her breath. The shot hits home. Cara has a point. Though Lorelei is furious at Casey right now, she can't imagine what it would be like to have gone through lockdown without him. Every day she looked forward to their nightly ZoomIn calls; all day she listened for the ping of his texts. Cara didn't have any of that. She's thirteen. Of course she wants a boyfriend.

"I get it," Lorelei says, "but you know we can't—"

Cara's lower lip wobbles. "The Sickness is awful. My life is over," she wails.

"No, it's not," Lorelei says wearily, not up for Cara's drama. "Go home. You've got Care Watch. And don't you dare keep trading with Tad. Show up when it's your turn—or I'll tell Papa everything you've been up to."

In a predictable snit, Cara leaves for home, and Lorelei continues her walk toward shore along the low beach road, thinking about Casey. Maybe she should forgive him. Cara's right—having a boyfriend is a wonderful thing.

Glancing up at the sun to track the time, Condi notes that it will soon no longer be a surfer's tide. Though right now the waves are big and friendly, horizon line waves are pulling back, running low and flat. There's a strange lassitude in the air. The day is beautiful, but the wind is shifting.

Making a final run, Condi points her board toward shore. Gliding on top of a glorious swell, she is filled with the energy of the sea. The pain lets go, emptying her heart and setting her free—at least for a little while.

On the shore, she lifts Aquamarine to her shoulder and heads up the beach to the Billabong, eager to talk to Andy

Marshall before she meets Lorelei.

"Hey, Andy," she calls as she swings open the screen door to the surf shop and steps inside.

"Hey, my girl." Bent over the long counter, white hair in a ponytail, the old man is polishing a rivet on the nose of a sky-blue board. Straightening up slowly, he rocks back and forth on his heels, working a kink out of his back. "How is it out there?"

"Punchy," she answers, smiling.

The surf master chuckles. "Lucky girl." He wags a warning finger, eyes growing serious. "Turn of the seasons is mighty good surfing—but no telling what may happen. An equinox tide is unpredictable." He sniffs the breeze. "I can smell the changes coming. We're going to have a whopper of a storm in the next few days."

"I know," she says darkly. "I never trust this time of year."

Awkwardly, he pats her shoulder. "How's Grand Ella doing?"

"She's good now," Condi answers, "but it was super scary when she was sick." She tries to smile. "Thankfully, the Beachlings helped."

"Those fine old ladies show up when things are at their worst." Andy strokes the grizzle on his chin. "Always in the right place at the right time. Hard to believe they used to be the outcasts of the town."

Condi nods. Funny how things have changed. After the storm, the people of Dipitous Beach rallied together and built bunkrooms for the Beachlings when their homes in the cliffs of Windy Hollow were swept away. Now the old women are dearly loved—though it wasn't always so.

The bell on the screen door jangles. A bug-eyed surfer

dude with blotchy red skin bursts inside. "Hey, Andy," he says. "Got any sunscreen? I'm burning bad. Lockdown sucked. I turned white as a ghost!"

"Sure thing, Jace." Andy bends to rummage through a shelf under the counter.

"Okay if I stash Aquamarine in the storeroom?" Condi interjects politely. She needs to escape. Jace is a talker. "I'm meeting Lorelei for gelato."

The surf master shoots her a conspiratorial wink. Condi hurries out to the porch, retrieves Aquamarine, and maneuvers her way down the hall to the surfboard storage room. Pausing in the doorway, she takes a moment to absorb the calming essence of the room. Sun pours from the bubble glass skylight and prisms of rainbow light dance across the beach wood floor. Built to house Andy's prized collection of vintage surfboards, the room smells like surfboard wax, blended with the clean, bright scent of the sea. Like Andy himself, the space puts out a peaceful vibe, swirling with good humor (and more than a little mystery). The room is the old surf master's home. At night, the space flows with tidal rhythms and the soothing scent of beach grass while Andy sleeps...and perhaps dreams...of the stories told in the shaper's marks of his precious boards, made by master craftsmen from times gone by.

Quietly, Condi slips Aquamarine into a rack next to Andy's cot in the corner of the room. Suspended above the old man's humble bed is a classic old-school longboard with rudders, a vibrant jade green with a brilliant blue shaper's mark. Briefly, she wonders at the surfboard's story and why Andy chooses to sleep beneath it. She figures the story contained in the shaper's mark is special.

The surf master knows better than to invite any old surfboard story into his dreams...

Surfboard stories hold great power.

If you believe–

The garage-style window at the back of the shop is rolled open to let in the sweeping breeze. Leaning against the window frame is a molten black board. Drawing in her breath, Condi gazes at the board–Trustin's longboard, the one he left behind the night of last year's awful storm. Recovered from the ruins of the oceanfront hotel where the Davis family was staying before they evacuated, no one understands how the board survived the violent winds, but somehow it did. During the beach clean-up, it was found and delivered to Andy for safekeeping.

Reverently, Condi lays a finger on the shaper's mark on the nose of the board–a blazing orange-red flame.

The surfboard tingles under her touch.

Hope flickers in her chest.

Everyone in town believes he'll come back.

"Why wouldn't he?" they say.

After all, Trustin Davis was the best surfer boy in town.

Spying Condi on the beach, Lorelei hangs back, resisting the urge to crush her best friend in a huge hug.

"Condi!" Lorelei cries. "I thought this day would never come."

"Same," Condi answers, smiling with every part of her body. "You look great, Lorelei. But what happened to your face? That's a mean-looking scratch."

"Later. Promise to tell you the whole story." Lorelei

rolls her eyes. “First, let’s grab gelato and head for the tide pool.” She waves her arm toward the gleaming red food truck parked in the high parking lot. “I’ve been dreaming about *Cones and Cream* for ages.”

“Me, too,” Condi answers.

At the food truck, a cute guy leans out of the pass-through window, raising a red-and white-striped awning.

“Hi guys.” His voice rumbles out in a deep baritone.

Condi’s eyes widen. Lorelei suppresses a giggle. The last time they saw Vinnie Maretti he was inches shorter, his voice nothing more than a squeak.

Keeping a straight face, Condi manages to say, “Hi, Vinnie. Are we ever glad to see you! It’s been ages.”

“Too long.” Twirling a silver ice cream scoop, he grins wickedly. “What’s it going to be today?”

“Roseberry coconut swirl gelato on an Italian cream cake cone, please,” Condi tells him.

“Same,” Lorelei echoes.

“Got it.” Swiftly, Vinnie scoops up gelato, packs the cones, and passes them to the girls.

Licking a trickle of scarlet and white ice off the cone, Lorelei groans with pleasure. The gelato is heavenly. Italian cream cake cones are Maretti’s specialty. “Mm, so good. How’ve you been, Vinnie?”

“Busy. Working ’round the clock. Grocery runs and all.” Shrugging, he flips the ice cream scoop into a tub of soapy water.

“It’s great how you and your dad kept delivering groceries during the Sickness. I don’t know what we would have done without you,” Lorelei tells him.

“Thanks.” Vinnie blushes. Looking over at Condi, he adds, “Sorry we couldn’t make it out to the yellow cottage after the road barricades went up."

Condi's brown eyes soften. "Hey, no problem. The yellow cottage is remote. Thankfully, Grand Ella had the pantry stocked and Sheriff Coodle made it out a few times with supplies. The Beachlings brought baskets of fish and Trippy's sea harvest medicines." She smiles. "Those elixirs really helped when Grand Ella was sick." Quietly, she slips a few bills across the counter. "My treat, Lorelei—and the change is for you, Vinnie."

"Thanks." Vinnie grins and tucks the bills in his pocket.

"Well, then, I guess we'll see you at high school in a few weeks," Lorelei says. "We're in ninth grade this year."

"You'll like Craggy Point High," Vinnie tells them. "Teachers don't treat you like babies." He shrugs. "Never thought I'd say it, but I'm glad school is starting up again. Thought I was going to spend my whole senior year in lockdown."

"You're a senior already?" Condi exclaims. "Wow."

"Yep," he says proudly. "Next year I'm going to chef school."

Licking the last dribble of roseberry coconut swirl from her cone, Condi says, "Well, you've got a great start on baking, that's for sure. This Italian cream cake cone is the best."

"Grand Ella helped my dad create the recipe," Vinnie tells her. "It's an original."

Condi looks surprised. "Really? I didn't know—but that's my grandmother for you. She loves to share recipes."

The girls wave goodbye, heading up the hill toward the high dune of Craggy Point.

Once out of earshot of the food truck, Lorelei whispers, "Seriously now, when did skinny little Vinnie Maretti get to be so hot?"

Condi laughs. "I know. Those shoulders..."

Lorelei moans. "And that *voice*."

"Wonder if he's still crushing on Kait Dooley?"

Lorelei shakes her head. "Probably. But that isn't a thing. Before Mama got sick, she said Kait told her Vinnie was only a friend."

Condi winces. "Too bad."

"Mama says Kait has a broken heart. A boy in Ireland." She sighs. "Maybe she'll get over him."

Sadly, Condi shakes her head. "Or maybe she won't."

At the tide pool, Lorelei sits on top of the high rock, examining cracks and fissures, while Condi stretches out below, dipping her toes in the gurgling water.

"Andy's starting junior surfing classes soon," Condi says. "Want to help out?"

Lorelei laughs. "I can barely stay up on a board."

"That's because you'd rather be floating around on Amethyst, poking your nose into sea caves, looking for your precious sea creatures."

"True," Lorelei giggles. "I like to be looking under water, not surfing on top of it." Growing serious, she adds, "Remember how Marissa Davis hated corralling the little kids when she was teaching junior surfing at the surf shop last summer? I miss her so much, Condi. She loved sea creatures as much as I do, and I can't believe she gave Amethyst to me. Imagine, giving away your first surfboard!"

"Yeah," Condi says, looking away. "When the Davis twins left after the storm, we lost two amazing friends."

Kneading her fingers, she stares down at her lap.

"Oh, Condi," Lorelei says. "I'm sorry. You lost way more than I did. Trustin Davis was more than just a friend to you."

"It's okay," Condi says sadly. "I miss him all the time. You're lucky you have Casey."

"You're the second person who's said that today. The first was Cara. I yelled at her this afternoon for making out with Dom Jacobs in the olive grove." Lorelei rolls her eyes. "I was so mad. When she started crying, she reminded me I have Casey. Cara thinks she'll never have a boyfriend."

"I get that," Condi says thoughtfully. "She hasn't been around other kids for nearly a year. And everyone is terrified of germs these days." Leaning back, she lifts her face to the sun. "Please, let's not think about any of that now."

Lorelei nods and stretches out on the high rock. "I missed this. Hanging out and catching rays. Being stuck inside for days on end was awful."

Condi feels for her friend. Lorelei had a rough time during the Sickness. People living in town had to stay indoors. Condi and Grand Ella were lucky, living in freedom at the yellow cottage overlooking the cove, breathing in clear, sweet air from the sea.

"How's your mom doing?" Condi asks quietly.

Lorelei's shoulders sag. Idly, she picks at the sand, eyes downcast. "Not good," she mumbles.

Condi exhales. "That's hard." After waiting a long moment, she says, "Grand Ella heard that experimental research is going on at the marine sanctuary. A famous scientist just flew in to research a cure for the Sickness. Something to do with sea creatures." Condi stops short and looks embarrassed. "But I guess Casey's told you all about it, since the new scientist is staying at Arondale's B&B."

Lorelei frowns. "No...Casey and I aren't really talking right now." Slowly, she lets out her breath. "Besides, experimental research won't help Mama. It takes years to test and prove these things." She lifts her eyes and looks at Condi, letting her pain show. "Oh, Condi, when you lost your parents, I don't know how you stood it."

Condi holds her friend's sad gaze, wishing more than anything that she could tell her all the extraordinary things she's learned since that awful day.

"Hey, listen to this." Lorelei's mood changes. "An awesome thing happened to me." She leans forward in excitement. "When I was exploring sea caves off Craggy Point, I fell off Amethyst and got sucked under. That's how I hurt my cheek. It was scary, but then I saw a beautiful octopus with colored arm lights. Like nothing I've ever seen before." She hesitates. "In fact, the octopus looked a lot like the shaper's mark on Amethyst. Ever since Marissa gave me her old board, I've wanted to find a multi-colored octopus like the one on my board."

Thoughtfully, Condi looks at her friend. "Andy says shaper's marks hold energy and power." When Lorelei looks puzzled, she adds quickly, "Marissa knew what she was doing when she gave you that board. There are tons of undiscovered sea creatures. Maybe your dream is coming true, Lorelei—maybe you discovered something new."

Lorelei hugs herself tight. "Oh, Condi, do you really think so? If I have, it's because Marissa made me see that my dreams aren't dumb. She made everything seem possible. And she wasn't scared of anything. When the octopus wrapped me up in those sparkling, colored arms, I thought of Marissa and told myself to be brave. Then I blacked out.

The next thing I knew I was safe on the dock at the marine sanctuary." She shakes her head, remembering. "Condi, I think that octopus might have saved my life somehow."

Condi's brown eyes sparkle. "Sounds like ocean magic."

Lorelei slowly shakes her head. "Naw...that's not exactly what I meant. No offense, but I'm sure there's a scientific explanation. Casey thinks I saw colored lights because I hit my head on the sea floor. We had a big fight about it."

"Well," Condi says softly, "you were the one who was there." After a long sigh, she gazes out at the horizon. "I can tell you one thing–a lot of mysterious things happen under the sea."

Tad is glad Lori is home from meeting Condi at the beach. Now she's in the shower. When she leaves the bathroom, he will go talk to her. He is feeling anxious and red. While she was gone, Papa got a phone call, and it made him upset.

Inching closer to the living room door, Tad peers into the kitchen where Papa is typing on his laptop. If Tad stands very still, maybe Papa will look up. Breathing in and out as loud as he can, Tad reminds Papa that he's here.

Shifting in his chair, Papa clears his throat. "Tad." His voice is a stern warning.

Tad retreats to the living room. Breathing loud was not a good idea. Papa does not want to talk. He needs space.

Going over to the couch, Tad sits down, staring at the wall, focusing on counting ticks of the clock. Thirty ticks are time enough for Lori to shower and wash her hair. Just in case, he waits for five more clock ticks.

At the door to Lori's room, he shuffles his feet and

knocks. Knocking is the polite way to enter a room. He knocks three times very loudly.

Lori flings the door open. "Not so loud, buddy."

Tad studies his big sister's face. The scratch on her face bothers him. Though it is healing, he does not like it. Tad is sure the scratch on her cheek is trying to tell him something. It looks red and mad.

"Are you angry, Lori?" he asks. Reading people's faces is hard for him. Often, he is wrong about emotions. When that happens, Mama says to ask questions.

"What do you mean, Tad?"

"Are you mad that the ocean scratched your face and almost drowned you?"

She bursts out laughing.

Hurt, Tad wrinkles his forehead. "Why is that funny?"

Lorelei hugs him to her. "Oh, Tad, I'm sorry. I fell asleep on my surfboard. It wasn't the ocean's fault." She sighs. "In fact, I think I discovered a new ocean creature. An octopus with colored arm lights."

Tad's face brightens. "Octopuses are smart."

"You bet they are!" Lorelei's lips curl up in a gigantic smile. After pulling her laptop off the dresser, she flops down on the bed, patting the space beside her. "Come here."

Pleased, Tad sits carefully on the bed, arranging both feet flat on the floor. Lorelei flips open the laptop. Her fingers fly across the keyboard.

Tad watches intently. She is smiling. He feels happy and peaceful, soft light blue and white, like clouds in a summer sky.

"Look," she says, pointing to the screen where an ocean video is playing.

Thoughtfully, he watches the video. A common octopus unfurls, closes tight, then blows out a cloud of black ink, disappearing into indigo water.

"Inking!" Tad exclaims excitedly. "Octopuses know how to protect themselves."

"Yes," Lorelei says thoughtfully. "I've been thinking about it...I think maybe the octopus with colored arm lights squirted ink in my face. It wrapped me up and then everything went black. I passed out. I think maybe it saved my life. I was in deep water, Tad. When I woke up, I was in the shallows by the dock." She leans forward and stares into his eyes. "Do you believe me?"

"I believe you, Lori." He wrinkles his brow. "Why wouldn't I?"

She turns toward the window, staring gloomily out at the catalpa tree. "It's awful when people don't believe you, Tad. Casey is acting like it didn't happen, like the whole experience was a figment of my imagination." She turns back toward him. "I'm starting to not believe it myself."

"People think I'm imagining things all the time," Tad says seriously. "They don't think I feel my feelings in colors, but I do." Awkwardly, he pats her hand. "Only you and Mama understand my colors."

Lorelei squeezes his fingers. "What color are you feeling now?"

"Blue," he says. "Slow and calm—like low tide." He snuggles a little closer. "And safe. I feel safe with you, Lori."

"You are safe with me."

Happily, Tad smiles. Maybe now is a good time to tell her. She is a good big sister, and she will help him. "Lori?" he says softly.

"Yes, Tad?"

"I don't want to go back to school."

Her forehead gets a line in it.

"Kids make fun of me," he says. "I like being at home."

She lets out a long, slow breath. "Oh, Tad. I can't lie. In a few weeks, you must go back to school." Taking another breath, she smiles. The line on her forehead disappears. "But I'll figure something out. I promise. You just need something to give you confidence." Moving the laptop so he can look directly at it, she clicks on a link. "Today at the tide pool with Condi I saw a Nanny Poppins Sea Star." She pulls up the photo. "Blue with red stripes!"

Tad grins wide and leans closer. "Now that's a good one, Lori."

After she settles Mrs. Hardy for the night, Kait steps inside the library and gazes helplessly at the empty birdcage. The curtains flutter and swirl at the open casement window as a heady ocean breeze sweeps into the room, brushing across the beads of sweat on her brow.

The wrought iron door to the cage is flung wide.

The cage is still empty.

Oh, no.

Please, please, come home.

In despair, she limps across the room. The pain in her burned thigh is stealing her breath away. Gingerly, she slides into Mr. Hardy's desk chair in front of the big screen of the library's computer. The first day she arrived, the kind old man set up a password for Kait and gifted her an international ZoomIn account so she could make calls home to Ireland.

She notes the time as the computer hums to life.

A few minutes until she talks to Mam—

Anxiously, Kait shifts in the chair, trying to get comfortable. The burn on her thigh is beating in her blood, a deep, raw ache. No matter what, Mam cannot know that she's hurt. Entering the search engine, Kait pulls up a link. She needs something, anything, to distract her from the pain. She clicks. Instantly, his photo flashes on the screen—laughing blue eyes, unruly black hair curling over his brow. Her heart swells with love and grief. How could he be gone? They were in love—he was her best friend.

Surfing photos of Paddy McClain are all over the internet. That last glorious day, the world competition, surfing the biggest wave in Ireland off the Cliffs of Moher. Everyone in County Clare was there that day—along with the great wave, Aileen—rising off the Cliffs.

Paddy thought he was ready. Kait was confident, too. Standing on the high shore, hidden in the glade of oak trees at the top of the Cliffs, she was certain he would tame Aileen. Brave and fearless, Paddy McClain was one of the best big-wave surfers in the world. Rising on a sky-blue board, he dared to touch the sky, carving a path through a fifty-foot mountain of water.

In the end, Aileen broke him...

...and shattered Kait's heart.

Fiercely, she glances at the clock, then clears the screen. Sitting up straight in the chair, she ignores the throb in her thigh and waits for the ZoomIn call to connect. Soon, the full screen lights. Her mother's pale face beams out, backlit by soft gray dark. It is very late in Glengarry, Ireland.

"Hello, lovey," Mam says.

"Hello, Mam," Kait answers, smiling.

Peering into the screen, Mam wrinkles her brow. "Something's off with you, my Kait."

Kait glowers. No keeping secrets from Mam. In addition to a sharp tongue, her mother possesses the Second Sight.

"I'll not be discussing it," she answers firmly.

"Do not be lying to me, Kait," Mam declares. "My girl is hurting—an' 'tis not the Sight that tells me." She leans in close to the screen. "Tere's a wee pinch between your brows."

"I said we'll not discuss it," Kait repeats. "I'm blue. It's a curse to be never knowing when I can go home again."

For a long moment, Mam studies her daughter's face. "I canna fight with you tonight, Kaitlin Rose Dooley," she says slowly. "I'm missing my girl too much."

The pain on her mother's face tears at Kait's heart. Guilt washes through her. Why is it always hard to talk to Mam, even an ocean apart?

"How are things with Da and the boys?" she asks. Her father and brothers have been laid low with the Sickness.

"Da is better," Mam replies. "Rhys and Rory, too."

"And Pauly?"

Mam shakes her head. "Still weak."

"Oh, no," Kait murmurs.

Her mother's fiery eyes flash. "And you, my Kait, are not well. There's a mist of sweat on your brow. More than homesickness ails you."

Kait swallows. She's burning up, inside and out. How she wishes to sob out the truth, but she cannot let Mam guess how badly she is burned. Her mother has more than enough to deal with at home.

"It's warm here, Mam. I work hard. Mrs. Hardy keeps me on the run."

"Hmph," Mam answers. "You're telling a tall one. But I'll respect your wishes and leave it be—as long as you know I know." Her face softens, and she clucks her tongue.

"Rest, my girl, and close your weary eyes. I'll tell you a story. Twill help with heartache, and the aches of the body, too."

Relieved to let conversation go, Kait settles back into Mr. Hardy's leather chair, obediently closing her eyes. Listening to her mother's lilting voice is exactly the comfort she needs.

"Take yourself back to the oak grove," Mam murmurs, her voice a whisper of breath. "Remember the night we saw the faerie lights."

Kait sighs, falling back through time to remember.

Fresh and cool the breeze had been that fair spring eve. Fighting mad she'd been at Mam. After a foolish spat in the kitchen, Mam threw down her towel. "Come. This quarrel is borne of two fierce women in a wee small space. Let us take the air." Together, they held hands, going down the hill, the peat soft and springy, the mist soothing their heated faces as they made their way to the oak grove by the sea above the cliffs. There the sun was melting pink and orange, drowning in a bruised blue sea. On an old stone wall, they sat in the ancient forest of oak until all their anger was hushed. When the sun was gone and the ocean bled to ink, the faeries came out to dance. Sparkling pink, sprinkling blue, pricking gold and silver...everywhere and endless...the faeries spun circles of light around the eldest trees of the wood.

Lulled by her mother's voice, Kait dozes off, slipping into the place of dreams, the pain in her thigh a distant throb...

"...and so it is, when the faeries dance, under the crook of the moon, held in the magic breath of the sea." Mam clucks her tongue. "Time to rest now, my girl."

Kait's eyes flutter open. "I missed the story."

Mam smiles. "You know how it goes. It's the same one I've told you since you were a wee one."

"I love you, Mam," Kait says softly. "Give my love to Da and the boys...and a hug to Pauly."

"Remember the faerie lights." Mam places a kiss on a fingertip, touches it to the screen and whispers, "Light to dark, dark to light, the magic of the faeries binds us." Mam's eyes shine and sparkle, holding onto Kait's, enfolding her in an embrace of limitless love as the screen goes dark.

Kait stares forlornly at the monitor. Sweet ocean air wafts through the eucalyptus trees outside the window, spinning a comforting smell into the room.

"*Awk!*"

In a streak of light, the parrot dives into the room and swoops into the iron cage. The late evening sun glazes the bird's feathers, glossing them with silver.

"Praise be," Kait says softly. "You've come home."

Chapter Five

UNEXPECTED VISITORS

Casey couldn't fall asleep for hours last night. Now he's dreading going downstairs for breakfast. Though he's starving, he can't stand the thought of leaving his room. Leaving means facing endless prying questions from his mom and dad, who don't have enough to do these days.

All he wants is to talk to Lorelei. He's tried every way he knows to contact her, leaving messages on every platform.

No reply.

Ghosted.

Sitting on the side of his bed, he hangs his head, wondering how everything could have gone so wrong. All he wanted was to save her—and then to comfort her. She almost drowned, she hit her head, she got a concussion. Her story about the octopus doesn't make sense.

You always think you're so sure, Casey.

Lorelei's words fire in his head. He sits upright, flinching. Always being sure is what she's called him out for in the past. That—and not really listening to her.

Now he's done it again. He wishes he could take back everything he said about the octopus. There are hundreds of new sea creatures discovered every year.

Maybe he was wrong.

#

Without eating breakfast, Isaac grabs his guitar and heads out to the porch.

"Hold up, Isaac," his dad says from the kitchen. "I need your help at the aquarium this morning. There's a problem with the water filter in the turtle tank."

Isaac glowers. "Can't Heath help?"

His dad sighs. "Dr. Heath's out in *Limelight*. The turtles can't wait. Water's going bad." He eyes Isaac's leather boots. "Wear rubber-soled shoes. If you don't have any, I'll find you some."

Isaac storms to his room. Yanking off his leather boots, he throws them, one at a time, as hard as he can, against the back of the closet. All the stuff he brought from home is dumped onto the floor. Fishing through the pile, he finds tennis shoes, the ones he almost didn't bring. Classic Knicks high-tops, a gift from his mom's last boyfriend, an NBA basketball freak.

Swearing under his breath, he laces up the shoes. Electric blue and orange. Not his style, but better than whatever his dad might dig up.

He heads outside. Hot morning sun strikes his face like a blow. Squinting into the glare, he fishes in his jacket pocket for shades and stands at the top of the long stretch of stone stairs leading down to the aquarium building.

How he hates this place.

The marine sanctuary property is built into a cliff, the steep slope down to shore covered with trees. A path made of crushed shells connects two mismatched buildings—the huge one is the aquarium, the smaller one the cephalopod house, shaped like a domed beehive.

Tapping his ear pod to amplify the beat of a drum piece, he goes down the stairs to the aquarium and keys in the code. When he steps inside, his shoes squeak, announcing his arrival.

"Hey, Isaac. In here."

A chokehold of stale ocean stink grabs him. He tries not to gag as he squeaks his way down a long checker-board hall to the giant aquarium. The tank is a huge glass cylinder filled with cloudy water.

Frantically adjusting valves on a control panel, his dad's face is slick with sweat. "Clogged filter. Water's collecting algae." Jerking his head toward a coil of hose on the floor, he commands, "Let the slack out in that line, will you?"

Picking up the coil of hose, Isaac yanks out some slack. After wrestling with the stuck valve for a long minute, his dad resorts to banging on it with a wrench. When he cranks the faucet, only a small stream of water drizzles out of the nozzle.

"Knotted line," his dad observes.

Isaac extends the line by walking backward to straighten out the kinks. At last, with a huge burp, a long spurt of water sprays out over the cement floor, drenching his shoes.

"Got it!" Grabbing the hose, his dad points the geyser at a large filter next to the tank. Water rips away the clots of algae and muck, washing down a large hole in the floor.

"Check out the green sea turtle in the tank. He's a mighty sick animal. Thanks to you, now the water won't go bad."

Shrugging off the compliment, Isaac goes over to the tank and turns up his music. A huge sea turtle floats in the cloudy water, a listless, black blob. Though the turtle's skin is olive-colored, the domed shell on its back is shiny and black. Sprinkled into the dark surface are tiny speckles of white.

He leans his forehead on the glass. The carapace is as dark as late night, etched with colors, like lights shining on pavement after a rain in the city.

Cautiously, he taps on the glass with a finger, matching the drum beat in his ears. As the beat in his head grows more frenzied, Isaac taps harder and faster, imagining the great wall of glass breaking, splintering into jagged pieces, a single sharp one piercing his heart.

Wearily, the old sick turtle swivels his head and looks at Isaac with sad eyes.

The music drains away.

Isaac removes his finger from the glass and leans in to stare at the turtle.

I get it, buddy.

It's awful when you're hurting and everyone else is fine.

"Earth to Lorelei," Cara mutters. "Pass the milk, would you?"

Absentmindedly, Lorelei picks up the milk pitcher and hands it to Cara, accidentally sloshing some of it on Tad's plate.

Tad stares in horror at the spreading oval of milk leaking into his waffles.

"Oops. Sorry, Tad." Lorelei jumps up and mops at the milk on his plate with her napkin.

"He's going to freak out," Cara announces, pushing away from the table.

"I am not a freak," Tad says, looking at his lap.

"Of course not, Tad," Lorelei says. Whisking away his plate, Lorelei glares at her sister.

"I'm out of here," Cara says coolly, gliding to her feet and leaving the room without excusing herself.

"I am NOT a freak," Tad repeats in a loud voice.

Helplessly, Lorelei looks over at Papa. Cara is out of control. Why won't he do something?

But Papa is checked out, scrolling through his phone, and aimlessly shaking more salt and pepper on his eggs, pretending not to hear.

"You are not a freak," Lorelei tells Tad firmly. She goes to the toaster and drops in two more waffles. "You know how Cara is."

Tad's eyes are sad. "Everybody calls me freak."

"People are stupid," Lorelei says hotly. In frustration, she snaps the dishtowel on the table.

Alarmed, Tad reaches out to touch her arm. "It's all my fault. I don't like spilled milk in my food. Don't be mad, Lori."

"It isn't your fault, Tad." Lorelei sighs. "I'm not mad at you." Taking a deep breath, she reins in her temper. She wants to snap the towel at Papa, though she knows he's exhausted. Still...isn't he the grown-up here? "No one likes spilled milk in their food."

Tad follows her eyes over to Papa. "Papa isn't listening, is he, Lori?" he whispers loudly.

"No," she replies, even more loudly.

"What did you say?" Dazed, Papa looks up. But before Lorelei can reply, his cell phone buzzes. "Sorry, kids, got to take this call." Jumping up, he hurries out of the kitchen.

Instantly, Lorelei's anger fades. The incoming call was from Dr. Everett. Of course, Papa can't focus on his kids right now. His mind is on Mama. It's up to her to watch out for Tad.

"Tad, I have an idea," Lorelei says. "After breakfast, we're going on an adventure—to the marine sanctuary."

Tad's eyes widen. "Do I have to? There might be strangers there."

Lorelei smiles reassuringly and shakes her head. "I don't think so. It will be just you and me."

"Why, Lori?" Tad takes a long, quivering breath. "Why are we going to the sanctuary?"

"I want to thank Mr. Huddleston for fishing me out of the ocean. And besides, he's an expert on cephalopods. I want to find out more about octopuses. Maybe he'll know something about the octopus I saw."

Tad's brow wrinkles. "That doesn't make sense. You said Mr. Huddleston didn't believe you. He said your unconscious mind was playing tricks—just like Casey."

Lorelei sighs. Her little brother's memory is scary. "Okay, I did say that. But it doesn't matter. The thing is: both of us need to get out of the house today. I'm sure Papa will say it's okay. A trip to the marine sanctuary will be fun, don't you think?"

Tad looks uncertain. "I'm not sure it will be fun, Lori."

Lorelei sighs. Tad needs to get out. Having a positive experience in a new place will help his confidence. Her little brother loves sea creatures. Going to the marine sanctuary is a safe outing, though she thinks maybe Tad has a point–it's not a good idea to mention the octopus with colored brain lights to anyone else again.

When Lorelei and Tad leave for the marine sanctuary, he nervously counts each step aloud.

"Two hundred thirty-four. Two hundred thirty–"

"Tad," Lorelei interrupts. "It's a long walk to Craggy Point. Count to yourself, please."

"–five." The word pops out of his mouth anyway. "Sorry," he mumbles. Mama says Tad's mind is like a train speeding down a track; it takes a long time to slow it down.

Tad is proud that he manages to count his steps silently to himself the rest of the way. Five hundred and sixty steps later, Lorelei stops at the top of a hill. She puts a hand on his shoulder and together they look down the hill at the marine sanctuary, a sprawl of buildings above a rocky shore and a sea fluttering with whitecaps.

"Those are *really* big waves, Lori," Tad says.

"It's because it's almost autumn," Lorelei explains. "Tidal patterns are changing. It's called the equinox."

In the next instant the breeze kicks up, blowing in swirls and puffs, scenting the air with lavender and wild beach honeycomb, threaded with woodsmoke.

"The wind is shifting, too," she adds.

"Oh, Lori," Tad exclaims in delight. "I like beach smells!"

Lorelei smiles and Tad relaxes. Maybe the visit will be fun after all. Mr. Huddleston is a nice man. Once he visited Tad's second-grade class and told funny stories about sea creatures. Everybody laughed.

"Look at that little green boat!" Tad says excitedly. On

the rocky shore, a metal dock reaches into the sea like a giant tongue. Tied to the end of the dock is a small, lime-green bubble, bouncing up and down on the waves.

"That's not a boat, Tad. It's a dome-hatch submersible. Mr. Hardy bought it for the marine sanctuary last year. It's for ocean research."

"Who's that boy, Lori?" A skinny boy dressed in black has emerged from the aquarium building and is heading down to the dock.

"'Mr. Huddleston's son," Lorelei answers. "He moved here from New York."

Tad frowns. "The boy from New York looks upset—and he should not be wearing black. Black is not a good color for the beach."

"He'll figure that out soon enough, I imagine." Impatiently, she tugs on his hand.

"C'mon, let's get going."

"Wait." Tad pulls his hand away. Sometimes Lori is in too big of a hurry. "Something's wrong with that boy. He is looking sad."

"Tad—"

"Look, Lori. Please."

Lorelei glances down at the dock. The boy is slouched against the rail with his head down. "Oh." Her eyes grow soft. "I see what you mean." Quietly, she explains, "I guess it's because his mom died."

Tad nods. The boy on the dock is sad—because of death. Death is sad. Sad people do a lot of the same things. The way the boy looks with his drooping head is the same way Papa looks at night when he sits at the kitchen table. A rush of red anxiety floods through Tad. *Oh, no.* Is Papa worried Mama might die?

Panicked, he looks at Lorelei. "Is Mama—"

Firmly, she shakes her head. "No." She takes his hand. "Let's count and breathe as we walk down the hill."

"Okay."

Holding tight to Lori's hand, Tad counts his breaths. He is grateful that Lori answers his questions. Understanding is better than not knowing. His red feeling fades. Soon he is back to feeling his best color for times when things are new—green for curiosity.

When Lorelei pushes the door buzzer at the entrance to the aquarium building, it isn't long before Mr. Huddleston's startled face appears, and the glass doors roll back. "Lorelei. Your dad called to let me know you two were coming, but I thought you'd be here later. Casey's not here for his shift yet."

"We didn't plan to meet Casey." Lorelei sucks in her breath. Thank goodness Casey isn't here. "This is my little brother, Tad," she adds.

"Nice to meet you, Tad." Mr. Huddleston extends a callused hand.

Tad steps back and sticks his hands in his pockets. Lorelei shoots Mr. Huddleston an apologetic look. Tad doesn't like to be touched.

"Lori told me your wife in New York died," Tad blurts out suddenly. "You must be sad."

"Tad, Mr. and Mrs. Huddleston weren't married anymore," Lorelei explains quickly.

A furrow appears in Tad's brow. "What difference does that make, Lori?"

Mr. Huddleston smiles at Tad. "Thank you, Tad. I am sad. Julia and I were divorced—but I never stopped loving her."

Tad beams.

Before her little brother can steer the conversation into more unexpected places, Lorelei says, "Tad and I want to learn some fun facts about sea creatures."

"My favorite subject." Mr. Huddleston chuckles. "Come this way. Let's visit the sea turtles." He leads them down a long hallway covered with photos of giant sea creatures.

Thoughtfully, Tad studies each of the photos, his eyes growing big and round. "I'm happy you made me come, Lori," he whispers loudly when they enter the aquarium room.

"Shhh," Lorelei reminds him. "Remember to listen."

Mr. Huddleston steps over to a gigantic tank of curved glass stretching from the floor to a two-story-high ceiling, with a feeding platform in between. In the tank, a huge turtle floats on its back, hardly moving. "This fella is old. Look at his scars."

Tad's eyes dart from the turtle to Mr. Huddleston. "What is wrong with him?"

Mr. Huddleston sighs. "Poor guy is recovering from plastic poisoning."

"How did he get poisoned?" Tad asks indignantly.

Mr. Huddleston winces. "The usual way. There's a lot of litter in the ocean, Tad. A plastic grocery bag got twisted up in his gut."

"It is bad to litter," Tad announces. Two smaller sea turtles with olive green shells swim into view. "Are the little green turtles sick, too?"

Mr. Huddleston shakes his head. "Thankfully, no. They're healthy as can be."

Tad looks relieved. "I'm glad the big sick turtle has friends. That is a very big tank to be alone in."

The oceanographer chuckles and puts a hand on Tad's shoulder. "You're right. It is a very big tank." He glances at Lorelei. "Any questions yet?"

Lorelei shakes her head. The visit to the marine sanctuary is going exactly as she hoped. Tad is asking good questions and Mr. Huddleston is being kind. Her little brother is having fun. It's been a long time since she's seen him so happy.

"Lorelei wants to learn about octopuses," Tad declares.

"Is that right?" Mr. Huddleston gets an odd look on his face. "Well, now, that's a funny thing. We haven't had an octopus at the sanctuary since before the Sickness, but this morning I got a real surprise." Thoughtfully, he strokes his beard. "A male octopus was floating upside down at the end of the dock. Normally they resist captivity, but this one barely gave me a struggle when I hauled him in."

"That doesn't sound good," Tad says worriedly. "Is he sick?"

Mr. Huddleston shakes his head. "That's another funny thing. Doesn't appear to be." He smiles at Lorelei. "I haven't forgotten that you claim you saw an octopus when you got swept off your surfboard the other day, young lady."

Politely, Lorelei nods and decides to dodge any possible discussion about her octopus. She's glad Mr. Huddleston remembers she said she saw one, but she doesn't appreciate that he said *claim*. Sounds like he still has doubts.

"Casey said the last octopus you had at the aquarium died in an accident before the Sickness," she says.

Mr. Huddleston grimaces. "That's right. His name was Horatio. One night, he pulled out the drain plug in his tank and dried up. They can't be out of water too much more than thirty minutes." He shakes his head. "It's hard to keep octopuses from getting into trouble. They're crafty, the smartest creatures in the sea. Being in a tank bores them."

"Keeping them shut up in a tank is cruel," Tad proclaims righteously.

Lorelei shoots him a warning look.

Mr. Huddleston nods. "You know, Tad, I'm coming to believe the same thing. The lifespan of an octopus is short, only about two years. Shame for them to spend it in captivity. Horatio died before his time." His voice is serious when he looks at Tad. "I promise I won't keep this one in captivity long. I only want to identify him and take a few notes."

"That sounds like a good idea," Tad says, matching Mr. Huddleston's adamant tone. "He probably won't mind. After all, if he isn't sick, then maybe you caught him because he wanted you to. Like you said, octopuses are very smart."

Mr. Huddleston grins. "You may be right. Maybe he just wants adventure. Let's go to the Cephalopod House and take a look."

Though Tad is excited to meet a real octopus, the minute he steps inside the modest beehive-shaped building next to the aquarium, he feels pink. He doesn't like new places. This building is small and dark, different than the glass and light-filled aquarium. Sniffing loudly, he holds his nose at the funny smell. Lorelei nudges him in the ribs.

"Sorry about the stale air," Mr. Huddleston apologizes. Hurrying to the single small window, he raises the heavy blinds and opens it wide.

Right away, Tad feels better. Fresh air flows through the room. His head stops swimming. Light pours in, dappling the floor with sun splotches and shadow, revealing a large metal tank in the center of the room.

“That’s better,” Mr. Huddleston says. “Octopuses like the dark, but if we want to see our new guest, it’s best to have plenty of light.” He looks at Tad. “Want to help me slide back the tank cover?”

Lorelei comes to stand beside Tad. He feels yellow and happy. Together they assess the tank. The top is covered with a seamed lid made of a tightly woven mesh with handles on each side.

“Ready?” Mr. Huddleston asks, grasping one of the handles.

Suddenly, the tank looks big and scary. Tad’s yellow feeling turns to pink. His breath comes in fast gulps.

Quickly, Lorelei grabs ahold of his hand.

Tad looks at her gratefully. It’s hard to not be scared. Octopuses are unpredictable. Unpredictable is one thing he really, really doesn’t like.

Mr. Huddleston lifts the one side of the seamed lid off the tank, exposing a half-circle of water.

A gentle peace fills the room. Light from the window catches and shines on the nearly translucent body of a floating octopus. The creature rolls over, looking at Tad with soft, friendly eyes, gracefully opening into a shimmering golden eight-armed star.

Tad forgets about being scared. “You are beautiful,” he exclaims.

“What kind is it?” Lorelei’s voice sounds funny and surprised. Tad turns to look at her. Her forehead is wrinkled.

She is staring at the octopus, her mouth a surprised O.

"I can't get a good match in the database," Mr. Huddleston answers. "I need to do more research. Until then, he's a mystery."

"You keep saying 'he.' How do you know it's a boy?" Lorelei asks.

"When the third arm of an octopus has suckers all the way to the tip, it's a girl. If not, it's a boy."

"Amazing." Lorelei moves closer to the water, peering at the creature in the tank. Her eyes are big and curious. The octopus floats under her nose and looks up at her, widening his eyes.

"He likes you, Lorelei." Mr. Huddleston laughs. "See how he mimics your eyes. When octopuses are nervous, they narrow their eyes into a slit called an eye bar."

"Or change colors," Tad adds.

"That's right," Mr. Huddleston says.

"His skin is as clear as glass," Lorelei murmurs. "And his blood is gold instead of blue."

Tad leans in to study the veins of the octopus. Tiny delicate golden threads wind through the creature's nearly translucent body.

"I've never heard of a cephalopod with golden blood," Mr. Huddleston tells them.

"Maybe it's a new species!" Tad says triumphantly.

"Slow down, little buddy," Mr. Huddleston cautions. "Good scientists don't jump to conclusions."

Tad feels embarrassed. A twinge of pink creeps in. Maybe Mr. Huddleston thinks he doesn't know how to be a good scientist.

Lorelei slips an arm around him. "It's okay," she whispers. "You didn't do anything wrong. Look."

Slowly, a slender arm lifts out of the water of the tank. The octopus swivels its eyes, tentatively exploring the air, exposing a row of smooth, clear suckers. The arm rotates and reaches toward Tad.

Mesmerized, Tad meets and holds the creature's gaze. Tiny glints of light sparkle in the depths of the rectangular eyes; the inquisitive arm touches Tad's wrist, wrapping around it like a vine. Each sucker makes a sweet smacking sound, clamping down one at a time, as the octopus gently squeezes his forearm.

Thrilled, Tad looks at Mr. Huddleston.

"He's checking you out, taking your pulse," Mr. Huddleston tells him. "Relax."

Scrunching up his eyes, Tad counts his breaths like he does when he goes to the doctor. His heartbeat slows. Every part of him tingles. He feels calm and blue.

"He likes you, Tad," Lorelei murmurs.

"He likes me," Tad repeats in wonder.

After a few blissful moments, the tightness around Tad's wrist loosens and peels away. The slender arm lifts in a wave, then dips beneath the water.

"I'm glad he didn't squirt us with his funnel." Lorelei laughs.

"Or ink us," Tad adds. "That would be bad."

Mr. Huddleston shudders. "You're right. Inking is the most dangerous thing that can happen to an octopus in captivity. Ink contaminates the water with poison. The creature can die. It's called inking out."

Lorelei looks concerned. "That's odd. I didn't know they can kill themselves that way. Isn't octopus ink used for medicine?"

"Yes," Mr. Huddleston answers. "But it's not that simple. Octopus ink is used in heart and blood medicines for *humans*. Octopus ink is lethal to many sea creatures. When the octopus shoots ink as a stress response, the ink can kill smaller creatures of the sea in an instant."

Tad strokes the octopus's soft and silky head. "We can't ever let our octopus get scared." Leaning over the tank, he whispers, "We're your friends. We won't ever hurt you."

"Since you're his friend, Tad," Mr. Huddleston says quietly, "would you like to name him?"

"Would I?" Tad glows with pride. "My first friend."

"What about Flowy or Inkling?" Lorelei suggests.

"Those are names from my video games." Tad shakes his head. "I will need to think about it. A name for an octopus should be just right."

Mr. Huddleston smiles. "Take as much time as you need, Tad."

Chapter Six

THE SKY-BLUE BOARD

Andy glances out at the crisp lines of waves rolling in off the Point. Though the day is bright and clear, the waves are rolled tight, signaling a rising tide. Nasty weather ahead. Time to get busy baking the batches of treats for his beach bookmobile runs. Until school starts, a lot of kids are still stuck at home. No matter what, he won't let them down.

Carefully, he selects recipes for today's treats. Ella's coconut cloud cookies and strawberry chia macaroons are a must. Chocolate cayenne cupcakes for the grown-ups. He grins. Adults are beyond tired these days; a spicy jolt of pepper will pep them up.

After popping a tray of cupcakes in the oven, he goes to his workbench. At last, the repair is done. The gash blighting the shaper's mark on the sky-blue surfboard is gone. The custom board, of rare design, is fit to surf again. Satisfied with his work, Andy traces the unusual pattern of the shaper's mark...tiny colored lights, woven like a floating circle through a grove of giant trees, surrounded by silver mist.

It is a beautiful mark.

Magical–

A tingle of energy vibrates beneath his finger. Andy draws in his breath. The scene comes alive. Silver mist rolls away from the grove of great trees on a high shore; the ocean pounds, loud and strong; the salt air thickens with the smell of peat. In the tall trees, the circle of tiny lights twinkles in gem-hued colors as a sky-blue surfboard rises from the sea, carrying a dark-haired rider.

Sadly, Andy removes his trembling finger from the board and bows his head.

He knows the tragic story far too well.

Tad goes down the hall to Mama and Papa's room, feeling his emotions one at a time. For a long time, he didn't understand what the colors meant. When he was little, it was awful. The colors were mixed up, and they made him spin. Feeling all the colors, all the time, was confusing. Over time, Mama taught Tad that each color is a separate feeling, to be felt one at a time. Feeling too many feelings at once is scary.

Outside the bedroom door, Tad stops, feeling pink and nervous. He takes five long, slow breaths. He can't be anxious before he relieves Cara from Care Watch. Papa says Mama needs calm energy. Cara's energy is not calm. Nobody knows this better than Tad.

Tad's stomach clenches. The pink feeling darkens. Warily, he puts his hand on the doorknob, preparing to get his feelings hurt. The minute he opens the door, Cara will rush past him like he's invisible, pushing him aside. She will go put on her bikini, hurrying to meet boys at the beach. Cara loves boys.

Slowly, he opens the door to Mama's room. In the big comfy bed, Mama is asleep, surrounded by his favorite stuffed ocean creatures, looking peaceful. A warm rush of blue swirls around him, wrapping him up like a hug. The pink fades. His stomach unknots.

Cara surprises him. She doesn't jump up and rush out. Instead, she remains curled up on the cushions on the window seat overlooking the garden. Her head is bowed over a sketchbook. The only sound is a gentle scratching on the page.

Tad tiptoes into the room and slips into the rocker beside Mama. He likes to watch Cara draw. It is the only thing that keeps her from making drama. When she's creating fashion sketches, she is quiet and focused. The softness of blue spreads through him.

Nibbling on her pencil, she pulls back to study her work. Then she slyly looks over at him and smiles. Cautiously, he smiles back. She beckons for him to come closer. Biting his lip for courage, he gets up and joins her at the window. Keeping a safe distance, he looks over her shoulder at the drawing, a skinny girl in a fashion dress. The girl's shape is five lines, but the dress is too many wiggly lines to count.

"Charcoal," Cara says, holding up her pencil. "It smudges." With her pinkie, she smears the lines in the interior of the dress. The smearing brings the dress to life, making it look like it's filled with air and floating.

"Oh," is all Tad can think to say.

She frowns and narrows her eyes.

"I mean, it's pretty," he stammers.

Closing her sketchbook with a snap, she rolls her eyes

and stands up. "I'm going to the beach."

The flash of hurt is red, but he is not surprised. He tried to say the right thing to Cara. It didn't work. Mean Cara is back.

In an instant, he is smudged out.

When she leaves, Tad sits beside the bed in the rocker, watching Mama's breath rise and fall. Why can't she wake up? He needs her to be his mother again.

His eyes travel to the top of Mama and Papa's bookcase. On the top shelf is Mama's silver laptop, where it has been since she got sick. She used to let him use her laptop a lot. He knows her passwords and codes. She let him look at her files, except for the ones containing her research with Mr. Hardy.

For a long time, he sits in the rocker, watching Mama sleep. The red hurt feeling ebbs away. Soon everything is blue. Tad feels Mama's love for him, even more than when she's awake. Maybe love is easier to feel when a person is still and quiet.

Mama makes a little coughing sound.

Tad jumps up. Passing his hand over Mama's face, he checks to make sure there is air coming out. Her breathing softens. He sits back down, feeling pink. Worry is tickling his insides. He needs to do something. Not something that will make noise, but something that is calming.

Quietly, he creeps over to Mama and Papa's bookcase. The temptation to open Mama's laptop is overwhelming. But he knows it is not a good idea. Instead, he reaches for a book, one that is face down and open on the shelf. Carefully, he picks it up and smooths out each of the pages. Closing it, he places the book back in its proper space on the shelf. One by one he takes out the other books. Counting to himself, he smooths out each of their pages, then puts the books back on the shelf exactly as they were.

When he finishes, he feels calm, though his fingers still want to reach for Mama's laptop.

Papa will be mad, but...

Tap, tap.

The rattle on the windowpane startles him. He looks out. On the lowest branch of the catalpa tree, is the parrot that showers the garden with heart shaped leaves.

"*Awk.*"

The bird puffs out feathers of shiny turquoise, and silver exposing a red throat. Tad smiles. He's decided that the bird is the one Mama told him about, a Costa Rican parrot Mr. Hardy kept in his study to help with his research.

The parrot's name is Guardian.

Tad thinks Guardian is a good, true name.

The parrot is here to watch over Mama.

Outside the closed door to Mrs. Hardy's bedroom, Kait wipes perspiration from her brow. The pain in her burned leg is awful, making doing even the simplest of chores almost impossible.

"Stop fumbling around." The old lady's shrill voice cuts into the hall.

Balancing the lunch tray, Kait slips on the ridiculous lace mask, covering her flushed cheeks. With her good hip, she pushes open the door to the bedroom.

"Fresh chicken salad today, ma'am," she says cheerily.

The old woman glares. "It's stuffy in here."

After carefully placing the tray on Mrs. Hardy's lap,

Kait opens the window out to the garden. A burst of sea-washed air flows into the room, deliciously soothing on her hot forehead. She leans against the sill.

"Come away from the window," Mrs. Hardy snaps. Sliding her mask under her chin, she sniffs at the mound of salad on the carefully arranged plate, she asks, "Did you use thyme and dill?"

"Yes, ma'am."

Mrs. Hardy eyes the slice of crusted bread. "Sourdough?"

"French."

"I said sourdough."

"We ran out. A fresh loaf is arriving in today's grocery delivery."

"Hmph." Mrs. Hardy's finger taps the carafe of iced tea. "Pour."

Dutifully, Kait grasps the carafe and picks up a frosted glass.

"Don't spill." Mrs. Hardy purses her lips and studies Kait's face above the mask. "Are those beads of sweat on your forehead?" she asks suspiciously.

"No, ma'am." Without a single wobble, Kait pours the tea. "I've been baking," she improvises.

"Indeed." The old woman lifts the glass to her thin lips. "See that you stay well. I won't be having more sickness in this house." She nods imperiously. "Return to your baking."

"Yes, ma'am. It's banana bread. Your favorite." As soon as she can, Kait hurries back to the kitchen, yanks off the mask, and gulps down a glass of cold water. Then she mixes up a batch of banana bread and slides the pan into the oven, doing her best to keep her mind off the exploding pain in her thigh. The last thing she needs is to be caught in a lie. She hasn't been paid for months. She can't get fired on a whim.

Pouring another glass of ice water, she holds it up to her hot cheeks, glancing with bleary eyes at the bluebird clock over the sink. The grocery delivery should be here any moment.

Please—

Let it be Vinnie and not old Mr. Maretti on grocery delivery today.

When the bluebird clock chirps to announce the top of the hour, Kait limps out to the front garden. With the old lady's window open, she can hear Mrs. Hardy if she calls.

Slipping off her shoes, Kait sits on the bench under the shade of a twisted eucalyptus and stretches out her toes. The peaceful gurgle of the fountain is pleasant. Some of the pain eases.

It's hard to believe that the tranquil fountain was an anniversary gift from Mrs. Hardy to her husband. The basin is ocean-blue marble, rimmed with a ruffle of white-tipped waves. Inside the basin are onyx sea turtles, a tribute to Mr. Hardy's conservation work at the Craggy Point Marine Sanctuary. Kait shakes her head. The fountain is a marvel, though it's hard to fathom that such a sweet shrine of love was designed by the crotchety old woman inside.

Kait gazes at the white-tipped waves rising into a line of sky blue, the exact color of her Paddy's board. How odd that his lost surfboard ever landed on this foreign shore. Stranger still that a surf master named Andy Marshall recognized the board by the shaper's mark. The old man read about Paddy's accident in a surfing magazine. Since Paddy had no family, it was well publicized that what little he owned was left to Kait Dooley, his longtime girlfriend. A man of integrity, Andy tracked Kait down in Ireland.

Kait took the phone call from the surf master as a sign. Without a second's thought, she told Andy not to ship the board. She said she would come to Dipitous Beach instead. Crazy with grief, she'd fought with Mam. Without her mother's blessing, she ran away to America. Andy found her a job and a place to live with Frank and Mary Hardy. He promised to repair Paddy's board and teach her to surf. Then, not long after—the Sickness struck. The town shut down, and Kait was trapped in the Hardy mansion.

Weary, Kait closes her eyes and lets her mind wander back to that last blissful evening with Paddy. The night was misty and velvety dark, setting off the faerie lights twinkling in the hidden wood high on the cliff. Holding hands, they sat on the old stone wall, two hearts pulsing in time—to the relentless beat of an ancient shore. The night was filled with magic. Time stopped in the star-spun glade, as it often does for lovers.

"Kait?" A deep male voice rumbles through the courtyard.

The front gate rattles.

"Vinnie!"

Going to the gate, her fingers fly as she keys in the security code. When the gate rolls back, Vinnie's smoke-gray eyes are smiling above the mask covering his nose and mouth.

"Take off your mask," she cries. "I need to smile at another living soul."

Ripping off the mask, he grins broadly as he steps into the courtyard.

For a long moment, they smile at each other.

"I'm glad it is you today, and not your Da." She stops, embarrassed. "He's a lovely dear man, of course."

Vinnie throws back his head and laughs. "I insisted on making the run today. Dad's getting too old to pump his way up this hill on a tired bike, dragging a grocery cart."

Stepping forward, she reaches to take the grocery bag. Without warning, she stumbles as her burned leg gives out. Her vision blurs.

He grabs her arm. "Kait?" The worry in his voice is instant.

Pushing him away, she limps back to the fountain. Grasping the basin, she scoops out a handful of cool water, splashing it over her flushed face and neck.

"What is it?" he asks.

"I'm okay," she mumbles.

"Don't lie to me," he says gently. "Something's wrong."

Defiantly, she shakes her head, and wipes the tears of water off her cheeks, ignoring the pounding of her thigh. Sick at heart, she knows what she must do. Vinnie cannot know.

"Kait. Please." He comes closer and reaches out a hand. His eyes hold hers a beat too long.

Exhaling softly, she lifts her chin. "I canna talk...I'm sorry..." Her voice trails off. Resolutely, she slips on the lace mask, avoiding his eyes. "It's good to see you, Vinnie. But I forgot. I have bread...baking in the oven. I must go inside." She takes the bag of groceries.

The quick snap of his shoulders reveals how she's hurt him.

"Got it," he says brusquely. "I'll be on my way."

Turning, he strides back to the gate.

Hobbling toward the house, she tries not to sob. *How can everything be so wrong?* Vinnie is kind and good and smart. He was her first friend in Dipitous—before he mistook what she meant for friendship and fell in love with her. She had no choice but to push him away. Now, she can't let him know she is unwell. She dares not lose this job in such uncertain times. If she goes to a doctor, who knows what Mary Hardy may do?

Before she reaches the kitchen, she smells the smoke. The banana bread is char. A nasty burned odor is curling through the mansion. Mrs. Hardy is pounding her cane on the floor of her bedroom. Old lady has a nose like a bloodhound.

Struggling to remain calm, Kait finds her way down the hall.

"Whatever have you done?" the old woman demands.

"Scorched the bread, ma'am."

"Did you burn up the kitchen?"

"Only the bread," Kait answers meekly.

Mrs. Hardy flutters her hand. "Light my Frosted Cherry Blossom candle to cover that ghastly smell."

"Yes, ma'am."

After lighting the candle, Kait hurriedly backs toward the door.

Mrs. Hardy eyes Kate suspiciously. "Have you fed the exotic parrot?"

Kait's temper flares. The old lady's pretensions are too much. "The parrot has a name, you know," she snaps. The hot words fly out of her mouth before she can stop them.

"Indeed?" The old woman's eyes harden.

"I'm sorry, ma'am." Kait forces her tone back to meekness. "But you know that Mr. Hardy called the parrot Guardian."

To Kait's surprise, the old woman's eyes soften and shine with tears. "Yes. I believe that is so." Squaring her thin shoulders, she waves a knobby hand. "You are dismissed."

Outside the bedroom, Kait closes the door and leans against it. Ripping off the mask, she takes in gulps of clean, unscented air. One excruciating step at a time, she gropes her way up the stairs to the library and shakily pours food into the feeding tray, leaving the cage door open.

After pecking furiously at the seed, Guardian twirls up to the ceiling to perch on the rafters. Making her way to the cushioned window seat, she flops against the pillows, finding a moment of rest in the peaceful library. If only Mr. Hardy was still here, hunkered down among his books and papers, snow-white head bent over the notes spread across his desk beneath the photos of his beloved sea turtles.

"Sure, and he loved you, too," Kait says, looking up at Guardian. "Maybe as much as he loved her. That's why she was jealous."

After Mr. Hardy returned from an oceanography trip to Costa Rica with the rare parrot, Mrs. Hardy pitched an unholy fit. For sanitary reasons, she objected to having animals in the house. To appease her, Mr. Hardy solemnly promised to keep Guardian sequestered in the library. After that, the old man spent long evenings alone in his study, in earnest discussions with the parrot. If Kait hadn't known he was in there with a bird, she would have thought he was conversing with a friend.

One evening, as Kait served dinner to the couple on the veranda, Mrs. Hardy was in a temper and lashed out. "Frank, don't stretch the truth. That bird doesn't converse with you. He only mimics what you say."

Mr. Hardy had patted her hand and laughed. "Mary, dearest, believe what you wish. Guardian assists with my research. Exotic parrots like Guardian are savants."

Mrs. Hardy was speechless. She never nagged him about the conversations after that.

"*Awk!*"

In three dramatic silver-blue circles, the parrot dives off the rafter and soars out the open window.

Thump! Thump!

The old woman's cane echoes from downstairs. Cautiously, Kait makes her way down the hall to the top of the staircase. Holding tight to the rail, she grits her teeth at the first downward step. Pain shivers through her body. Her leg buckles. Pitching forward, she falls headfirst down the stairs.

#

When Lorelei peeks in on Mama, Papa is sitting on the bed, attempting to feed her.

"*Mi amor*," he croons. "Time for a few sips of broth." Supporting Mama's frail body, he cradles her in his arms. Lifting her chin, she gazes gratefully at him, trying to make words, but no words come.

"Eat," Papa whispers. "Don't try to talk." Lifting a spoon, he gives her a tiny sip of broth. She has trouble swallowing and coughs. Patiently, he gives her a sip of water, gently wiping dribbles from her chin. All the while he talks to her as if they were at the dinner table, catching up on the normal events of the day.

"Tad is helping around the house, Gabby," he says. "You'd be proud. I trust him to help me with cooking—as long as his feeling color is blue or green."

At the next spoonful of broth, Mama shakes her head.

"Love..." she murmurs faintly, before slipping into a

deep sleep.

Papa sighs. The cup of broth is not even close to empty.

Lorelei's breath catches. *She's not eating enough.*

Going to the door, Papa steps outside, motioning for Lorelei to join him. When she does, he puts his arms around her. "Stay strong," he whispers. "You know that's what she would want."

Lorelei buries her head in Papa's shoulder, sniffling into his sweater. "Sometimes I get so scared."

"We're all scared," Papa answers.

Isaac grabs a banana and hard-boiled egg off the kitchen counter, ignoring his father, working on his computer at the kitchen table.

"Morning," his dad says, dryly.

Ha. It's hardly morning. Isaac was up until three, playing his guitar in his room. If his dad hadn't banged on the door a few moments ago, he might have slept all afternoon.

Without answering, he carries the food out to the wide porch of the cottage, the only place in this stupid house he can breathe. The morning mist has burned away, revealing a good view of Craggy Point and the south cove, though gray clouds are gathering on the horizon. Slouching into a wooden rocker, he peels the egg and tosses the shells into the flowerbed.

The screen door creaks open. His dad steps out onto the porch. "Dash of vanilla, cream and sugar, the way you like it," he says, holding out a mug of coffee.

"Not interested," Isaac says flatly.

Defeated, his dad sits down beside him.

Isaac hurls the uneaten banana into the bushes and stands up.

"Where are you going?" his dad asks.

"Anywhere but here."

"Be home for dinner." His dad holds up a warning hand. "There's a bad storm brewing—"

Shooting his dad a pity glance, Isaac sets off for the main gate and turns onto the high beach road. At the top of the hill, he stops and looks down at the cove. The waves are high and coming in fast. Despite the press of angry clouds, a few surfer kids are out on the Point.

He randomly chooses to take a rough path off the road, where a rutted path is protected from view by a pocked sand dune covered with scrub. With any luck, he can bypass the town without being seen and find his way to the far north side of the cove, to the tall tower of rock known as Windy Hollow. Seems like a good place to hang out alone.

Shoulders hunched, he taps an ear pod and turns on a ragged steel guitar solo that suits his mood. The guitar squeals, vibrating to a screech as a clap of thunder rolls and rumbles in the distance. A wind gust tears at his jacket. Swearing, he stops to zip it up. Bowing his head to the wind, he walks on.

After she cleans the dishes, Lorelei goes to sit in the garden under the catalpa tree. Mama has had a rough day and Papa didn't say a single word at dinner. The thick scent of rain is in the air, the evening oppressively stuffy and growing darker by the second. A bad storm is on the way.

The phone on her lap buzzes. *Casey*. Impatiently, she clicks the phone to silent. After the visit to the marine sanctuary yesterday, she's spent most of the day researching octopuses. So far, she's found no record of cephalopods with golden blood *or* ones with different colored arm lights. Identifying a new kind of sea creature is all she wants to think about. Anything to get her mind off Mama.

"*Awk*."

A silver-blue parrot spins out of the softening dusk and settles in the top of the catalpa tree. Leaves in the shapes of hearts flutter down. Idly, she wonders if the bird will stay in the tree all night, hiding from the coming storm.

The porch light flickers.

"Lorelei!"

She jumps up, blood beating in her throat. The urgency in Papa's voice terrifies her. "Is it Mama?"

"No, hija." Papa hurries toward her and puts an arm around her shoulder. "Mama is the same, but I must take you up to the Hardy mansion. Kait Dooley fell down the stairs today. She's in the hospital. There's no one else to care for old Mrs. Hardy. Mary Hardy knows you've had the Sickness. She asked for you because she thinks you're immune. You must go."

"Me?" Lorelei's hand flies to her throat. "I don't know how to care for a sick old lady."

"You know how to care for Mama," Papa answers. "Hurry. Go pack a bag. A wild storm is on the way. I must get you up to the mansion."

#

LaLa. LaLa. LaLa.

LaLa's gone.

Tad chants his baby name for Lorelei, repeating it over and over. He doesn't know what he's going to do without Lori.

Tad's arms twitch at his sides. Everything is terrible and red. Papa works all the time and Cara is mean. A big storm is coming. What will he do without Lori?

LaLa's gone. LaLa's gone. LaLa's gone.

Tad's arms lift away from his body.

He spins.

On the high terrace of the yellow cottage, Condi looks longingly out at the tall tower of Windy Hollow, wondering if she should chance it. The sun is a red-orange glow, blazing beneath cast-iron clouds gathering in the south. The ocean is lit with trickles of golden-pink light, the eerily lovely kind that precedes a significant storm. The tide is low, though it will turn soon. If she's going, she's got to hurry.

Wind whipping at her hair, she flies down the zigzag stairs to the beach where the wash of light falling across the slippery stones of the tower is beckoning. Picking her way through the broken shells and pebbles of the rugged north shore, she keeps her eyes fixed on the tower until she reaches the waterline. Slipping out of her sandals, she steps into the water. The tug of the tide is more ferocious than she expected, but the sand dune under the waves supports her like an old friend, providing safe passage over to the stone stairs.

When she takes the tentative first step to climb, a giant wave breaks, showering her with foam. The tide is rising, but time is on her side. The sky is sunset rose, the wet stairs mirrors of inviting light.

Resolutely, she climbs. A rumble of thunder shakes the tower. Unexpected lightning splits the sky, dazzling the Hollow in light. Maybe this wasn't such a good idea after all.

At the top of the ledge, she looks longingly toward the two half-moon rocks, blinking into the light.

What?

Wondering if her eyes are playing tricks, she blinks again. Huddled beside the orange-red kayak between the rocks is a boy, a glaze of mist in his onyx hair, beads of moisture clinging to his black wetsuit.

Ducking into the wind, she joyfully runs toward him.

The figure raises his head.

Abruptly, she stops.

Shock whirls, screeching like sea birds, ripping at her heart.

Of course it isn't him–

How could she make such a mistake? The boy's eyes are dark as night, not the turquoise of the sea. What she thought was a wetsuit is a black leather jacket. And he is wearing black leather boots. Fighting for calm, she steadies her breath. Wrapping her arms across her chest for courage, she strides over to the rocks. "Who are you?" she demands.

He looks at her and shrugs. "What's with you? You look like you've seen a ghost."

"Never mind," she snaps, shaking her head. The resemblance is eerie, though she wonders how she could have been confused. This boy is nothing like Trustin.

Another cut of lightning flashes in the distance. Bored,

the boy turns his attention to the clouds.

"The tide is rising," she tells him. "Lightning strikes up here all the time. Soon it will be impossible to cross to shore."

Expressionless, he doesn't move.

Her disappointment turns into a terrible coldness.

This time she's the one who shrugs.

Squaring her shoulders, she turns her back and heads for the stairs.

Tapping his pods, Isaac turns up his music. Another gash of yellow lightning bellows in the sky.

Whatever.

Chick confused him with someone else.

The next crack of thunder vibrates the kayak, pitching him to the ground. Abruptly, the music switches tracks to one of his mother's favorite songs. The pour of sound is like a gentle hand between his shoulder blades.

Keep going, Isaac.

The very last thing she told him—

Honey-gold, the music loosens the taut muscles of his neck. A gash of lightning strikes the tip of the north cliffs, shaking the tower. Alarmed at last, he struggles to his feet. A piercing wind blows back his hair as he stumbles to the stairs. Cursing his leather boots, he makes a precarious descent, trying not to look at the churn of wild water around the jagged rocks.

At the bottom of the slick stone steps is the girl, huddled into a crevice, curls lifting off her shoulders in a sweep of wind and tide.

"See? It's bad."

He stares at her. A few hours ago, the step where she is crouched was midway up the tower, the water he crossed to get here from shore was not even knee deep. Now the waves are twice as high, tipped like flames, straining to touch a crackling sky.

Terrified, he slides and gropes his way down the last few steps.

"I can't swim," he tells her.

"Seriously?" Her eyes flare wide. She eyes his clothes. "Lose the jacket and boots."

Kicking off his boots, he watches them spin into the tide. "Not the jacket. My mom gave—"

Exasperated, she says, "If you want to protect it, stash it under the kayak," she answers. "Hurry."

He hesitates, reluctant to make the treacherous climb again.

"Go back up. You need a paddle anyway."

Barefoot and shaking with cold, he crawls back up the stairs. After shoving the jacket under the kayak's hull, he grabs a paddle. When he starts down the stairs, a vicious spear of ragged light is hurled from the sky.

With a terrible groan, the orange-red kayak splits in half.

Grasping one end of the kayak paddle, Condi shoves the other into Isaac's chest. Plunging into waist-deep water, she shouts into the wind, "Hold on!"

The second she tugs him into the water, she feels him flounder. Like most people who can't swim, he's petrified.

Shouting encouragement over her shoulder, she watches him nearly go under. The resigned look in his eyes scares her. Gripping a jagged rock, she uses all her strength to sweep his end of the paddle wide, pushing him out of the powerful center flow of water. Forging ahead, she drags him toward the shoreline.

In the shallows, the tension on the paddle stops and she nearly face-plants in the water. Shaking the kayak paddle in fury, she whirls to face him. Wide-eyed, floating on his back, he is several paddle lengths away, disappearing into the waves.

This can't be happening.

Not again.

Stumbling to shore, she dashes for the zigzag stairs leading up to the cottage.

Merciless water, cold and black as ice, closes over Isaac like a lid. Every part of his body gives in, releasing everything that's bound and held him for so long. He wonders if he'll soon be with his mother. Opening his arms wide...he welcomes her embrace. In his ears there is a riff playing on an old-school guitar, a Black Strat, the words of the song the story of his life:

"I have become comfortably numb." [1]

In relief, he closes his eyes.

At last.

Chapter Seven

CANDLES AND CREAM

On the front porch of the Billabong, Andy warms his hands on a hot mug of cider, squinting out at the cove as rain spits fat drops into the irregular line of waves pounding on the shore. Who knows what strange surprises may wash ashore tonight. High circular winds, churned to a froth by the equinox, lure the deepest of ocean currents out of their foreboding sleep. After such storms, Andy's found many a bizarre sea creature gasping on the sand, types that haunt only the darkest zones of the sea.

He sighs and takes a sip of cider, trying to savor the tang. The truth is, he used to love violent storms, but not anymore. Nights like this are when he misses Frank the most. Lost stormy nights...when being young and bold and foolish was all that mattered. He and Frank—old enough to know better and too young to care—sneaking out to ride the big ones under a lightning-riddled sky.

Grief tightens Andy's throat. Frank Hardy was his oldest and best friend. Hard to believe he's gone. Flinging the last drops of cider into the wind, he paces back inside. After lighting the old ship's lantern kept for emergencies, he sits on the creaky cot in the corner of the surfboard storage room. Flames from the lantern set the jewel-toned vintage boards sparkling in the soft light, the wood shining, thick and rich and sleek. Andy relaxes into the comfort of the room. He guesses he feels about this space the same way some people feel about libraries. The ancient boards hold sacred energy, protecting the stories contained in the shaper's marks.

A high-pitched wind wails outside the surf shop. Andy gazes at the jade-green board suspended over his bed. Frank's old board. The shaper's mark: two foam-topped waves cut from cerulean blue. When they were kids, Frank said the double wave was a symbol of his never-ending bond to Andy—though that boyhood promise didn't hold. After high school, Andy stayed in Dipitous Beach, and Frank went away to college. After graduation, Frank married Mary. The marriage was a shock, a thing Andy never could understand. Though Frank and Mary made their home in Dipitous, and Frank often stopped by the Billabong to hang out with Andy, it took a lot of strength for Andy to endure those conversations. His heart had been well and truly broken.

When Frank knew he had the Sickness, he sent for Andy and asked him to come right away. When Andy pulled up at the front gate of the mansion, Frank was waiting, leaning against the gate, eyes dark and hollowed. With a shaking hand, he passed Andy a leather book through the iron bars of the gate.

"Keep this in a safe place—in case I don't recover." His eyes had held Andy's for a long precious moment. "Give the book to Gabby Finch. She'll know what to do with it."

#

The iron gate of the Hardy mansion creaks shut. Lorelei waves goodbye to Papa, blinking away tears as the old car chugs out of sight. Crossing the cobblestones in the courtyard, she dodges water from the fountain, now throwing up vicious plumes of spray. In the doorway of the mansion, an old woman, bent like a gnarled root, is leaning on her cane. Behind her, the mansion looms huge and cold.

"Come along, child. I'm cold." Impatiently, Mrs. Hardy taps her cane. "Hurry. Before the storm breaks."

When Lorelei steps inside, she fights a surge of panic as the door clicks shut behind her. The empty front hall of the dark house is too warm, overhung with the lonely scent of household cleaner.

"Take off your shoes," the old lady orders.

Obediently, Lorelei slips off her sandals.

"Bare feet are unsanitary." Mrs. Hardy thrusts a pair of slippers toward Lorelei and impatiently taps her cane. "Can you cook?"

"A little," Lorelei stammers.

The old lady flourishes the cane toward a pair of swinging doors. "Kitchen's there."

Helplessly, Lorelei looks at the swinging doors.

"Gas stove," the old lady tells her. "If the power goes out tonight, you'll manage fine in the morning." She points to an arched doorway beyond a grand sweeping staircase that dominates the end of the hall. "My bedroom is there. Knock before you enter. Always wear a mask. Tomorrow morning, eight a.m. sharp. Toast and coffee."

"Yes, ma'am."

"I shall retire now," the old lady announces, "though

I won't sleep a wink." She jabs her cane toward the staircase. "Feed the parrot in the upstairs library first thing in the morning. Second door on your right at the top of the stairs. A bag of seed is under the desk." Lowering her chin, she slowly taps her way toward the long hall.

"Wait," Lorelei calls after her. "Where do I sleep?"

Without turning around, Mrs. Hardy shakes her head. "Upstairs. Maid's room is down the hall to the left. Don't mess anything up."

"I don't mess things up," Lorelei mumbles under her breath.

"Indeed?" Mrs. Hardy turns to face her. Her thin lips curl. "I shall hold you to that."

Embarrassed, Lorelei stares down at the ugly slipper socks, wishing she could take the hot words back. *Old lady's hearing is excellent.*

Bursting through the door of the yellow cottage, Condi dashes inside and gasps out the story of the boy's disappearance to Grand Ella. Through a wild rush of tears, she describes him the best she can. "I don't know his name! I went up to the top of the Hollow and he was there."

"I know his name," Grand Ella says grimly as she tries to get a signal on her cell phone. "From your description, his name is Isaac Huddleston, Abe Huddleston's son from New York City. Clive called to say Abe reported him missing when the storm warnings broke." Jumping to her feet, she heads for the door. "Cell service is spotty. I'll drive into town." Yanking her yellow rain slicker off the hook, she grabs the keys to the old gray van and disappears into the rain.

The power snaps and pops. Lights in the cottage flicker, then go out. Groping her way to the hall closet, Condi retrieves an emergency flashlight. Teeth chattering, she climbs up the ladder to her loft bedroom, strips off her wet clothes, and pulls on a pair of sweats and a warm sweatshirt. Descending the ladder, she throws herself on the sofa and hugs a yoga blanket around her, praying the simplest prayer she knows.

Please, please, please.

Even as she says the words, she knows it's no use. Everything's gone horribly wrong. Isaac has drowned, and now Grand Ella's life is endangered, too. It is a hard journey to Sheriff Coodle's house in town. If she gets there safely, he will call out rescue crews...and send someone to tell Mr. Huddleston the bad news that his son is likely dead.

At the B&B, Casey pushes roast chicken and garden peas around on his plate. His dad went all out on the meal tonight, but Casey can't taste a thing. He puts down his fork. Everything sucks. Lorelei still isn't responding to him.

"Son, eat your food," his dad says patiently.

Taking a methodical bite of chicken, Casey starts to chew.

A deafening thunder roll shakes the table, rattling the water glasses. His parents look to the window in alarm. Wind buffets the broad red awning outside the window. With the next great gust, there's a ripping sound. The awning tears off, twisting upward like a flame.

"Great," his father mumbles. "Another expense."

Calmly, Casey's mom takes a sip of water. "At least we got the umbrellas off the outside tables."

"True. Could be worse." Standing up, he clears the plates and carries them into the kitchen. The chandelier lights above the table sway, flicker, and pop, going out with a single dramatic *poof*. The room falls into darkness.

Casey groans. Never fails. Every time a major storm hits Dipitous, the old aerial power lines give out. Something's got to be done, but the small coastal town isn't high on the power company's maintenance list. In the dry days of summer, the old lines are a power hazard, a risk for fire. In wet seasons, they can't handle high winds and rain.

"Do you need help disconnecting appliances?" his mother calls to his dad in the kitchen.

"Nope. Got it handled," his dad calls back. During last year's big storm, a power surge did a job on the big appliances in the B&B's kitchen. Both the dishwasher and refrigerator blew out.

Going over to the sideboard, Casey's mom picks up his grandmother's silver candlesticks. "I enjoy getting the chance to use these," she says softly, smiling at Casey. Retrieving a box of matches from a drawer, she lights the tall red tapers, infusing the room with a gentle glow and shadow.

The doors to the kitchen swing wide. Casey's dad returns to the table and sets down three heaping bowls of vanilla ice cream drizzled with hot chocolate sauce and cinnamon.

"Eat up," he tells them, chuckling. "If the power stays out long, it will melt anyway. Besides, an equinox storm calls for a special dessert." He winks at Casey's mom. "I call this one Candlelight and Cream."

"David." Casey's mom giggles.

Casey sighs, trying not to wince at his parents' goofiness. Why can't his parents admit when things totally suck?

Still, the combination of sweet and spicy cheers him. Cold chocolate sauce and ice cream crackle down his throat, filling him with a sudden hope. Maybe Lorelei will be in touch tonight.

A loud sound of stamping boots rumbles on the porch.

"What in the world?" His mom startles and puts down her spoon. The door to the B&B flies wide, letting in a blast of wetness.

Dr. Heath leans against the doorframe, panting to catch his breath. Water runs off the hem of his pristine lab coat. His dark hair stands on end, damp and wild.

Ignoring his parents, the doctor fixes a steely gaze on Casey. "The emergency generator at the marine sanctuary is on the blink. We need to operate the manual pump." The doctor snaps his fingers. "You need to come with me."

Casey jumps up. If the generator isn't on, the oxygen circulators in the aquarium won't be working. The sea turtles will die.

"Hey." Annoyed, his dad steps in front of Casey. "I don't want my son out on a night like this. Can't you and Abe handle things?"

The doctor glares. "Huddleston's son's gone missing up the coast. Some place called Windy Hollow. He wants you and the rest of the men in town to join the search party."

Casey's mom gasps, "Missing?" Her hand goes to her throat. "But how—"

"Dad, Mom, I've got to go!" Casey interrupts his mother and heads for the front closet to grab flashlights. The sea turtles won't last long without proper aeration. Saving them is what matters right now.

#

Tad can't stand Cara's wailing. With Papa joining the search party for Isaac Huddleston and Lorelei up at the Hardy mansion, there's no one to stop her. Cara's never gotten over her fear of storms. Tad likes them. Tucked snugly in their house, he thinks the wind and rain feels like a weighted blanket, his favorite kind, the kind that keeps you grounded.

A booming clap of thunder shakes the house and Cara shrieks again. Tad feels a flash of red. Why does she think yelling is going to help?

Concentrating on counting, he pads down the hall to Mama and Papa's room. A storm like this will rage all night. With Papa away, Cara will continue to wail, so it's his job to take care of Mama. Even though he's not supposed to get on Mama's computer, he's going to anyway. That's the only way he can play Mama's favorite music. Maybe the music will cover up Cara's screaming.

When he goes into the bedroom, he quietly shuts the door behind him. Putting his fingers close to Mama's mouth, he feels for the softness of breath. Despite the noise of the storm, she's deep in sleep. Pink anxiety creeps over Tad. After the storm is over, Papa says she'll probably have to go to the hospital.

Unplugging Mama's laptop from the wall, Tad carries it back to the rocker beside her bed. He knows the password—each of her children's birthday months. When the computer home screen comes up, Tad clicks on the music icon and searches through Mama's favorite classical playlist; Beethoven is a good choice for tonight. A lot of his music sounds like storms and rain anyway.

The music chases away the last of pink and red. As Tad pulls his legs up into the rocker, he is surrounded by the peace of blue. Though Papa had to rush off to help look for Mr. Huddleston's son, Tad is content. He isn't worried about a little wind and rain.

His mind drifts to his new friend. The octopus liked him a lot. Sitting up straight, Tad claps his hands. He's just thought of the perfect name for his octopus! Lorelei will think it's funny. Tad hopes she will tell Casey. It might make Casey think before he decides to not believe Lorelei about something again. (Tad likes Casey, but sometimes Casey thinks he knows a lot more than he does.)

Tad smiles. He's going to name his octopus Figment. Lorelei said Casey thought the octopus with colored brain lights was a figment of her imagination. Casey deserves to be wrong about something. After all, he hurt Lorelei's feelings.

Dragging her suitcase into the maid's room, Lorelei fumbles for the light switch and then shakes her head. Why, in this whole huge house, did Mrs. Hardy give her Kait Dooley's bedroom? What an invasion of privacy. Kait's belongings are everywhere, personal photos on the desk, clothes tossed on an overstuffed chair. Kait would not want her here, Lorelei's sure of that.

Resigned, she sets down her suitcase. On the small wooden dresser in the corner, there's a lamp with a faded shade. When she clicks it on, a shimmering cone of muted yellow pours out. The gentle lamplight changes everything, the spooky shadows in the eaves vanishing to reveal a bedroom more spacious than Lorelei's porch-sized room at home.

Tucked under the high eaves of the mansion's witch's-peak roof, the slanted walls of the cozy space are a soft blue, the color of a summer sky. A can of paint sits atop a neatly folded pile of plastic sheeting in the far corner, alongside two clean paintbrushes and a roll of blue painter's tape.

Kait must have painted the room herself before the Sickness. When the Sickness shut down the world, how awful it must have been for Kait—she'd only been in the States a month. What a terrible way to start a new life in a strange country. Lorelei sighs. Beautiful, lost days...those days before the Sickness when everything seemed possible. Things with Casey were good, Mr. Hardy was alive... Mama wasn't sick.

Tentatively, Lorelei sits on the bed, an old-fashioned four-poster carved with vines and flowers. Laid neatly across the foot of the bed is a well-worn quilt of many colors, carefully pieced with fraying blocks of faded fabric, each embroidered with a delicate ring of circles.

I bet she brought this from home. Lorelei fingers the quilt, soft from many washings.

On the orange-crate desk under the far eaves is a framed photo of a surfer. Lifting the frame off the desk, Lorelei takes it to the dresser lamp and holds it beneath the light.

Paddy McClain, Big Wave Surfing Champion
Cliffs of Moher, Ireland

In the photo, a handsome surfer boy is riding a wave

higher than any wave Lorelei's ever seen, cutting a swath of foam through a dark teal sea.

Lightning cracks madly across the night sky, lighting up the room. Quickly, she closes the curtains and unpacks her bag, pulling out a robe, pajamas, and a toothbrush. After a visit to the bathroom down the hall, she slides into bed and takes out her phone to text Papa good night. Disappointed when he doesn't text back, she kills time by doing an internet search on Paddy McClain.

The name comes up at once.

Paddy McClain is dead. Killed in a surfing accident.

Heartsick, she stares at the handsome headshot. Laughing blue eyes...poor Kait.

Lorelei pores through the surfing articles about Paddy and his Big Wave Surfing championships. Toward the end of the internet listings, there is a small article from the Burren Brag, a small local Irish paper. Andy Marshall, owner of a surf shop in the States, recovered Paddy's sky-blue board in a cove in America one morning, recognizing its unique shaper's mark, a ring of colors in oak trees, representing the famous faerie lights of Ireland.

Respectfully, Lorelei touches the ring of tiny colored beads stitched onto the quilt. Each bead sparkles and turns like a twinkling light among a silhouette of trees. The quilt pattern must represent the faerie lights, too.

The low battery warning on her phone glares red. Lorelei winces, then turns the phone off. At least she doesn't have to feel bad about not communicating with Casey.

A crash of thunder shakes the attic room. The lights go out as the power blows. Getting out of bed, she puts on her robe and gropes her way down the dark hallway to the library. Repeated crashes of thunder rattle the old bones of the house. In the library, she waits for her eyes to adjust to the dark, then makes her way over to the heavily draped window and forces the curtains wide. To her surprise, the casement window is partially open, letting in splatters of rain. A grand view of the storm over the sea greets her. Lightning illuminates the waves, throwing up startling white arcs of spray.

After closing the window, she waits for lightning flashes to illuminate the room, a large space with floor-to-ceiling shelves stuffed with books and an ornate iron birdcage in the corner.

The door to the cage is open. A large parrot sits proudly on its perch.

"Hello," she murmurs, recognizing the creature at once. "You're Mr. Hardy's parrot. No wonder you come to the garden and sit by Mama's window."

In the dim light, the bird's eyes gleam like shards of green bottle glass.

Thunder rumbles; the lights blink, then flicker back on. The change is startling. Lamplight catches on long rows of titles set among bookshelves shimmering with honey-scented polish. The fine collection of oceanography books amazes her. No wonder Mama loves doing research here. There's even an antique glass cabinet packed with the goldenrod-yellow covers of *Ocean Geographic* magazines, dating back to the 1920s.

At Mr. Hardy's desk, Lorelei sits down primly in the leather chair and runs her hand over the gleaming wood. Above the desk is a framed certificate embossed with the seal of a sea turtle swimming in an azure sea. The certificate recognizes Mr. and Mrs. Frank Hardy as founders of the Craggy Point Marine Sanctuary.

On a small table next to the desk is Mama's logbook. Lovingly, Lorelei puts her hand on it, imagining Mama sitting at the research table next to the desk, happily taking notes beside Mr. Hardy, doing the work she loved.

A ferocious clap of thunder shakes the windows.

She picks out a book on endangered sea creatures and curls up in a chair by the window.

Might as well read. It's impossible to sleep.

At the aquarium, the air smells stale. Casey tries not to panic as he looks at the cloudy water of the big tank. The sea turtles are hardly moving. The tank needs to be aerated quickly.

"Get to it," Dr. Heath says tersely.

Casey doesn't waste a moment. He rushes to the storage closet and drags the heavy manual pump over to the tank. Once the hose is hooked up, he uses all his strength to press down on the rusty pump handle to get it started. After a few pumps, the hose shudders, and a spurt of air bubbles flows into the tank. Almost immediately the small sea turtles swim eagerly toward the bubbles. The large turtle jerks awake, makes a lazy turn, and floats in the wake of freshly streaming oxygen.

"Well, you seem to know what you're doing. I'll be in my office. Keep pumping." Dr. Heath heads toward the administrative wing, leaving Casey alone.

Casey frowns. Operating a manual pump to aerate a huge aquarium is a herculean task, usually requiring two people at least. It's obvious now why the doctor brought him to the lab. He never planned to lift a finger. Using Casey for manual labor was the plan.

After a few hours, Casey's whole body is tired. Operating the ancient manual pump is exhausting, especially when there's no one to switch out with. When the tank is less cloudy, he takes a brief break to conserve his strength. Shaking out his tired arms, he goes over to the emergency generator and randomly flips the switch. The machine makes an odd choking noise. Quickly, he checks the fuel gauge. *Full.* Yanking the generator away from the wall, he kneels and opens the generator's engine box. Thing is flooded with gunk. After retrieving an old rag from the mop closet, he carefully wipes out the fuel compartment and uses the handle of a small fish net to clear the inside of the fuel line. After scraping out a few clots of oil, he closes the engine box and flips the switch again. The generator whirs to life. Smiling in satisfaction, he wipes his fingers on the rag, thankful he once watched Mr. Huddleston clear a clog in the fuel line in the same way.

Excitedly, he goes to tell Dr. Heath. After he types in the security code to the offices that are off limits to the visiting public, the glass doors roll back. Casey steps inside. His shoes squeak as he walks down the hall.

"What are you doing here? This is a top security area." Dr. Heath is standing outside the open door of Mr. Huddleston's office, glaring at him. Behind him, file drawers are open, piles of folders stacked on the floor, a topography map of the sea floor spread across the desk.

"You don't have permission to be back here," the doctor snaps.

Do you? Casey bites back the hot words. Dr. Heath shouldn't be going through records in Mr. Huddleston's office.

"Got the emergency generator working. Fuel line clog," he answers curtly.

Angrily, the doctor firmly shuts the office door and strides down the hall. "I'm taking you home."

Chapter Eight

AURAS

Isaac opens his eyes. Dazed, he tries to understand where he is. Far, far above is the rocking surface of the ocean, glazed with tantalizing light. A monumental ocean current has flung him to the sea floor. Sprawled on a mound of sand, tiny shells cutting into his palms, he is trapped under the weight of tons of water. Next to him, a girl with shining amber hair and sculpted shoulders is holding onto his arm, shaking him awake.

Confused, he pulls away from her. His heart pounds. Stunned, he looks down at his chest, watching the rhythmic rise and fall.

I'm trapped underwater. How am I breathing?

"You've landed in Ki's Circle."

"Ki?" His voice echoes in his head.

The girl nods, pointing to the white clam shells surrounding the pallet of sand. "Ki is the breath of the sea. Shells in the Circle carry the ebb and flow of the life force. They are breathing for you."

He stares at her. Her voice resonates between his ears, though her lips are not moving. How is this strange girl tapping into his thoughts?

"Who are you?"

"I am called Auramar."

"How am I alive?" He wonders as his lungs inflate with air.

"Why do you care?" she counters. "You tried to kill yourself."

"I let go of the paddle," he agrees, "but I wasn't trying to k–"

"Coward." She rolls her eyes. "You didn't fight. You gave up."

He shakes his head. "I'm dreaming, right?"

"This is NOT a dream." Exasperated, the girl tugs him up and off the sand. Sweeping her fingers over the sea floor, she picks up a small white shell. "Put this in your pocket."

"What for?" he asks.

Her eyes, a clear blue-green, assess him coldly. "Don't ask questions. There isn't time." Impatiently, she closes his fingers around the shell. "Do as I say."

Puzzled, he opens his hand and looks at the shell, then back at her.

"We're not staying," she tells him. "If you don't have one of Ki's shells, you can't breathe outside the Circle."

Her voice is fierce, and her eyes bore through him like lasers. He slides the shell into the pocket of his jeans.

Grabbing his arm, she tugs him upward, pulling him away from the sand and swimming toward the perimeter of clam shells. When they break out of the Circle, the temperature drops, the light dims, and the water changes from lavender to indigo.

Isaac shivers. The girl is swimming with terrible urgency. Her powerful frog kicks propel them upward despite the downward pull of the current. Helpless, he is pulled along in her wake. All around him flickers of electrical light in neon colors buzz through the dark waters, twisting into eerie patterns without shape. There is no identifiable source of light. It is terrifying.

At the crest of a ridge, the darkness lifts, fading from indigo back to violet.

"We made it through the Dark Zone," the girl says, smiling for the first time. "Things get easier from here."

A giant sea turtle, moving in the slow rhythm of a prelude, swims out of a dense cluster of algae and hovers in front of them.

"Climb aboard," the girl says, nudging Isaac forward.

Isaac hesitates. She can't be serious. The creature's carapace is as shiny as a polished jewel and looks twice as slippery.

"Grab the neck of the shell."

Awkwardly, he stretches out and reaches for the turtle's powerful neck. The turtle rolls slightly, allowing him to throw a leg over the broad domed back. As soon as Isaac balances his weight, the turtle rolls to center and lurches forward, moving with slow, thrusting power.

"Hey, aren't you coming?" he cries, looking back over his shoulder at the girl.

"I'll be along."

The ponderous body rises through the bruised blue water. Making a sweeping turn, the creature throttles upward, heading toward a dusky purple ridge in the distance. At the end of the long climb, the turtle bursts up and over the high summit of a great sea mountain.

Again, the light changes. Though tinged with strands of amethyst, the water here is much lighter, a clear aquamarine. Sun streams down from the surface waters, illuminating a vast colony of golden-green kelp swaying like underwater trees in a fluid forest.

"We made it."

Isaac looks over. Auramar is beside him, straddling an indigo surfboard. Her sculpted shoulders shimmer with radiant light. She is beautiful—in a dazzling and totally unbelievable way. He grins. This is one of the best dreams he's ever had.

Wryly, she shakes her head. "Isn't what you think." With an elegant toss of her head, she flops onto her tummy. "Follow me." Catching the beat of the current, she paddles away.

With a surge of strength, the turtle takes off, swimming steadily behind the girl on the indigo board. For miles, they travel through the sunlit sea toward an underwater volcano towering in the distance, oozing a filmy silver mist. Isaac grows tired and sleepy. By the time they arrive at the base of the steaming mountain, he is clinging to the slick carapace in quiet desperation.

Silently, Auramar points to a cleft between two hardened rivers of ancient lava, where jewel-colored lights bounce off long oval shapes. Isaac squints unto the cleft. Trapped in a fissure at the foot of the sea mountain, caught in a blinding ray of the sun, two surfboards sway in the tide, one cobalt blue, the other ruby red.

"This is the Place of Lost Surfboards. Tucked in the arms of the mountain, they float in the twilight waters... waiting for the volcano to rumble," Auramar explains.

"Sometimes, though not always, lost boards are set free and returned to shore."

Isaac stares at her. "I don't care about surfboards."

She arches a brow. "You will care about these."

Defiantly, he raises his chin. He is over this crazy dream. "I want to wake up."

She looks at him with pity. "This is NOT a dream."

"Fine," he grumbles. "Whatever you say, but I want to go home."

She laughs. "You should have thought about that when you tried to kill yourself."

"I wasn't trying to kill myself," he answers hotly.

"You weren't trying to live. That's all that matters. If you want to get home, you have work to do. If I were you, I'd pay attention." Stretching out an arm, she places a fingertip on the nose of the cobalt blue board. The board shimmers. Slowly, a familiar beach scene comes into view.

Isaac's heart pounds. *Can this be happening?*

Rising from an azure sea, surrounded by the jagged stand of rocks, is Windy Hollow. Weaving through the rocks and wading through the frothing surf is a man, black-haired and roped with muscle. It is his father, years younger, but essentially the same, deep-set green eyes and heavy beard unmistakable.

"That's my dad," he mumbles.

"Yes." The girl moves her finger to the ruby-red board. "Watch."

The scene on the blue board fades. Under her touch, the red board brightens. Again, the scene that appears is Windy Hollow, though this time there is a rock bridge stretching from tower to shore. An old mansion is perched on a cliff, crumbling into the sea...

"That's the way the Hollow looked before last year's hurricane," Auramar explains. "The storm swept the mansion and most of the north cliffs into the sea."

He leans in to look closer. High stepping through the tide is a dark-haired young woman, moving toward his dad. The scene zooms in, and Isaac looks directly into her face.

"Mom?"

Those eyes...he'll never forget them...clear and gray, like pebbles in a mountain stream.

With a shaking hand, he reaches out a finger to touch the board. His finger tingles. At once, the scene expands and shimmers, transforming into a whole new scene. His parents, young and lithe and strong, are surfing together. His father is riding the cobalt blue board, his mom the board of ruby-red. Laughing into the wind, they make synchronized turns, cutting matching paths through a sheen of silver water.

Isaac is mesmerized. His mom (who knew she was ever that young?) is beautiful. When she rides the last gentle pulse of a wave to the shore and wades through the shallows, his father is waiting there to catch her by the hand. She smiles at him. He scoops her up in a giant hug.

Isaac shakes his head, unbelieving. "My mom said she hated the ocean. I didn't know she could surf."

"We don't know what we don't know," Auramar answers. "Especially when it comes to our parents."

"You don't get it," Isaac says bitterly. "My parents' relationship was awful. They couldn't stand each other."

"You only knew one part of their story."

"Yeah. The bad part," he mutters.

"Endings are only part of a story, you know," Auramar

says kindly. "Your parents loved each other once. Choose to remember what you've seen, and the good part can last forever."

Puzzled, Isaac lifts his finger off the ruby-red board. The smiles on his parents' faces crack and blur.

"I don't understand," he tells her sadly.

"Give it time." She looks at him with empathy. "We must move on."

The last of the scene fades away and the steamy mist around them thickens. The water grows hotter and wilder, and the sea turtle bucks in the crazed pendulum swing of the tide. Turbulent waves thrust them toward a knobby chain of caves in the stern face of the volcano. Isaac is filled with foreboding. One cave, the mouth much bigger than the others, flickers with an unsettling orange-pink light.

"Hang on!" Auramar shouts.

A giant wave rises from behind, lifting the turtle like a raft on a swell, tipping and pouring them into the mouth of the cave. Swept along in a mighty current, the steady flow of water pushes them into a high-domed cavern.

"Stay low." Auramar lies down flat on her board as the turtle banks, descending into a narrow, winding channel. The light fades, the walls of the cavern shrink, tightening into the spiral of a shell. Like toothpaste squeezing from a tube, they are pressed through a dark tunnel toward a small opening of light.

A huge surge of water smacks them from behind, flushing them forward—

"Hold on!" Auramar cries.

Isaac bucks and jerks, but he cannot hold on.

The sea turtle's body drops from beneath him.

For a time that feels like forever, he falls through a

vaporous cloud of steam. At last, he lands in a pool of silky warm water. Tasting beads of saltwater on his tongue, he kicks wildly, thrashing and tossing up spray. Frantically, he looks around. An arm's length away is a slick lip of rock, overhanging the steaming pool. Pawing through the water, he lunges for the edge of the pool and grabs ahold of the rock. Awkwardly, he pulls himself up over the slippery lip and flops his way to a seated position.

"Nice moves."

Peering through steam, he looks up. High on a clamshell balcony, under a rock crystal ceiling, is Auramar.

"Where are we?" he calls up to her.

"Air pocket in a steam vent," she says matter-of-factly, tossing back her hair and letting her legs dangle off the balcony. "Volcanos are living, breathing things. Sometimes they hollow out a pocket of steam and create an underwater cavern with an air pocket."

Looking around, he steadies his breath. It's wonderful to be breathing normally again. The cavern is miraculously filled with air, contained somehow within slick ebony walls. The great sea turtle that delivered him to the cavern is resting on a ledge. Auramar's indigo surfboard is leaning against a ribbon of hardened lava. The mirrored surface of the surfboard is clouded, drizzled with warm beads of moisture. Isaac is drowsy, the pool is popping with air bubbles, the warm water spinning in circles. Idly, he lazes back on his elbows, wondering if Auramar's indigo surfboard also has a story to tell...

"Maybe someday you'll know," Auramar interrupts his thoughts. "But trust me, you'll have to work for it."

"What's that supposed to mean?"

"You don't know what you don't know," she answers.

"Fine." Frustrated, he decides to ignore her. Leaning over the pool, he peers into the water. Beneath the bubbles and spinning circles, a pebbled basin is studded with glowing phosphorescent rock. The water clears and stills. One section of the pool is draped with suckers and webs of a sticky something, odd little hanging white blobs, like the gunk in strep throat.

Yuk.

Auramar laughs. "Octopus nursery."

Hurriedly, he backs away from the edge.

"What's with you? Isn't your dad an oceanographer? Brooding octopuses aren't dangerous. Octomoms turn themselves inside out to protect their eggs."

Cautiously, he eyes the contents of the pool.

Flash!

One of the white hanging blobs detaches from the sticky web and unfurls, exploding in a star of multi-colored light, stuttering across the pool, then diving into a crack.

The light dazzles him with sound, vibrating in his ears like an epic guitar solo.

"I see you appreciate miracles," a voice booms out from behind him.

Isaac whirls around.

On a slippery ledge, sprawled over the hardened molten rock, is a huge octopus, eight arms spread wide, like a colossal king on an ebony throne.

"Miracles?" Isaac stammers.

"You witnessed the birth of a baby octopus in the Metamorphosis Pool," the booming voice says kindly. "I'd say that was a miracle, wouldn't you?"

Isaac's mouth falls open. "I'm dreaming, right?"

The creature lets out a loud guffaw. An arm, heavy

with glistening suckers, lifts into the air and ripples down to the rock (a movement strangely like slapping a knee). The great body shakes, rolling with laughter. "Oh, my dear boy, is that what you think? How typically human, explaining my world on your own terms."

Irritated, Isaac glares up at Auramar, still swinging her legs on the clamshell balcony. "Can I get some help down here?"

She grins down at him. "Welcome to Metamorphosis Cavern, home of Koan, the Riddlemaster of the Sea." Shaking back her hair, she slides down a ribbon of black rock, joining him at the edge of the pool.

Isaac shakes his head. *How did I get stuck in a dream with a talking octopus?*

"NOT a dream," she reminds him.

Elegant plumes of steam lift off the pool, swirling up to the domed ceiling of the cavern, dripping beads of water on the dark crystal of the ebony throne. The octopus' great head expands, shimmering with a glowing white light. Eight arms flash with color, brilliant and blinding, each one different. As each color flashes, a pure musical note sounds, vibrating through the cavern with perfect pitch.

Isaac looks at Auramar. "What is going on?"

Her lips curl in a mysterious smile. "You don't know what you don't know," she murmurs.

"Tell me."

Nodding, she points to the orb of white light in Koan's head. "Octopuses have a complex nervous system with *nine* brains. The white light is the master brain." Lightly, she touches the lights at the top of each of the octopus' arms. "Purple, blue, green, red, yellow, orange, pink, and aquamarine. Each colored arm is a smaller brain. All nine brains work together, making the brain power of an octopus powerful and complex."

The brain lights flash, and more enthralling music plays. Isaac closes his eyes. Dazed with color and the perfection of the tones, he is having trouble listening to Auramar's words. Whatever tune the creature is creating with its multi-colored brains is the most beautiful thing he's ever heard. Lost in a river of sound, he is floating, experiencing a synchronicity of frequencies he never knew existed.

Isaac stares at Koan. The creature's head is blazing with a blinding light, while eight rippling arms lift and drift from ceiling to the floor like a great symphonic conductor at the climax of a musical score.

Auramar nudges him. "Why do you look like you're in a trance?"

"Isaac hears the various colors of my brains as musical tones," Koan explains. "He is a musical synesthete. His brain is wired to associate musical notes with color." Koan taps Isaac's shoulder with a green arm. "What note do you hear, Isaac?"

"Middle C," Isaac answers, shivering with awe at the perfection of the tone.

"And this?" A blue arm lifts.

"G."

Koan lifts a red arm, pointed at the tip.

"D sharp."

"Now for the true test." Koan winks at Auramar. Eight octopus arms lift and ripple, twinkling and flashing, in a complex show of lights. "What piece am I playing, Isaac?"

"Bach's Cantata 78." Isaac grins.

Koan chuckles. "Yes! That's my boy! Cantata 78 is one of my favorites, a musical riddle, a conundrum of light and dark."

Thoughtfully, Auramar studies Isaac. "You're a classical music guy? Had you pegged as punk rock."

"I like it all. My mom was a musician," Isaac answers. "She was amazing."

"I see," says Koan. "So...you choose to honor her talent by making yourself small?"

Confused, Isaac looks at Auramar.

"Think about it," she says.

As the last of the music fades away, the white orb in Koan's head dims, the colors in the creature's arms lose sparkle, shrinking into the gelatinous body. In seconds, the octopus morphs into a non-descript blob spread over the black rock.

A disturbing transformation–

Falling on his knees, Isaac begs, "Please, don't stop the music."

To his relief, the arms of the great octopus expand and fill with color. A haunting cello solo flows through the cavern, thick and golden, rich with the sweet and sticky ache of memory. Bowing his head, Isaac cradles his face in his hands. "My mom played every instrument...but she loved the cello most of all."

"Isaac, Isaac, my dear, dear boy," Koan says softly. "Look at me." Mournfully, the octopus shakes his head. "You must go on, learning to love what she left behind."

"I don't know how," Isaac says despondently.

Wearily, the octopus sighs. "You are stubborn."

The circles in the Metamorphosis Pool spin faster, producing a dense cloud of steam. When the mist clears, a boy with turquoise eyes surfaces from the vortex and pulls himself out of the water. Flipping a lock of onyx hair off his forehead, he flings himself down on the shelf of rock.

"Who are you?" Isaac stammers. Except for eye color, this boy could be his twin.

Thoughtfully, the boy gazes at Isaac. "I'm a friend of Condi's," he answers quietly. "The girl you met on the top of Windy Hollow—the one who tried to save you."

Isaac's eyes go wide. "You know that girl?"

"Yes." The boy looks sad. "The top of Windy Hollow was our special meeting spot."

Impossible.

"Nothing's impossible." Koan's stern voice echoes through the cavern, bouncing off the ebony walls.

Isaac studies the boy, trying to process what he just heard. The girl on the top of the Hollow *was* surprised to see him the night of the storm. She ran to hug him. It was obvious she thought he was someone else.

Nothing's impossible.

"I love Condi," the boy says quietly. "I'd give anything to be you."

Koan plays a wistful melody, rolling through sparkling light and frightening shadow, sounding the poignant notes of love and loss and yearning. Isaac cannot deny the powerful message of the music. It is where the truth lies. If you dare to love, you will someday lose...and yearning is what is left.

"Tell Condi I miss her." Slipping back into the water, the boy sinks into the spinning circles and disappears into the steam cloud.

Isaac looks at Koan. "What just happened?"

"No more questions," Koan replies firmly. "It's time for you to return home. I've provided all the help I can. Now you must face your future—whatever you choose to make of it."

"My home is not that stupid beach town," Isaac blurts out. "I hate living there."

"Isaac." Koan's voice is chiding. "Like many misguided humans, you are focusing on what you hate. Learn to focus on what you love." The octopus waves a golden arm, and a trumpet sounds. "I shall leave you now." A fissure opens in the black rock. In a shiver of light, Koan fades into a steam vent.

"Wait!" Isaac shouts.

His voice reverberates off the cavern walls...ricocheting aimlessly for what seems like forever...descending at last to silence.

In despair, Isaac turns to Auramar. "I don't get it. Nothing makes sense."

"Of course not." She raises a brow and looks at him, amused. "In Koan's world, things don't make sense–until they do."

Lifting its great head, the sea turtle lumbers over to the pool, slides off the ledge, and floats over to Isaac. Auramar gently pushes him forward. "You know how it works. Climb on."

When Isaac straddles the turtle's shell, he looks at her. "Will I see you again?"

She smiles. "That, too, is a riddle."

In a great whoosh of water, the turtle dives deep, sweeping Isaac into the heart of the spinning circles of the Metamorphosis Pool.

Chapter Nine

TINCTURE OF SAPPHIRE

Condi huddles in front of the window of the yellow cottage, clutching the blanket. Outside, the storm rages. Huge waves are pounding the shore, gnashing, gnawing, beating, breaking. It's too terrible to think about. No one can survive this.

Pressing her nose to the glass, she squints anxiously into the dark. Electricity illuminates the sea. A gash of lightning strikes, flinging foam over the shore, lighting up the beach where a lone figure is staggering out of the water. Afraid to believe but hoping with all her might, Condi rushes out to the terrace, unwinding the blanket and holding it like a sail. As swirling rain slashes her face and yanks her hair, she runs down the zigzag stairs.

Trudging through wet sand, Trippy rises out of the dark mist, a limp body slung over her muscular shoulders. On the sand at the base of the stairs, she kneels, laying Isaac's body on the sand and sagging against the low railing, gasping to catch her breath. Condi tucks her blanket around the boy. A stutter of moonlight exposes his face, ashen and beaded with rain.

"Is he—"

"No!" After a great intake of breath, Triponica lowers her mouth to Isaac's, pinches his nostrils, and exhales deeply. Taking another breath, she presses on his chest with the heels of her strong hands. The boy's chest rises and falls. The steady rhythm of *breathe, press, breathe* seems to go on forever. At last, with a jerk, he flails and turns his head, spewing seawater onto the sand.

Triponica sits back on her heels, pewter hair loose, water dripping from her exhausted face. "Help me get him up to the cottage," she says calmly.

Isaac hangs onto their shoulders as they half-walk, half-drag him up the zigzag stairs to the terrace. Inside the cottage, Condi rushes to light candles and hands the emergency flashlight to Triponica. Swathed in the blanket, Isaac staggers into the living room and collapses on the sofa, eyes panicked and watchful.

Trippy extracts a leather bag suspended from a cord around her neck and takes out a small indigo vial. Looking at Condi, she asks softly, "Do you remember?"

"Tincture of Sapphire," Condi murmurs, recognizing the familiar vial from last year's hurricane. The vial contains one of Trippy's medicines, a calming potion made from sapphire kelp, a rare sea plant that can only be harvested during the equinox tide.

"Who is this boy?" Trippy asks.

"Isaac Huddleston. His dad reported him missing. I saw him go under. Grand Ella went for help," Condi tells her.

At the mention of his name, the boy lurches forward and tries to stand.

Trippy waves the vial under his nose. Wild-eyed, he grabs it from her hand and flings it across the room, spilling deep purple liquid on the wooden floor.

A soothing scent of sea salt and blooming beach grass fills the room.

Triponica laughs. “We all need a bit of calm this evening.” She winks at Condi as the tincture takes effect. Panic recedes from the boy’s eyes.

Condi smiles. How well she knows the potion’s remarkable power. Last year as the hurricane ravaged the town, Trippy’s Tincture of Sapphire kept a roomful of fretful Beachlings calm, even when the frightened old women knew the violent storm was destroying their homes in Windy Hollow.

The boy’s shoulders relax and his eyelids droop. Closing his eyes, he falls back on the sofa, one bare arm exposed, falling to the floor. Glaring in the candlelight is a ladder of scars, silver, pink, and red, lacing the boy’s forearm from wrist to elbow.

Horrified, Condi looks to Trippy. Putting a gnarled finger to her lips, Trippy shakes her head. Rising, she goes to the sofa and tucks the boy’s arm back into the blanket, wrapping him tight. Gently, she says, “Scars. We all have them, my dear. Some are best left unseen. Let him sleep.”

The lights of the dashboard cover Dr. Heath’s face with shadows as he drives Casey back to the B&B. The wind is howling, rain pounding the windshield, the wipers slashing at top speed. The drive is precarious, mud flowing over the road. Casey shivers. Things are getting uglier by the minute.

When Heath pulls into the driveway of the B&B, Casey puts his hand on the door handle, ready to jump out. The work at the aquarium was hot and sweaty. He can't wait to get inside and take a hot shower.

The jeep rolls to a stop. "Tomorrow I'm changing the password to the hospital and offices," Dr. Heath tells him. "You'll not be allowed in the administrative area again."

"Fine." All Casey can think about is that he really hates this guy. And he doesn't care if he can't get into the office area. He only cares about the aquarium. No telling what would have happened if he hadn't aerated the tank tonight. He doubts if Heath would have bothered to try to activate the manual pump. The turtles would be dead by now.

Casey yanks on the door handle. Stupid fool has the child lock on. Furious, he says, "Unlock the door."

"In a moment." The doctor clears his throat. "I need you to tell me something."

Why should I?

"I've heard you see a lot of Lorelei Finch."

Casey can't believe it. "That's none of your business."

The doctor snorts. "I don't care about your little girlfriend. I want to know how her mother is. Is she getting better?"

The question comes out of the blue and makes no sense. With a set jaw, Casey clenches his teeth and stares out the window.

"You're not getting out of this car until you answer me, young man. I asked you a simple question."

Annoyed, Casey swivels his head. "No comment."

The doctor glares at him. He glares back.

The porch lights flash at the B&B. In the doorway, his mother is anxiously peering out into the rain. Inwardly,

Casey groans. She is waiting up, ready to pester him with questions.

"Mrs. Finch is really sick," Casey says coldly.

"Conscious? Able to talk?" the doctor probes.

Casey shrugs. "Don't know."

"Do you know what kind of research Frank Hardy and Gabby Finch were doing in *Limelight*?"

Another wild question. What kind of an interrogation is this? Even if he did know, he wouldn't tell. All he knows is that during the Sickness, Mrs. Finch and Mr. Hardy took *Limelight* out for underwater explorations. Casey's pretty sure even Mr. Huddleston didn't know what the expeditions were about.

"No."

"Where is Hardy's exploration logbook?"

"No clue." Casey locks eyes with the doctor. "Why don't you ask Huddleston?"

"You think I haven't? He claims to know nothing about Hardy's missing logbook. He swears Frank Hardy always kept his expedition records at the mansion—which is apparently as impenetrable as a fortress." Slyly, he glances over at Casey. "I understand that's where your little girlfriend Lorelei Finch is right now. Helping Mrs. Hardy at the mansion."

What?

Casey gulps. Lorelei hasn't answered his texts for days. He didn't know she was at the Hardy mansion.

The porch lights flash again.

"Go on in." An irritated click announces the release of the child lock. "And take care what you tell your mother about this evening," the doctor warns, "or I'll make certain you never work at the sanctuary again."

Casey jumps out, slams the door as hard as he can, and dashes for the porch. Over the howl of the wind, he hears the wheels of the jeep squeal away through the night.

#

Across the dimly lit room, Isaac stares at the girl he met at the top of the Hollow. Intermittent lightning exposes the corner where she sits, wrapped in a blanket, hair falling in damp curls over her shoulders. Her name is Condi. The name sounds familiar, but he can't think why. She watches him with dark, unreadable eyes. This is her grandmother's house.

The low buzz of male voices comes from the tiny cottage kitchen. His father is here, talking with the sheriff.

The girl's grandmother enters the room, carrying two steaming mugs of tea. Going to the corner, she hands a mug to her granddaughter.

"Thank you, Grand Ella."

The girl's voice is soft but strong. He remembers her fierceness. The bold way she thrust the kayak paddle at him and told him to hold on. He owes her. She was trying to save him.

Grand Ella gazes at the girl for a long, tender moment, then comes over to the sofa and offers the second mug to Isaac. He breathes in the warmth of cinnamon and cloves.

After taking the mug, he kicks the blankets piled on top of him to the floor.

"Feeling better?" she asks wryly.

He looks at her through narrowed eyes. This woman called Grand Ella is not at all like what he expects a grandmother to be. Though there is silver spun through her dark hair, she moves gracefully as a girl.

He takes a loud slurp of tea.

She laughs and turns away as his dad emerges from the kitchen. The strong old woman who rescued him follows, looking ancient and scary.

"He's doing fine, Abe," Grand Ella tells his father.

"Trippy..." His dad looks at the ancient old woman. "How can I ever thank..."

"No thanks needed, Abe." With shocking speed, the old woman strides over to the sofa. Her thick fingers reach out and tighten around Isaac's shoulder like a talon. "Your boy learned an important lesson today."

Scowling, Isaac pulls away and stands up. Without a word, he goes into the kitchen where the sheriff is doing paperwork at the kitchen table.

"Isaac—" The sheriff looks up.

Isaac ignores him. Opening the door of the cottage, he dashes into the rain, runs to his dad's van, and throws himself into the back seat.

He doesn't have to wait long.

Within minutes, his dad appears and the van sputters to a start, jerking through the deep, muddy ruts of the saturated beach road.

Isaac wishes he had his ear pods, but they're in the pocket of his black leather jacket, under the split shell of the kayak at the top of the Hollow. He'll never get them back.

Exhausted, he sinks back into the seat.

A sea turtle...a girl with red hair...a talking octopus... some dude who could be my twin?

Impossible.

What happened under the sea must have been a dream.

Chapter Ten

THE BLACK LEATHER JACKET

At breakfast the next morning, Condi spreads a spoonful of blackberry-lemon jam over a slice of Grand Ella's almond bread and gazes out the window. The weather is glorious, bright, and clear. The rough-and-tumble storm is gone. And somehow, thanks to Triponica, Isaac Huddleston managed to survive it.

"When did Trippy leave last night?" Condi asks Grand Ella. "I couldn't keep my eyes open." After Isaac and the men left last night, Condi had fallen into bed, leaving Grand Ella and Trippy in the cottage kitchen, drinking countless cups of tea.

"As soon as the storm blew through," Grand Ella replies. "She insisted on getting back to Francie. I offered to drive her, but she said she wanted to walk the shoreline to see what the storm washed in."

"Don't you think it was a little crazy that she was out swimming during a lightning storm?" Putting down her knife, Condi looks at her grandmother. "And why was she on Windy Hollow when she usually dives off the Point?"

Her grandmother takes a meditative sip of cocoa. "Oh, I don't know. Trippy's an expert free diver. She can swim from Craggy Point to Windy Hollow as well as anyone. Besides, the autumn equinox is the only time of year she can harvest sapphire kelp from the waters around the Hollow."

Condi nods. It's true that Trippy needs the kelp to make Tincture of Sapphire. Last year, during the autumn equinox, Trustin helped Trippy harvest sapphire kelp from the rocks off the Hollow—but it sure wasn't in the middle of a lightning storm.

"I can't believe Isaac Huddleston didn't drown." Condi shudders. "The waves last night were wicked."

Grand Ella smooths a lock of hair off her granddaughter's face. "You mustn't dwell on what *didn't* happen, Condi." Getting to her feet, she does a gentle back bend, then begins to clear the table. "Today I'm going into town. There's a pressing matter I must discuss with the sheriff." At the sink, she turns on the tap, filling the basin to the brim with lavender-scented bubbles.

"I'm going to run up to the top of the Hollow. Tide's out. I'll only stay a moment."

"Oh, Condi." Grand Ella looks concerned. "You took a big chance yesterday when you climbed the tower knowing a storm was brewing."

"I know," Condi mumbles. "I'm sorry I risked it—but, oh, Grand Ella, the tower looked so safe, sparkling pink and orange against the sunset. I thought the storm clouds were far away."

Grand Ella lifts one hand from the soapy water, turns her head toward Condi and blows gently on her palm.

A stream of tiny iridescent bubbles flows through the kitchen. "The Hollow is like these bubbles, Condi," she says softly. "What happens there cannot be foreseen. You of all people should understand that."

"I do," Condi answers earnestly. "Isaac's jacket is under the orange-red kayak. I want to get it, then walk over to the sanctuary. He said his mom gave him the jacket."

"Ah." Grand Ella nods. "All right then. I agree that you should go. That poor boy could use a friend."

"Thanks." Condi gives her grandmother a peck on the cheek. "By the way, what do you need to talk to the sheriff about? He was just here last night." She tries to sound off-hand, but it's hard. Grand Ella's growing relationship with Sheriff Clive Coodle worries her. He's not good enough for her grandmother.

"A private matter," Grand Ella answers casually. Dropping a baking pan into the sink, she scrubs at it hard, sending another flurry of bubbles into the air.

A flush creeps over Condi's cheeks.

Oh, no.

Grand Ella swivels her head. "My dear, it's nothing personal. Not what you're thinking. I need a favor from Clive. And trust me, he's not going to like it. You know how hard-headed he can be."

Relieved, Condi grins and pops a few bubbles. "Sheriff Coodle won't say 'no' to you."

Grand Ella chuckles. "We'll see."

As Grand Ella prepares to leave for town, Condi flies down the zigzag stairs, kicks off her sandals and runs barefoot across the beach to Windy Hollow. Slowing to a careful walk, she picks her way through clusters of drying seaweed and pearly shells...treasures left behind by the storm.

Today the tide is rocking soft and low among the jagged rocks of the Hollow. Relaxed, she steps into the sparkling teal waters and wades over to the stone stairs, eyeing the slabs of glistening stone, slick with moss from the storm. Mindfully, she climbs the tower, every toehold intentional, each step an ascent into the tower of remembering.

Mama.

Papa.

Trustin.

Marissa.

Whispering their names, she makes every step a prayer. The Hollow is the place that belongs to them, where she feels their presence the most. Here on this high, flat ledge, she sat on the orange-red kayak and waited for the green sail of Mama and Papa's sailboat, until the day it never returned home. Here, gazing out at the high rollers on the horizon, she sat and watched Trustin and Marissa surf. And who would have ever thought that yesterday she would have encountered a strange boy in a black leather jacket in this same spot, a boy who looks strangely like Trustin?

Grand Ella is right; what occurs on the Hollow cannot be foreseen.

When she sees the upside-down orange-red kayak, she draws in her breath. A gash from a lightning strike has split the hull cleanly down the middle. The twin pieces of the kayak are baking in the sun between the two half-moon rocks. Remarkably, though soggy from last night's rain, Isaac's leather jacket is unscorched.

Picking up the jacket, she shakes it, letting the water droplets fly.

Slinging it over her shoulder, she goes to the stone

stairs and hurries down to the beach.

Isaac Huddleston has a lot of explaining to do.

#

Today Isaac wears a black short-sleeved T-shirt, intentionally not covering up his scars. At breakfast, his dad is abnormally silent, though the tension in the air between them is the same. He knows his father wants to ask about the scars but is afraid to upset him after last night. Squirming around in his chair, his dad does everything he can to avoid looking at Isaac's bare arms.

"I have something in my office I want you to see," his dad says when the awkward meal is over. "Will you come?"

"I guess."

Without bothering to clear the dishes, his father pushes away from the table and heads out to the porch.

Reluctantly, Isaac follows him. Outside, the day sparkles, as days after storms tend to do. Sun glitters on water, too bright for Isaac's sleepy eyes. Hunching up his shoulders, he wishes he had his shades. Not having his jacket on feels weird, but at least his tennis shoes make a satisfying destructive crunch on the broken shells on the path down to the aquarium.

Nervously, his dad looks at the security pad that opens the big glass door, then looks apologetically at Isaac. Heath is standing inside the doors, glaring.

"I'm not watching," Isaac says sarcastically. Turning away from the door, he looks out to sea. Heath is a stickler about security, and a control freak about everything at the aquarium. Smirking, Isaac listens as his dad keys in the numbers of the code, easily memorizing it by hearing the frequency tones on the keypad.

The glass doors slide open.

"What are you up to today, Luther?" his dad asks carefully.

"I'm taking *Limelight* out. Collecting more specimens."

His dad inhales sharply. "I don't think that's a good idea. The depth gauge is acting up."

Dr. Heath burns his dad with a look. "I ran a safety check. It's working fine." Abruptly, he stalks past them and heads down to the dock.

His dad shakes his head. "Can't stand that guy," he confesses to Isaac. "The government sent him. He's got access to everything."

For the first time, Isaac feels a pang of sympathy for his dad. Heath is creepy, locking every door and pacing around the marine sanctuary grounds like he's looking for a dead body or something.

At the large aquarium tank on the way to his dad's office, Isaac stops and taps lightly on the glass. The large sea turtle looks healthier and more alert than the last time he was here.

His dad adjusts the aerator hose, increasing the bubble rate of oxygen into the tank.

In the fresh stream of bubbles, the turtle contently rolls from side to side. Isaac gets a déjà vu feeling in his chest watching the gentle rhythmic movement. A wisp of a stray melody hovers on the edge of his mind...reminding him of something. Thoughtfully, he studies the creature's marred shell. Large and shiny, the high dome is covered with a design of scars, looking oddly like a constellation of stars.

His father says softly, "Survivors have scars, Isaac."

Isaac snorts. "Is that why you brought me here?"

"No." His father wipes his hands on a towel. "What I wanted to show you is in my office." Going to the steel door protecting the public aquarium from the administrative wing, he keys in the security code.

The door squawks.

Swearing under his breath, his dad clenches and unclenches his fists. "Heath again. Nerve of that guy. He's changed the code again and locked me out of my own office." Pacing, he yanks out his cell phone and fires off a text.

"Are we done here?" Isaac looks pointedly at the front door. Dr. Heath is not his problem.

Running his fingers through his hair, his dad sighs. "You can go, but tutoring's in an hour," he answers glumly. "Be on time, please."

Isaac rolls his eyes. "What does it matter if I'm behind in school?"

"It matters," his dad says, with surprising firmness.

"Fine."

Hurrying back to the house, Isaac goes into his room. Kneeling by his bed, he pulls out his guitar case. Guitar in hand, he leaves the house and takes the stairs down to the dock two at a time. The strands of music he heard in his head when he looked at the turtle were complex. It won't be easy to find the notes and chords in the guitar strings, but he wants to try.

On the end of the dock, he sits in the sun, the warmth surprisingly comforting on his scarred arms, rarely exposed to the light of day. Beneath his thumb, a chord plays itself, shivers and holds...shimmering indigo.

Plucking out another note, he lets it vibrate...until it fades to violet. Picking out random sets of chords, he holds down strings, trying to remember. The sounds are sweet, the colors flowing in waves...but none of them are right.

Discouraged, he gives up, and puts away the guitar.

#

With the damp jacket slung over her shoulder; Condi takes the overgrown path above the cove to the marine sanctuary. The high road keeps her well out of sight. No chance of running into kids she knows. The last thing she needs is questions. She bets everybody has heard about the new boy from New York...and that he almost died at the Hollow last night.

At the gate to the marine sanctuary, she pauses under the high iron arch, draped with ivy and wisteria. Purple coneflower and salvia peek through the trees, sheltering the sloped path to shore. The beauty here is bold and tangled and wild—exactly like her mood.

Goodness knows, she doesn't *want* to see Isaac again—

But something strange happened last night.

He should be dead.

At the top of the stairs leading down to the metal dock, she gets her first view of the sea. Even the air smells different than the air on the north shore. At the yellow cottage, the breeze is heavy with the nostalgic tang of citrus, though the old orange groves that once covered the Hollow have long since washed away. Here, on the south shore of the cove, the air smells purple and rich, laced with the scent of wisteria and lavender.

Gathering her courage, she starts down the long flight of stairs to the shore. Isaac is sitting alone at the end of the metal dock.

Good.

Hurrying past the high hedge shielding the Huddleston's house, a familiar female voice startles her.

"Abe," a woman is saying. "What are you going to do?"

"What can I do? Mary Hardy is threatening to cut funding to the sanctuary."

"Can't you explain to her that the pump to the big aquarium is failing? Frank Hardy's life was built around protecting sea creatures. Surely Mary wants to protect the legacy of the Hardy Foundation."

"Mary Hardy doesn't care a hoot about marine life," Mr. Huddleston answers.

"She's grieving, Abe. Give it time."

Condi pauses. She knows she shouldn't be listening, but she can't help it. The woman speaking is Miss Dennison, her favorite English teacher at Craggy Point Middle School.

"I don't know, Amanda," Mr. Huddleston goes on. "We're running out of time. The Sickness sent everything into an economic spiral. Everything at the sanctuary needs maintenance, and that takes money."

The news makes Condi sad—and a little mad. For years, Craggy Point Marine Sanctuary has been known for its world-renowned research on sea creatures, funded by the Hardy Foundation. Mr. Hardy was a good, kind man and a brilliant scientist—though everyone in town knows his wife is an old grouch.

The murmur of voices fades.

There is a gentle rustling behind the fence of wisteria.

Condi sighs. The faint sound, not quite silence, is the same one she hears when she's in the kitchen of the yellow cottage and Sheriff Coodle is outside with Grand Ella on the high terrace.

Miss Dennison and Mr. Huddleston are more than friends.

#

Resting his cheek on the warm metal of the dock rail, Isaac listens to the soft lap-dub of the sea. He feels weird. The elusive music is gone, but so is his protective armor—anger at his dad.

"Hey."

Startled, he lifts his head. Standing on the dock, looking dead serious, is Condi, holding out his black leather jacket.

Instantly, he jumps to his feet. "Uh, thanks," he says lamely, extending his scarred arm and taking the jacket. After fishing around in the inner pocket, he pulls out his saturated electronics and winces. "Figured," he says. "I saw the lightning strike."

"At least your jacket didn't burn," she says flatly.

Slinging the jacket over his shoulder, he nods. For the first time, he really looks at her. She's pretty, with a cloud of dark curls, big brown eyes, long legs.

"Thanks for bringing it."

"That's not the only reason I came." She crosses her arms. "You shouldn't be alive."

He raises a brow.

"Hey, I don't care that you wanted to die," she goes on bluntly. "What I care about is what happened to you when you almost drowned."

He glances up at the house, where Miss Dennison is

sitting in the big porch swing next to his father. "I can't talk about this now. I've got tutoring with my dad's girlfriend. I'm behind in school."

Turning, she eyes the house. Mr. Huddleston is waving at them, pointing at his watch. Awkwardly, she waves back.

"Miss Dennison's okay," she tells him. "I had her for English." Letting out her breath, she points to the high sand dune above the steep cliffs of Craggy Point. "Meet me there tomorrow. If you follow the high beach road past the Point, there's a tide pool hidden behind that dune, in a patch of tall seagrass. It's private."

Isaac assesses the ominous dune buttressing the steep side of the Point. He wonders if maybe she's into him. He shoots her a little grin.

She glares. "I only want to *talk*." Stepping aside, she clears his way up to the house. "Four o'clock tomorrow."

For a moment, he hesitates. Then thinks better of it. After all, what else does he have to do?

"Got it," he tells her. "See you then."

Chapter Eleven

CITRINE MAR

"Let's walk the shoreline and visit the Beachlings," Grand Ella says to Condi early the next morning.

Concerned, Condi scans her grandmother's face. "Is it Francie?"

"No," Grand Ella says quickly. "Triponica says Francie's holding her own, but it's time to visit. Come, help me pack the basket with baked treats. I made Francie's favorite angel wing shortbread last night."

Walking the shoreline, Condi matches her grandmother's steps, keeping pace with her sure strides. As they pass the Billabong, Mr. Marshall spies them and hurries across the sand. "How good it is to see you, Ella," he exclaims. "You look strong and well."

"I am, Andy," Grand Ella answers. "Grateful, too. The Sickness is not to be taken lightly." She reaches for his hand. "Please know how sorry I am about Frank. You two were lifelong friends."

Tears glaze the old surf master's eyes. "Thank you,

Ella." Awkwardly, he clears his throat. "Where are you off to?"

"To see the Beachlings." Reaching into the basket of goodies, she pulls out a delectable-smelling muffin crowned with a spongy gold top.

Swooning dramatically, Mr. Marshall takes the muffin and sniffs in appreciation. "Perfect muffin top, Ella. How do you do it?"

"I'll let you in on a little secret." Grand Ella smiles. "Always let the batter rest before baking muffins. See you soon, Andy. Come along, Condi."

They wander the shoreline in comfortable silence. When the high deck of the Beachlings' bunkrooms looms in the distance, Grand Ella stops at the waterline. Pointing to a place on a dune where a pair of smooth, dry rocks face each other like chairs, she says, "Let's sit. Before we see the Beachlings, I want to tell you a story."

Sitting cross-legged on one of the rocks, Condi breathes in the soft scent of wild beach roses. Grand Ella passes Condi the braided grass basket. Condi selects a ginger crinkle scone and Grand Ella takes a raspberry-molasses cookie for herself. "Do you remember the day we visited the orphanage, the one on top of Spiral Mountain?" she asks, holding Condi's gaze.

"How could I forget?" Before the Sickness, Grand Ella volunteered at the Overlook Home, teaching kids' yoga and organizing art projects. Condi shudders. "If it weren't for you, I would have ended up a foster kid."

Grand Ella takes a pensive bite of her cookie, then crumbles the rest of it and tosses the crumbs to the sea birds. "The Sickness caused a terrible disruption to the foster care system, Condi. People got scared. Some of the foster parents returned the kids they were caring for to the Overlook."

Condi stares at Grand Ella. "Returned them? Like the kids were things they didn't want anymore?"

"I'm afraid so," says Grand Ella, staring out to sea.

"Those poor kids," murmurs Condi.

"It's pretty awful, especially what happened next. The directors of the Overlook abandoned the children and returned to their own families."

"That's the cruelest thing I've ever heard!"

"It's terrible," her grandmother agrees. "The Sickness brought out the worst in many of us. We returned to tribal ways...protecting our families and hiding within our own little social bubbles." She pats Condi's knee. "But this story has a happy ending, my dear. Three of the abandoned kids found their way to Craggy Point, and the Beachlings took them in."

"How did the kids ever find the Beachlings?" Condi exclaims.

"The oldest boy at the Overlook is sixteen, and the son of a fisherman. He learned at an early age that you can never go hungry if you can find the sea. When food ran out on Spiral Mountain, he led the younger children down the old coastal road until they reached Dipitous Beach." Grand Ella's brow furrows. "Of course, they found the town shuttered and closed. When a heavy fog rolled in, they couldn't see a thing, but they kept going toward the sound of the surf. At last, they reached the waterline below the Beachlings' bunkrooms. That's where Triponica found them, hungry and scared, the next morning. The Beachlings took them in. They have cared for them all these long months, even though they hardly have the room for three more bodies." Her grandmother sighs. "Triponica shared this news with me the night we rescued Isaac."

"Why didn't Trippy bring them to stay at the yellow cottage?" Condi asks. "We have room."

"Oh, my dear." Grand Ella presses her lips together. "I've been struggling with that question." Her shoulders sag. "Triponica didn't bring the children to the cottage because of my friendship with the sheriff. Clive would have been obliged to report that the children were with us." Grand Ella's eyes cloud over. "Oh, Condi...I'm having such trouble forgiving myself. I always hated that horrible group home." She rubs her fingers over the worry line in her forehead. "As sheriff, Clive would have had no choice but to act on what he knew—or turn in his badge." She shakes her head, a wing of silver hair falling over her cheek. "The children would have been returned to the foster care system."

"That's horrible," Condi says hotly.

Grand Ella gets to her feet. "I'm determined to do right by those dear children now. Let's go meet them. I'm sure they'll be glad to see another young person."

In minutes, they are climbing up the steep stairs leading to the open-air decks where the Beachlings make their homes.

"How I've missed teaching here," Grand Ella murmurs, standing in the dappled light of the yoga pavilion, a latticed dome draped with ivy, white climbing roses and iris-blue wisteria. She slips an arm around Condi. "I start sunrise yoga classes on the beach next week, but resuming yoga classes here in the pavilion will have to wait. We can't let the town know about the children."

"I can't wait for yoga to start again," Condi says. "Sunrise yoga will help people stop being scared of one another."

Before the Sickness, Grand Ella's sunrise yoga classes on the beach below the yellow cottage were open to everyone. They were a healing balm, bringing rich and poor together.

Maybe sunrise yoga will work a little magic again.

Feeling hopeful, Condi sticks a sprig of ivy behind her ear as the two of them head toward tiny bunkrooms.

"Shh," Grand Ella whispers, pointing to the sweet scene unfolding on the deck facing the sea, where a small boy in tattered overalls and a tiny old woman with cotton-puff hair are kneeling under a wizened lemon tree. Flung down beside them is an orange knitted sock, spilling shells and sea glass over the sunbaked wood.

The tiny woman senses their presence and turns. "Ella, Condi!" she cries, spryly jumping to her feet.

"Charlene!" Grand Ella rushes forward.

The old woman's face splits into rays of light. She pulls the small boy to his feet. "Malcolm, these are my friends, Grand Ella and Condi."

"Hello, Malcolm." Grand Ella drops to a knee beside the shell and glass mosaic laid out on the deck. "Did you make this?"

"He most certainly did!" Charlene says proudly. "Mal's a born artist."

Thoughtfully, Grand Ella studies the intricate design for a long moment. "How original."

A smile nudges the corner of the boy's mouth.

Condi holds out the basket. "Would you like a sweet treat, Malcolm?"

Furtively, the boy glances at Charlene.

"It's fine," she assures him. "Grand Ella's baking is out of this world."

The boy's hand darts into the basket. Clutching a puffy-topped muffin bursting with berries to his chest, he looks at Charlene. "S-s-s-save...for...C-c-c-issy."

"Malcolm shares everything with his little sister, Cissy," Charlene explains.

"As it should be," Grand Ella says, smiling at Malcolm. "There's a special treat in this basket for your sister, too."

"Let's go see her. Cissy can pick out her own treat," Charlene suggests. "She's reading with Francie."

Malcolm exposes a partially toothless smile.

"Want to help me carry the basket?" Condi asks him.

Grasping the handle proudly, the small boy trots beside her, taking dramatic bites out of his muffin. Condi finds it hard to look at the top of Malcolm's head. There's no doubt he's been through a terrible time. Oozing sores blight his scalp, and he's lost a lot of his hair.

Poor little guy.

Walking ahead, Grand Ella and Charlene are deep in conversation. Charlene, spine curled like a shell, cranes her neck to look up at Grand Ella, talking animatedly while Grand Ella listens, eyebrows knitted together in a worried frown. Outside the door of Francie's bunkroom, they pause, waiting for Condi and Malcolm.

"Don't worry. She'll be ecstatic to see you," Charlene says, patting her arm.

"During the Sickness, I read all of Francie's favorite books, Charly," Condi says sadly. "The old-fashioned ones she loved when she was a girl."

"How lovely. She'll be pleased." Charlene smiles. "I must warn you; Francie is greatly changed since you saw her last—though her heart and mind are the same." The tiny woman touches Condi's cheek. "Are you prepared?"

Condi nods. "I think so."

Gently, Charlene pushes open the door, and they step inside.

On a low bunk, leaning against a pile of clean, ragged pillows, is a frail old woman. Her eyes are closed, and she is breathing heavily. Curled in the crook of the woman's arm is a tiny girl with braided caramel-colored hair, reading a book aloud.

The little girl stops reading. Her eyes travel anxiously to Malcolm.

Marching over to the bed, he lifts the basket so Cissy can see inside. Tilting it, he stammers, "T-t-treats."

The girl's eyes light up. Excitedly, she reaches into the basket, grabs a cookie, and crams it into her mouth. The old woman's eyes flutter open. After a long, shuddering breath, she smiles—a glorious spring morning smile.

Condi goes to kneel beside the bed. "Hello, Francie."

With a quivering finger, Francie reverently touches a lock of Condi's hair. "My child," she says weakly. "You've come." Struggling with a pillow, she fights to prop herself up.

Grand Ella comes to help, but Francie shakes her head. "I must use what strength I have, Ella." Once settled, she pulls Cissy close again and gestures to the foot of the bed. "Malcolm, come and sit on the bed with Cissy."

Shyly, Malcolm slides up onto the foot of the bed, holding the treat basket in his lap. Cissy stares at Condi, clutching the book she was reading to her chest.

"What are you reading?" Condi asks, smiling.

Cautiously, the little girl shows her the book cover.

"*Charlotte's Web* is one of my favorites," Condi tells her softly.

"Charlotte is going to die," the little girl announces. "Like Francie."

"C-c-cissy." Malcolm looks pained.

"I don't like the dying part," Cissy declares.

"Me, either," admits Condi.

"When Charlotte dies, a part of her stays with Wilbur," Francie says, looking into the little girl's amber-brown eyes. "People you love stay with you, no matter what."

"Well, I guess I know *that*," Cissy answers. "But I'm still sad about it."

"Sad is the hard part of love," Francie answers.

Cissy puts down the book and the rest of her uneaten muffin and lays her head on Francie's shoulder.

Charlene goes to the door. "Come along, children. Francie's energy is waning. Let her visit with Grand Ella and Condi. Firth and Trippy are arriving with the sea harvest soon. Come and see what they found!"

Cissy gives Francie a gentle kiss with a mouth covered with crumbs, then hops off the bed. "C'mon, Mal, let's go."

Happily, the children rush out to the deck. Charlene blows a kiss to Francie and softly shuts the bunkroom door.

"How the children love you, Francie," Grand Ella says, stroking the old woman's hand.

Francie smiles tremulously. "I've taught them how to read, Ella–they'll never be lonely again. Thanks to Andy's bookmobile visits, we have had plenty of books. In some ways, the Sickness has been a time of richness–the world's busy ways were paused–and we were given the gift of time."

"Yes, the Sickness has brought some hidden blessings." Grand Ella sighs. "But oh, Francie, how I wish we could have been together! Condi and I could have helped you with the children."

"We were fine, Ella," Francie answers. "The children

gave us joy. Caring for them was easy. Triponica harvested our meals from the sea. Andy faithfully delivered books. And that kind boy, Vinnie Maretti, brought a basket of fruits and vegetables from his father's grocery each week." She nods thoughtfully. "You know, I'm pretty certain Vinnie saw Malcolm playing on the shore one day—but he never said a word." She smiles. "Somehow he knew it was important to keep our secret."

They sit together quietly, Condi patting Francie's hand and Grand Ella gently rubbing her feet. When Francie's breathing deepens, Grand Ella rises to her feet and plants a kiss on the old woman's forehead. "We'll leave you to rest now. Is there anything else we can do?"

Francie shakes her head. "I'll be saying goodbye to all of you soon—but I have a little time left." She squeezes Condi's hand. "Run along and go on outside. Meet Firth. He's sixteen. I'm hoping you'll all become friends."

As they slip outside the bunkroom, Condi's heart is heavy. Watching gentle Francie let go of life is hard. A world without her feels bleak indeed.

Grand Ella hugs Condi close. "Francie is the frailest of the Beachlings. She's survived much. Soon we must let her go—so she can be free again."

Condi nods. It is amazing how much Francie has survived. After a bad fall many years ago when she was living in the high caves above the Hollow, she never regained the use of her legs. Yet she managed to live a bold, bright life in the caves. The other Beachlings cared for her, and she sustained them with the loving kindness of her spirit.

"Francie's body is broken, but her spirit is whole," Grand Ella murmurs.

Heading toward the railing overlooking Craggy Point,

they pass by the yoga pavilion. For a moment, they stop to watch as Glinda and Pippa, a pair of ancient sisters, practice yoga. Grand Ella smiles as knobby-kneed Glinda lifts her arms to the sky, bending into a graceful side stretch. Following her lead, wild-haired Pippa raises her arms, waving them frantically from side to side. Grinning broadly, she spies Grand Ella watching. Standing on one leg, she grasps the inside of her opposite foot with her hand and leans forward, posture regal as a dancer's.

Grand Ella chuckles. "Would you look at Pippa. Who knew she could do that pose!"

"Hurry, hurry!" Cissy calls to them from the front deck. "Firth and Trippy are bringing in the catch!"

Grand Ella and Condi rush to where Cissy and Malcolm are hanging over the rail, waving their arms. A tall, muscular teenage boy is emerging from the sea, with a bulging net of spiked grass and kelp tubes slung over his shoulder. Beside him, Trippy trudges through the foam with two smaller nets, each glistening with the sparkle of the sea harvest. Staggering under the weight of the nets, they make their way up the stairs to the high deck and lean against the rail, gasping for breath.

The boy is the first to recover.

Dropping the net, he clenches his fists and glowers at Grand Ella.

"Firth." Triponica fixes the boy with her powerful gaze. "This woman is to be trusted."

"She is called Grand Ella, and this is her granddaughter, Condi," Charlene adds. "They are two of our dearest friends."

Raising piercing green eyes, he pushes salt-matted hair off his forehead and nods curtly to Grand Ella.

Triponica empties one of the small nets and stoops to

grasp a twisted ribbon of yellow-green crystals, holding it high. "Look what Firth harvested. A chain of Citrine Mar." Proudly, she nods at Firth. "These rare crystals can only be obtained in the deepest hollow of the salt cave off the Point, the one I can no longer reach."

"Citrine Mar," Charlene explains to Condi and Grand Ella, "is a deep-sea healing gem."

"It's pretty!" Cissy claps her hands.

"Citrine Mar has many uses," Trippy tells them. "Pounded into powder and dissolved in seagrass chowder, it will loosen a tight chest. Sprinkled on the skin, Citrine Mar cures many difficult afflictions."

"Citrine Mar might heal Malcolm's scalp," Cissy announces. "He doesn't like his bald spots."

Triponica laughs. "I believe it may, Cissy."

"His hair will grow back!" Excitedly, the little girl looks around for her brother, but the small boy has slipped away.

"We shall see." Holding up more clusters of glittering golden brine, Triponica declares, "I've never seen such a bountiful gem harvest. Firth can hold his breath for over ten minutes–the time it takes to access and return from the deepest of the salt caverns."

"Ten minutes?" Condi looks at Firth. "I didn't know that was possible."

"Firth is a master free diver," Triponica answers. "A skill few possess nowadays."

"Firth's mama was a mermaid," Cissy confides to Condi.

"Cissy." Firth shakes his head.

"What Cissy means is that Firth's mother was one of the legendary Ama of Japan," Charlene explains. "For centuries, the Ama have gathered seafood to feed their villages. They are skilled free divers, said to be the original mermaids."

Grand Ella gazes at Firth in appreciation. "Free diving is an honored ancient practice. Most of us can only hold our breath for thirty seconds to a minute without panicking. A free diver must train his mind as well as his body."

Turning away, Firth busies himself with the nets.

Gazing at the glittering ribbons of crystals strewn across the deck, Condi asks Trippy, "Is there any chance Citrine Mar can save Francie?"

Triponica shakes her head. "I cannot save our Francie."

"Goodness me, where *is* Malcolm?" Charlene asks suddenly. "It's not like him to miss the bringing in of the nets. The boy loves the sea harvest."

Jerking his head, Firth points to the high ledge above Craggy Point. Silhouetted against the sun is Malcolm, his skinny form hunched over a book.

Smile lines crinkle around Trippy's eyes. "Malcolm practices reading to the old black dog that lives up on the high ledge. When he reads to the dog, he says his stutter vanishes."

"I don't see a dog," says Condi, squinting into the light.

"Oh, he's up there alright," Cissy reassures her. "The black dog is our friend. The night we found the Beachlings was cold and foggy. We got lost trying to find the sea. The black dog found us and led us here."

Smiling, Condi turns to gaze up at the high ledge. "Why, I know the dog you mean, Cissy." Condi's eyes shine. "He comes and goes as he pleases and likes to play in the waves off the Hollow. The folks around here call him Lucky."

Cissy giggles. "We named him Misty Black. He came out of the dark mist." She looks at Condi. "I like the name Misty Black better than Lucky—though I guess we're lucky he found us."

Condi laughs. "Well, it's alright if he has two names, don't you think?"

The small girl grins broadly and flips her caramel braids over her shoulder. "I like you."

"Cissy." The tone contains a warning. Going to the girl, Firth kneels and whispers something in her ear. Cissy's eyes grow large and concerned.

Squaring his shoulders, Firth stands up, sets his jaw, and addresses Grand Ella.

"We won't go back," he tells her fiercely. "Not ever. Do you hear me?"

"Firth," Trippy admonishes. "Heed your words."

"It's alright, Trippy," Grand Ella says, stepping forward and looking him in the eye. "You most certainly will not return to the Overlook. You have a home here in Dipitous Beach." She puts an arm around Cissy's shoulders. "I intend to see about that."

Chapter Twelve

TRUTH AND LIES

At three o'clock, Isaac leaves the house without telling his dad where he's going. Today the wind carries a chill, though the air is golden. Feels like autumn, though the weather is nothing like the fall blasts in New York. Shoulders up to his ears, he's glad to be wearing the black leather jacket. With a little help from his hair dryer, he got it dried out last night, no worse for having been soaked in the rain.

When he turns off the beach path, he ducks his head into the wind and sticks his hands in the pockets of his jeans. His fingers close around a small lump in the right pocket. Surprised, he stops and draws out a small white shell.

Strange.

He was wearing these jeans the night of the storm.

Confused, he shoves the shell into his jacket. The storm is a disturbing memory he wants to forget. He's kicking himself for agreeing to meet Condi at the tidepool. She clearly wants to talk about what happened, and he does not. It's a bad idea to meet her. He's bound to make her mad, though he's not sure why he cares.

Climbing through hard-packed sand, he crests the steep dune and pushes his way through the thicket of dense seagrass. At once, the wind falls to a hush. The noise of the waves lessens, and it feels ten degrees warmer. Choosing a spot on the highest rock overlooking the pool, he looks around. The place is ruggedly beautiful. The pool is a cupped palm of rock, with gushes of seawater flowing in and out. At the bottom of the pool are shiny black rocks and a glaze of sand.

Leaning back, he closes his eyes. A few lines from a poem float into his head.

I always thought that I was me.

But I was you and never knew it.

The lines come unbidden, making his heart ache. His mom loved Rumi's poetry. "But what does it mean?" he'd asked her. "It makes no sense. Everybody is their own person, right?"

She'd smiled at him, her eyes gray pools of light. "Think of music, Isaac," she'd answered. "The different notes vibrate together to create melody, blending and becoming the same."

At the time, he hadn't understood what she meant—but then he hadn't really tried.

At the thicket of tall grasses surrounding the tide pool, Condi pauses to brush away the sand stuck between her toes. Her hair is flecked with the little flowerets of lavender wisteria spinning in the wind. She's nervous about meeting Isaac. *What if he won't tell me?* Taking a deep breath, she sucks up her courage and steps boldly through the circle of grass.

Isaac is sitting on the high ledge of volcanic rock above the tide pool.

"Hey," he calls down to her.

"Hi," she answers. Avoiding his eyes, she slips out of her sandals and dips her toes in the cool water.

Now that she's here, she finds she can hardly bear to look at him.

He looks so much like Trustin.

It hurts.

#

Sliding down from the high rock, Isaac sits across from her. "Why did you ask me here?"

It is a long moment before she looks at him. When she does, her luminous brown eyes contain an emotion he doesn't understand. "I want to know what really happened to you," she says at last.

"Why?"

Looking miserable, she lets out a long breath. "I can't tell you."

"Seriously? That's your answer?" Annoyed, he starts to stand up and leave. But the truth is, he doesn't want to.

"Please," she says quietly. "Tell me what happened."

She has a lot of nerve. He doesn't owe her anything. But still, she did try to save him. "I'll answer questions if you play a game. Truth or Lies."

She tenses. "How do you play?"

"We each ask a question. The other person answers, but they can lie if they want."

"What's the point?" she asks. "I only want the truth.'

He shrugs. "Take it or leave it. Those are the terms."

She thinks for a long minute, then nods. "Alright then."

"I'll go first." He watches her face. "Who did you think I was when you saw me at the top of the Hollow?"

"A boy I knew last year," she answers, holding his gaze. "You look a lot like him."

"Truth," he concedes. Impulsively he pulls the white shell from his pocket and hands it to her. "Your turn."

Thoughtfully, she bounces the shell in her palm. "Where did you get—" She stops abruptly. "Never mind. That's not my question. Why did you let go of the kayak paddle?"

The question irritates him. She sounds accusing. "You wouldn't understand."

"Is that your answer?"

Curtly, he nods.

"Lie. You don't know what I can understand." She dips her fingers into the pool, picks up a smooth black rock and coldly tosses it his way.

"Is the boy who looks like me your boyfriend?"

"No." Her eyes cut away.

"Ha." He flicks the black rock back into her lap. "Lie."

She surprises him and doesn't deny it. "What happened to you under the sea?"

He hesitates.

"Please tell me."

Her desperation is real. It rattles him. "I had a dream," he says finally. "Or I was hallucinating—"

She studies his face for a long moment. "Truth," she says and hands over the white shell.

"Where is your boyfriend now?"

Something that looks like pain crosses her face. "I don't know."

"Lie."

"It isn't!" she blurts. "I don't know for sure."

He nods and gives her the white shell. Whatever is going on with her, she's telling the truth.

Clutching the shell, she closes her eyes and murmurs something. The intensity in her face makes him wonder if she's praying. When she opens her eyes and speaks, her voice is shaking. "What happened in the dream?"

Instantly, he's embarrassed. This is getting way too weird. "Usual dream stuff," he says flippantly. "You know, hot girl, giant sea turtle, talking octopus."

"You're not being serious."

"Fine." Irritated, he scoops up the black rock and tosses it into the pool.

"This is not a game," she tells him.

"What is it then?" he demands.

High color flushes her cheeks. "Strange things happen at Windy Hollow. People have died there. A lot of people, in a lot of strange ways. I thought you were next. You were underwater an *impossibly* long time."

Her expression is piercing. He drops his eyes.

"I lost my parents a few years back," she says. "An accident off Windy Hollow." "I get what it's like to lose someone—" Gently, she hands him back the white shell. "I'm sorry about your mom."

Slowly, he nods. His fingers close tightly around the shell. "I don't know what happened to me when I went under. I wasn't lying. The whole thing felt like a dream."

"Truth at last," she says, cracking a wry smile. Standing up, she brushes sand off her shorts. Looking out over the top of the whispering sea grass, she fixes her eyes on the horizon. "Maybe your dream was not a dream."

Speechless, he gawks at her.

It takes her a long time to look at him. When at last she does, she says simply, “I know it’s a lot. Think about it. If you want to talk again, let me know.”

Parting the seagrass, she steps through the circle, leaving him alone.

Chapter Thirteen

PATTERNS

A whispering morning breeze ruffles across the high terrace of the yellow cottage, nudging the sea lilies on the trellis awake.

"More coffee, Clive?" Smiling at the sheriff, Grand Ella leans forward in her favorite wicker chair. Lifting a lemon-yellow carafe from the outdoor table, she lets it hover invitingly over his ceramic mug.

"Please," he answers, reaching for the sugar bowl. Propping a boot on the railing of the terrace, he relaxes into the outdoor sofa. "It's been a tough morning. I just spoke to Abe Huddleston. He's worried about the marine sanctuary. Place needs maintenance. The aeration system at the aquarium is acting up. I don't know what will happen without Frank Hardy's financial support."

"Poor Abe. He's been through it," Grand Ella murmurs.

"At least his boy survived, thanks to Trippy."

"Trippy is a marvel." She reaches over and pats his hand. "I trust you'll remember that as you ponder your decision about what to do about the children from the Overlook Home."

"Ella..." The sheriff sighs. "You know I can't let my respect for the Beachlings influence my actions as sheriff."

"Hush," Grand Ella says. She passes a plate to him. "Try a strawberry and basil muffin."

Wrinkling his nose, the sheriff scrutinizes the suspicious green flecks in the puffy top.

"Trust me, Clive, you won't notice the taste of herbs."

Timidly, he bites into a muffin. "By jingo, you're right, Ella. It doesn't taste a bit like nasty green stuff."

She laughs. "Basil adds flavor, without overpowering the salty sweetness of Trippy's sea strawberries." Lifting a slender foot, she does a few meditative ankle circles.

The sheriff clears his throat. "Ella."

"Yes, Clive," she answers sweetly, circling her other ankle.

"What you want me to do..." Uncomfortable, he lets his voice trail off.

Putting both feet down, she sits up straight and looks him in the eye. "My request is quite reasonable, Clive. The actions of the Beachlings are understandable, given the extenuating circumstances of the Sickness." Placing her mug firmly on the table between them, she adds, "Everything they did to help the children was justified. What else could they do?"

The sheriff winces. "Ella, I know what you're saying... but it's still against the law. I don't see any way around it. I'm going to have to report it."

"I cannot accept that answer. Sometimes the law is wrong." Standing, she gracefully picks up the plate of muffins. "Please do whatever you can, Clive. Anything. Buy them a little more time."

Helplessly, he looks into her soulful eyes. "All right, Ella," he says at last. "I won't do anything yet."

#

Papa is on the phone with Dr. Everett again. They are talking about the hospital. This is bad. Tad is feeling pink. Mama isn't getting better.

More than anything, Tad wishes Lori was home. Counting his breaths, he goes into her room and stares out the window. A flutter of leaves in the top of the catalpa tree catches his eye. He studies the tree hopefully. In the tip top of the tree, among the heart-shaped leaves, is Guardian.

He smiles at the parrot.

In a flurry of feathers, the bird zooms down from the treetop and perches on the windowsill, looking in at Tad. He can hardly breathe. After researching the parrot on Mama's laptop, Tad has identified the bird as a Turquoise Exotica, identified by its blue and silver top feathers and flaming scarlet throat.

No matter how hard Tad tries, he can't stop looking at the parrot. Swirling in a diamond and emerald pattern, the Guardian's eyes remind him of a kaleidoscope. Kaleidoscopes make countless patterns of light. Tad likes patterns. The patterns in the parrot's bottle-green eyes are comforting, though they make him a little dizzy.

After a little while, Tad feels blue and calm. He knows he has made a new friend, just as he did with his octopus. He is glad the parrot is not afraid of him. The Turquoise Exotica is rare. People of the rainforest say it is a protector and a keeper of secrets.

In a friendly way, Guardian watches him.
Tad feels purple, safe and protected.
He hopes the parrot is keeping Mama safe, too.

Isaac can't stop thinking about the encounter with Condi at the tide pool. The thought that the dream might not be a dream is terrifying. Anxiety snakes up his neck, making him shiver. Pulling his battered guitar case from beneath the bed, he opens it and lets his fingers hover longingly over the torn fabric of the lining where the knife he swiped from the kitchen is hidden.

No.

Not today.

Taking out the guitar, he shuts the guitar case with a snap. Before he can change his mind, he rubs a thumb over the guitar strings in one quick strum. The random vibrations thrill him in a way they haven't for a long time. Jumping to his feet, he grabs his guitar, kicks the case under the bed and heads toward the porch.

At the end of the dock, he yanks off his shoes and throws himself down, letting his legs dangle over the edge of the dock. Funny, the ocean doesn't scare him anymore. In fact, it calms him. He leans back, savoring the way his toes play in the waves. This spot on the dock is nice, especially when the submersible isn't making slurping noises, bouncing against the dock. Heath is out collecting specimens again.

Breathing deeply, he closes his eyes, feeling the warmth of the sun.

Music will get you through anything, Isaac.

He smiles at the sound of her voice.

Opening his eyes, he reaches for his guitar.

Feels like his mom is right next to him—present as she ever was.

#

"Paddy...love..." Kait hears her own voice from somewhere far away. The fog in her head is heavy. She manages to partially open one eye, blinking into a room bright with yellow sun. A room she doesn't recognize.

Chirp.

The sound is familiar. Straining to open both eyes, she is horrified to see an IV drip. *Jesus, Mary, and Joseph.* She's in hospital. Lifting her head off the pillow, she sees her leg, elevated and swathed in bandages. Exhausted, she falls back into the pillow.

"Kait?"

"Vinnie?" Swiveling her head, she looks at his kind face, shadowed with fatigue.

"Sure not Paddy," he answers gruffly.

"Paddy was a boy I knew in Ireland," she says, turning her head to the wall. "He's dead."

He inhales sharply. "Aw...Kait. I'm sorry. You've been talking in your sleep."

She doesn't answer.

"Guess that's why you came to the States. It was more than running away from home." Vinnie clears his throat. "I didn't know."

"I didn't tell you." Taking a deep breath, she asks, "What happened to me?"

"You fell down the stairs. Do you remember?"

She shakes her head. "How did I get here?"

"That crazy parrot you told me about chased me down, squawking 'Call 911.' I was out making deliveries and called for help. When the ambulance came, I followed it to the hospital." He clears his throat. "I've been here every day... since you don't have family close by."

She tries to smile. "How long have I been here?"

"A few days. You were delirious with fever." He grins. "You missed one heck of a storm. The night you fell down the stairs, power was out all over town."

"Look who's awake." A nurse pokes her head in the doorway and moves to Kait's bedside. "Hello there," she says gently.

"What's wrong with me?" Kait whispers.

"Concussion and a nasty blood infection." The nurse points to the IV bag. "You've had multiple rounds of antibiotics. You're recovering well." She smiles and looks at Vinnie. "This young man's been here every chance he could. Night and day."

Blushing, Vinnie looks away.

The nurse detaches the empty IV bag from the pole and moves to the door. "The doctor will be in shortly. You'll be released in the next few days, possibly tomorrow."

After the nurse leaves, Vinnie says quietly, "Lorelei Finch has been up at the mansion since the night of the storm. She's been taking care of Mrs. Hardy."

"Poor kid," Kait mutters. "Lucky for her, I'll be home soon."

"Mrs. Hardy says you must quarantine in your room when you get home."

Kait sighs. "Of course she does."

"Lorelei will stay until you get out of quarantine. She'll

bring you meals and stuff. I'll check in with her to see if there's anything else you need."

"Thank you, Vinnie. For everything." Kait smiles. Vinnie has shown up for her as he always has. Soon she'll be getting out of this place and returning to her own comfortable sky-blue room under the eaves. She doesn't mind being quarantined. Lorelei is the one who has it tough. She knows better than anyone—putting up with Mary Hardy is a whole lot worse.

Chapter Fourteen

DISCOVERIES

"Bring me a fresh candle," Mrs. Hardy whines. "Plumeria and Sweet Pea. It will cleanse the room of germs."

"Yes, ma'am." Lorelei sets down the breakfast tray with a sigh. Mrs. Hardy burns her horrible, scented candles day and night. Who thinks about candles first thing in the morning?

Going to the French armoire, she opens the door, thankful to be wearing a mask. An avalanche of heavy perfumed smells rushes out. Mrs. Hardy may be afraid of germs, but she doesn't mind assailing her senses with imported candles—the kind with fake scents that give people headaches.

"I've changed my mind. Bring me the Arvani Rosette," Mrs. Hardy demands.

Lorelei reaches into the candle cabinet, letting her gaze linger on the row of candles in tinted bell jars on the top shelf, a precious collection of Grand Ella's handmade candles, infused with natural smells from the sea. Last year, Mama gave the candles to Mrs. Hardy as a gift, but she said the old lady complained that the delicate candles had no smell at all.

Lorelei carries the candle to Mrs. Hardy's bedside and lights it. Outside the window, she is surprised to see Maretti's food truck, *Cones and Cream*, pulling up to the front gate, with Vinnie at the wheel.

"Ma'am?" Lorelei asks timidly. "Mr. Maretti's red food truck is idling outside the gate. Vinnie Maretti is driving."

"That dratted boy," Mrs. Hardy sniffs. "Constantly making eyes at Kait. I'm sure he conned his father into letting him bring Kait home from the hospital."

"Kait's out of the hospital?" Lorelei's heart leaps with joy. "Does that mean I can go home today?"

Mrs. Hardy raises a brow. "Certainly not. Kait will quarantine in her room for five days." She glares, as if Lorelei should have known this all along. "In the meantime, I shall have to tolerate your abominable cooking." Waving Lorelei toward the door, she adds, "Open the front gate. Stay outside while that boy helps Kait up to her room. Keep away from him. He may have caught some horrible disease at the hospital. Foolish boy—rushing to Kait's aid like he did."

"My things are up in Kait's room," Lorelei reminds her.

"For heaven's sakes, girl, hurry up! Move your things into the library. You can sleep on the window seat."

Lorelei flies upstairs, taking the stairs two at a time. Poor Kait. Locked in her room for five days. After filling her suitcase with the clothes she's strewn around, she hurries to put her belongings across the hall in the library.

"I'll be sleeping in here with you," she tells Guardian. "On the window seat." She smiles at the bird. "If Kait needs anything, I'll be close by." Tossing blankets and a pillow on Mr. Hardy's desk chair, she pushes back the curtains and cranks open the casement window.

"Go on," Lorelei says, motioning at the open door of Guardian's cage. "You're free. Have some fun. It's a big-sky day."

"*Awk!*" With a goodbye peck to the bar of his cage, the bird soars out the window, shooting up and over the eucalyptus trees.

Hurrying over to Mr. Hardy's desk, Lorelei picks up Mama's logbook. Since the night of the storm, Lorelei has studied Mama's notes, growing more and more confused. The logbook records Mama and Mr. Hardy's expeditions in *Limelight* during the Sickness. Mama never mentioned the expeditions at home. Something doesn't feel right. Mama's not usually secretive about her work. And the notes in the logbook are odd. The entries lack precision, not at all like the ones she taught Lorelei to make in her tide pool notebook. The location names are vague, lacking GPS coordinates—like Mama was nervous about recording too much data rather than not enough.

Lorelei stuffs the logbook into the bottom of her laundry bag, beneath her dirty clothes. Thoughtfully, she slings the bag over her shoulder and goes down the stairs, heading out to the courtyard where the food truck is idling outside the gate. Vinnie's arm is slung over the back of the seat, as if he longs to touch Kait's hair, but doesn't dare.

At the iron gate, Lorelei keys in the security code. The gate rolls back. Lorelei slips off her mask and smiles as Vinnie helps Kait out of the truck.

"Welcome home!" she cries.

A weary-looking Kait limps toward her, leaning on Vinnie's arm. Beside the fountain, she pauses and grins. "Glad I am to see you, Lorelei Finch."

"Same here," Lorelei answers, beaming. "I wish you weren't quarantined."

Kait's eyes twinkle merrily. "We'll find a way to have a bit of fun, I'm sure. Even if it's just talking through the bedroom door. Things can be bleak in this old place, and well I know it."

Vinnie surveys the foreboding peaked eves of the mansion. "You'll be sure to help Kait, won't you, Lorelei?" he asks worriedly. "Check on her a few times a day?"

"Vinnie." Kait sighs pointedly. "It isn't Lorelei's job to wait on me."

"Oh, but it is!" Lorelei assures her. "I'll get you whatever you need. I'm sleeping across the hall in the library."

"Are you now?" Kait murmurs. "The library...now that's a magical place if there ever was one." Glancing over at Vinnie, she explains, "Mr. Hardy's parrot is a knowing creature."

The tender expression on Vinnie's face makes Lorelei shiver. His dark, curly head is bent protectively over Kait, and she is gazing up at him solemnly, like he's someone she's never met before. A plume of spray from the fountain lifts in the breeze, showering them in mist. They look at each other and laugh.

Embarrassed, Lorelei retreats to the garden bench in front of the fountain. She doesn't want to intrude on something that feels private. Suddenly, more than anything, she misses Casey. Maybe it's time to make up with him. The past few days, he's stopped texting her. He was hurt that she didn't tell him she was at the Hardy mansion. But it seemed to get his attention. He promised to give her space. Hard as it is, she thinks that not communicating for a while is a good idea. It's given her time to remember all the things she likes about him, rather than the things she doesn't. Right now, the fight over the octopus seems stupid.

Vinnie walks Kait toward the heavy front door. Gently, Lorelei hears him say, "Let's get you up to your room."

While the two go upstairs, Lorelei hangs out in the garden. She stretches out on the bench, the laundry bag with the dirty clothes and hidden logbook in a heap at her feet. She hopes Kait and Vinnie won't hurry.

It's a beautiful day. A clean rush of sunlight pours through low-hanging branches of eucalyptus and pine. Gurgling and popping, the flowing water of the fountain plays in the clean ocean breeze. A rainbow of spray glances off the carapaces of the onyx turtles on the bottom of the basin of the wave-tipped fountain.

"*Awk!*" Guardian dives through a lacy curtain of eucalyptus and flies several looping circles around Lorelei's head.

Giggling, Lorelei playfully wags her finger at the bird. "Yes, I know. It's wonderful to be free."

After another wild cry, the parrot flies off over the trees.

Leaning back, face to the sun, she smiles. With Kait here, she won't be alone anymore. Mama loved Kait. Kait knows more than anyone else about Mr. Hardy's last days—and maybe she'll have an idea why Mama's expedition logbook is a puzzling bunch of coded notes.

Minutes pass. She smiles. As she'd hoped, Vinnie is hardly rushing away from Kait's side. It's obvious he's got it bad, though Lorelei isn't so sure about Kait. Losing Paddy McClain might make it impossible for Kait to feel anything more than friendship for Vinnie. Watching Condi miss Trustin this whole long year has taught her that. When you love someone deeply, you don't easily move on.

Lifting her arms up to the sky, she stretches. When Vinnie comes back out to the courtyard, she'll send the laundry bag with Mama's logbook with him and ask him to drop it off at home. Papa will bring her clean clothes.

She's not going to tell Papa about Mama's logbook. Not until Tad sees it first.

Her little brother understands codes and patterns better than anyone.

Thankfully, it's one of Tad's chores to do laundry.

"Can you take Care Watch for a while, Tad?" Papa asks. "Vinnie Maretti just stopped by. He dropped off Lorelei's laundry. She needs clean clothes. I need to run up to the Hardy mansion and do a few quick errands in town. I won't be gone too long. Please don't tell Cara I've left the house."

Tad studies Papa's tired face. Papa is worried about many things. One is that Cara sneaked outside during the storm. When Papa returned from searching for Isaac Huddleston, he found her on the front porch kissing a boy in the rain. Now Cara is grounded. Tad hates it when Cara is grounded. She makes awful howling noises. She doesn't care a bit that Papa wants to keep her safe. All she cares about is that she can't go to the beach and kiss boys.

"I will help you, Papa," Tad answers, "and I will do the laundry, too." He takes the laundry bag from Papa's hand, standing up straight and tall.

"Thank you, son." The furrow in Papa's brow loosens. "Lorelei is staying with Mrs. Hardy another few days." He pats Tad's shoulder. "I'll be back soon."

After Papa leaves for Mrs. Hardy's, Tad carries Lorelei's laundry bag into the laundry room. He likes doing laundry. He loves the way the washer sounds, filling the tub with water and fresh, clean smells. Dryer sounds are even better...big circles of *whoosh, whoosh*...comforting and warm.

Turning the bag on end, he dumps it on the floor. To his surprise, there is a book at the bottom of the bag. Tad recognizes it right away. Mama's red leather logbook. The special one with her name in gold letters; the one Papa gave her for Christmas last year. Tad picks up the book. Holding it tight to his chest, he closes his eyes, feeling the colors, yellow for glad and brown for sad. He is glad to have the logbook home where it belongs, but he is sad that Mama is not awake to be glad about it, too.

After he starts the washing machine, Tad carries the logbook into Mama's room. Sitting down in the old rocker, he holds the book reverently in his lap. There must be a good reason Lori put the logbook in the laundry bag and didn't tell Papa. She knows Tad does the laundry. She must want Tad to look at it. Cautiously, he opens the logbook. Lori always has good reasons.

At the mansion gate, Lorelei tries not to feel sorry for herself when Papa leaves. He didn't stay for more than a minute. After giving her a quick hug, he said he needed to get going.

"What is going on?" she'd demanded.

"Cara is totally out of control." Papa had shaken his head. "She's been sneaking out to meet an older boy named Dom Jacobs."

Lorelei is furious. Her little sister is a royal pain. Because of Cara, Papa couldn't stay to talk. All because he can't trust Cara not to sneak out again.

Dragging her feet, she walks back to the house. Two people are depending on her now. Reluctantly, she returns to the gloomy interior of the mansion. Later, she'll call Tad and tell him to look at the strange codes in Mama's logbook. And she'll text Casey. Holding a grudge about the octopus is silly. Besides, maybe the octopus with colored brain lights really was a figment of her imagination. The more time passes, the more impossible everything that happened that day seems. Casey is always so certain. Right now, Lorelei feels certain of nothing at all.

Tad cannot believe what he's reading. The numbers in Mama's logbook match the confidential file numbers in her laptop. Each file is password protected. The strange notations next to the logbook entries might be the passwords. Cautiously, Tad goes over to the bookshelf and gets Mama's laptop down from the top shelf. Then he returns to the rocker, watching Mama sleep.

He opens the laptop. "Mama?" Tad says loudly. "Is it okay if I open your files?"

No answer. Only a shallow exhale.

Tad reassures himself that Mama wouldn't be mad. Finding the logbook entry that matches the first computer file, he types in the numbers, letters, and symbols next to it. The file opens. A video appears. Eyes wide, he clicks on it.

A shadowy scene comes into view, narrated by the excited voices of Mama and Mr. Hardy. The video is underwater photography of a volcanic shelf with glittering webs, hanging upside-down like open umbrellas. *Thousands of brooding octomoms, Gabby! Who would have believed it, just a few miles from Dipitous! Look at all the steam vents...a huge nursery... near the Ring of Fire.*

Trying to hide his excitement, Tad peers closer at the screen. He knows all about the Ring of Fire! Octopuses are attracted to the warmth of steam vents. A delicate webbed shadow floats into view and hovers in front of the camera. Slowly, it unfurls eight magnificent arms, sparkling in different colors.

Lori's octopus!

One arm lifts and flashes, matching the exact color that Tad is feeling inside—aquamarine—for wonder.

Casey stares into his computer screen. He can't keep his mind on anything, not even watching his favorite oceanography videos. His frustration is at a max.

When Casey served the doctor pancakes this morning at breakfast, he politely asked whether the pump at the aquarium was still working. "No concern of yours," Heath had answered. Then he demanded more caramelized syrup.

But that's not the worst thing. The worst is that Lorelei still isn't communicating. He told her he'd give her space and she seems to be fine with that. Casey thinks he might go out of his mind if she doesn't reach out soon.

In his pocket, his phone buzzes.

Yanking it out, he dares to hope. Disappointed, he clicks the phone to speaker. "Hello, sir."

"Casey, I need your help." The urgency in Mr.

Huddleston's voice snaps him to attention. "A few hours up the coast there's been a green sea turtle stranding, caused by the odd currents during the storm the other night. Sea turtles are washing up on Everwood Beach. Many are injured. I need to help with the rescue and transport wounded turtles to the aquarium. You in?"

Casey leaps to his feet. "Yes sir!"

"Ask your mom and dad."

"I will," Casey tells him with confidence. "But it's fine. They know how important sea turtle rescues are."

Sun-washed sea air plays with Condi's hair, tugging it up and into the breeze as she slides smoothly into the back door of the next wave. The high rollers are spectacular today. The aquamarine surfboard sparkles, catching light, blending with the color of the ocean in midafternoon.

Despite the flowing moves of her body, her thoughts are in a tangle. She doesn't know how to process what she learned from Isaac at the tide pool yesterday. The trouble with knowing and not being able to tell is that you can't be sure what other people know. Isaac surprised her.

As the nose of Aquamarine carves into another roller, a flick of foam flies off the crest of the wave and tickles Condi's nose. Hopping off her board in the shallows, she glances toward the beach. Afternoon light blinds her. Her heart jumps...then crashes. Looking totally out of place in his crazy black leather jacket and jeans, Isaac is leaning against the railing at the top of the beach stairs. When will she stop imagining he is Trustin?

Slowly, she walks out of the surf and picks up her beach

towel. Lifting her board, she trudges through the sand and makes her way to the beach stairs. Isaac descends the stairs to meet her on the sand. He is wearing shiny black rocker boots with thick heels. She tries not to laugh.

"New boots?" she asks, grinning.

"Second pair." Flushing, he tries to scuff them up in the sand.

"What are you doing here? Thought you hated the beach."

He pauses and squints at the horizon. "Yeah," he says when his eyes return to hers. "I really, really do."

She laughs. "Truth."

Tapping his sunglasses nervously on the rail, he says, "I thought about what you said yesterday. Couldn't sleep. I want to talk."

She studies him carefully. "Are you sure you're ready?"

He takes a deep breath. "Here's the thing. When I was underwater, I met a dude who looks a lot like me. He asked about you."

She sucks in her breath. Nervously, she glances around the beach. Surfer kids are arriving to catch late afternoon waves. "We can't talk about this here."

"Meet me at the tide pool?" he asks. "Promise not to let you down."

"You'll tell me everything?"

He nods.

"Tomorrow at two o'clock." She picks up Aquamarine and shoots him a steely stare. "No more games."

When Mr. Huddleston picks Casey up at the B&B, he tells him to hop in the front seat. "Only the two of us, I'm afraid." Mr. Huddleston shakes his head in annoyance. "No idea where Heath is."

Casey shrugs. After Heath's rudeness at breakfast, he's got no desire to see the CDC doctor for a long time.

"Heath's going to get himself killed," Mr. Huddleston mutters under his breath. "Something's off with *Limelight*'s depth gauge measurements. The remote programming software is acting up. Every time I check it, it defaults to the wrong depth charts."

"Yes, sir," Casey says politely.

"Everything's a mess at Everwood Beach. There's a slew of stranded turtles. We really need more manpower." Mr. Huddleston sighs. "Isaac's not around either. Today of all days, he decided to go to the beach and watch the surfers." He rolls his eyes at Casey. "Go figure."

"We can handle it, sir," Casey says confidently. Neither Isaac nor Heath would have added an ounce of legit muscle to the turtle rescue team.

Mr. Huddleston flips on the radio to listen to the news. They ride along in silence for a while, until Casey can't stand it. Though it may be a mistake, he takes out his phone and shoots off a message to Lorelei.

On my way to Everwood Beach with Mr. H. Sea turtle stranding.

As usual, he gets no reply. But it makes him feel better. He wants her to know he's never going to stop trying. After all, she's his best friend.

Typing furiously, he kills some time by telling Lorelei about Heath and the night of the storm when he aerated the aquarium. *Top secret bigwig from CDC is a mean dude. Doesn't care about the turtles.* For a moment, he considers telling her how Heath questioned him about her mom's research with Frank Hardy. But the news might feel manipulative, a trick to get her to talk to him. He's damaged her trust enough.

When a sign announces that they are entering Everwood Beach, Mr. Huddleston turns the radio off. "Time to review sea turtle rescue procedures. Almost there."

Casey sends the long text off to Lorelei, hoping he's got a signal. Cell service on the coastal road is tricky.

At least, she'll know he's thinking of her.

Chapter Fifteen

SECRETS

After serving Mrs. Hardy dinner and setting a supper tray outside Kait's door, Lorelei wanders into the library. A light fall breeze is spinning into the room from the open casement window. Mauve and crimson light pools beneath the overhanging eucalyptus leaves on the broad, sloped lawn. She pauses to say a prayer for Mama. How she would have loved this view...lacy silhouettes of trees against the sunset, backlit by a silver and teal sea.

Carefully, she fills Guardian's food tray. The parrot hasn't returned, but Lorelei isn't worried. Each evening, in the dwindling minutes of deep dusk, the bird faithfully flies through the window and returns to his cage.

With Cara acting out, Lorelei wonders how Tad is getting along at home. Now that Mama is sick, Papa doesn't notice when Tad is struggling. Her little brother is sensitive. He relies on Lorelei. Cara's never taken the time to understand him. Curling up on the window seat, she calls home and asks Papa if she can talk to Tad.

"Lori!" Tad's excited voice lifts her spirits.

"Hey, Tad," Lorelei says, "I miss you a lot. How's Mama doing?"

"She is the same, Lori," Tad answers. "And Papa is mad at Cara. He makes her sit with him, even when he is on Care Watch." Tad is indignant. He raises his voice. "I *really* don't like it that Cara is making drama. I wish you were home."

"I wish I was, too, Tad," Lorelei tells him. "But I have good news. Kait Dooley came home from the hospital today. She's in quarantine for five days, but soon she'll be out, and I'll be back home. In the meantime, I need a big favor. Can you empty the laundry bag I sent home today with Vinnie?"

"I already did, Lori! When I did the laundry, I found Mama's logbook." Tad's voice tells her he is smiling. "I knew you wanted me to find it." He takes a deep, proud breath. "I am doing all the laundry now, Lori. All by myself."

"That's wonderful, Tad," Lorelei says carefully. "Did you put the logbook in a safe place?"

"On your dresser, with your tide pool notebook, under the starfish mirror," Tad answers.

"That's a great place for it, Tad." Lorelei smiles. "Can you help me with something else?"

"I will help you, Lori."

"Did you look in the logbook?"

Tad hesitates. "Yes, Lori."

"It's okay, Tad," she tells him quickly. "I'm glad you did. Mama's logbook has a lot of confusing notes and number patterns in it. Can you–"

"You are wrong, Lori," Tad interrupts.

Lorelei fights for patience. "What do you mean?"

"The notes are not confusing, Lori."

"The notes are in code—"

"The numbers in Mama's logbook are not a code," Tad answers firmly.

"What are you saying, Tad?"

"If I tell you why I know, I don't want you to tell Papa. He will be angry."

Tad sounds worried. Lorelei bites her lower lip. She can't imagine what Tad might tell her. She can't promise to keep something secret from Papa—at least not until she knows what it is.

"Please tell me, Tad. I promise I won't get mad at you—but I can't promise not to tell."

"I am thinking, Lori."

Lorelei takes a long, deep breath. Tad cannot be rushed.

At last, Tad says, "Okay, I will tell you, Lori. Even if I get in trouble, you need to know."

"Thank you, Tad. Where is Papa right now?" she asks gently. Tad needs time when he has something big to explain. If he is worried about getting in trouble, he might take even longer.

"Papa is talking to Cara," Tad says sadly. "She is yelling very loud at him."

Lorelei sighs. There's no reasoning with Cara when she's acting crazy. Poor Papa. "I'm sorry about Cara, Tad, but there's nothing you and I can do. Let Papa handle it." She pauses, speaking slowly and carefully. "Tell me what you know about Mama's logbook."

"Lori," Tad begins. "Please don't be mad. I have been doing something sneaky."

"What, Tad?" Lorelei feels a nudge of fear. Surely her shy little brother has not been sneaking out of the house?

He's always been too scared to even venture out of the yard alone.

"I've been going on Mama's laptop without permission."

"Oh, Tad," Lorelei murmurs. "That is not a good idea." But she lets out her breath in relief. There are worse things. Tad loves computers, and Mama's laptop is the ultimate temptation. "How do you know her passcode?"

"It is easy," Tad answers solemnly. "Our birthday months."

Unexpected tears spring to Lorelei's eyes. Sweet, loving Mama, her children never far from her heart. *Please, please get well.*

"The numbers in Mama's logbook match her computer files." Tad's voice is triumphant. "Mama and Mr. Hardy made an important discovery, Lori. They found a big octopus nursery in the steam vents off the coast!" He pauses. "Mama's files tell all about it. One has an oceanographer's video, one has a letter, and one has a GPS map of a volcanic shelf marked with red dots."

"Oh, Tad," Lorelei says, hardly able to breathe.

"And Lori, I saw an octopus in the video—just like your octopus! Every arm was a different color."

Lorelei gasps. "That is amazing news."

"There's even more news," Tad goes on. "The key on the map says the red dots are 'melanin pools.' Do you know what that means, Lori?"

"A little," Lorelei mumbles, her mind abuzz with shock.

"Melanin," Tad says seriously, "is the dark pigment in octopus and squid ink. I read all about it."

"That's right," Lorelei answers.

"The file that has the letter in it is to the United States Center for Disease Control," Tad goes on, speaking carefully, making sure he says the words exactly right. "In the letter, Mr. Hardy and Mama say they made an important scientific discovery that might save lives."

"About the octopus nursery?" Lorelei asks eagerly.

"The letter didn't say. They said the discovery is top secret. Mr. Hardy asked for a marine biologist specializing in biomedicine to come to Dipitous Beach right away." Tad sounds puzzled. "Lori, I don't understand. Why didn't Mama tell us about the octopus nursery in the steam vents? She tells us everything."

"I think it must be because the discovery is important to the government, Tad. The Center for Disease Control is part of the government. If the discovery is top secret, she isn't allowed to talk about it—and it explains why her logbook isn't easy to understand." Lorelei's mind whirls with possibilities. "I don't know a lot about melanin, but I know it's used in medicines. Maybe Mama and Mr. Hardy discovered a special kind of melanin." Lorelei's heart races. Another wild thought occurs to her. "Tad, I just thought of something. When I saw the octopus under the sea and it reached for me, everything went black. What if I didn't pass out? What if the blackness was a squirt of melanin ink? What if the melanin is what helped me breathe?"

"That is a lot of what-ifs, Lori," Tad says seriously.

"Oh, Tad," Lorelei groans. "You sound like Casey. It's only a hypothesis."

Tad is quiet for a long moment. "I don't always like Casey," he says at last. "But sometimes he is right. When you are a scientist, it isn't good to rush to conclusions."

"Fine," Lorelei agrees with a sigh. "But it *is* a reasonable hypothesis, Tad."

"Yes, Lori," Tad concedes. "Scientists use melanin in medicines...but I am worried. Did you know that bad scientists hurt squid and octopuses to get it?"

"How do you know all this?"

"I read online articles about melanin harvesting. A lot of the cephalopods die. Lori, melanin harvesting is very wrong!"

"Tad, take a moment to breathe."

Obediently, he pauses to count and take long breaths.

While Tad calms down, Lorelei checks her phone for messages. There are two new ones. Lucky Casey. He's on a sea turtle rescue. The second message is disturbing. The new doctor at the CDC sounds awful. What in the world is going on?

"Tad, Casey thinks something is up at the marine sanctuary. The new doctor is not a nice guy. He doesn't care about sea turtles."

"Oh, no!" Tad cries. "Maybe he is a bad scientist!"

Too late Lorelei realizes her mistake. She should have never told Tad about Casey's message. With his fears about melanin harvesting, her little brother is letting his imagination run away. "Tad. Listen to me. Stop thinking about the doctor."

"I can't." Tad's voice is fast and pitchy. "Casey says the doctor is not nice. Casey is sometimes right." His breathing quickens. "I feel red, Lori."

Lorelei flinches. Red spells trouble. "TAD," she says in a low, clear voice. "Breathe with me. Sit up straight."

"I don't know if I can do it!" Tad wails.

"Yes. You. Can," Lorelei says firmly. "Inhale—two-three-four. Pause. Exhale. Two-three-four."

Slowly, they count and breathe together. "Thank you, Lori," Tad says at last. "Red is pink now—and I can handle pink." He lets out a long exhale. "But I am still *very* worried. I wish you could come home."

"Me, too," Lorelei answers. Downstairs, a demanding Mrs. Hardy is persistently thumping her cane on the floor. "I'm sorry, Tad, but I've got to hang up. Mrs. Hardy is signaling."

"Okay," Tad replies. "Thank you for calling, Lori."

Her brother's quaint courtesy touches her. "Sure you're good now?"

"I'm good, Lori."

"I love you, Tad. Stay positive. Don't worry about the sea creatures. I'll ask Casey to check on them. Promise."

After saying goodbye, Lorelei takes her sweet time responding to the banging of Mrs. Hardy's cane. Giving herself a minute to stand at the casement window, she breathes in the cool night air. Guardian is late. Still, she refuses to worry. Tad's news has blown her mind. What does Mama and Mr. Hardy's discovery mean? She longs to talk to Casey. How could she have stayed mad at him so long?

The banging of the cane is louder and faster. *Okay, okay, I'm coming.* Leaving the library, she notices the untouched supper tray outside Kait's door. She stops and knocks three times, this time louder than when she left the tray. "It's me, Lorelei," she calls. "Your dinner is outside the door, Kait."

A rustling comes from inside the bedroom. "Thanks, Lorelei," a sleepy voice mumbles. "Goodness me. I slept away the afternoon!"

"When I get Mrs. Hardy to bed, I'll check on you," Lorelei assures her, relieved that Kait sounds fine. "I'll bring dessert. Vinnie brought two kinds of gelato!"

"Of course he did!" Kait's laugh ripples through the closed door.

Smiling, Lorelei makes her way down the staircase and hurries toward the sound of furious thumping. Will Mrs. Hardy never let up? The old lady is relentless.

Slipping on her mask, Lorelei touches the golden knob of the bedroom door. The knob is hot. Cautiously, she places an open palm on the wood. Warm to the touch. She glances down. A faint wisp of smoke is seeping under the door.

"FIRE!" she screams.

Inside the bedroom there is the sickening sound of exploding glass. The window opening into the garden—

Running down the hall, she shouts at the base of the stairs, "Fire! Fire!" hoping Kait will hear. Tearing out the front door, she rushes into the garden and over to the shattered bedroom window, praying she's not too late.

Chapter Sixteen

HEART-SHAPED LEAVES

After dinner, Tad wanders out into the garden. Counting his breaths and steps, he walks in circles around the small courtyard. Awful red thoughts buzz in his head. A new doctor is at the marine sanctuary, probably because of Mama and Mr. Hardy's letter. Tad is sure Mama and Mr. Hardy expected the new doctor to be smart and good—but the new doctor is stupid and mean. This is bad.

The sun is sinking, glowing bronze and copper on the horizon. Deepening shadows fall over the garden.

"*Awk.*"

The catalpa tree shakes, sending down a shower of heart-shaped leaves. Tad looks up, squinting into the draining light. On the top branch of the tree, swaying above the roofline, is Guardian.

"*Awk.*" The parrot swoops to perch on the limb of the shrub next to Tad.

Tad is motionless. He stops counting his breaths. As the last glints of sunset catch and hold, he stares into the parrot's sparkling kaleidoscope eyes. Glistening shards of color spiral in a hypnotic pattern. Mesmerized, he cannot look away. Slowly, the fragments of light cease to spin. Coming together, they interlock like puzzle pieces, uniting in a design.

Tad leans in, staring. The pattern is familiar...a creature with eight long arms and a glowing orb of a brain. The octopus sparkles, glowing brightly in the black pupil of the parrot's green eyes.

Startled, Tad blinks.

The octopus flashes orange. One arm lifts, glowing like a torch.

"Go to the sanctuary."

Tad jumps to his feet, but the bird says no more. Soaring upward like an arrow, it pierces the canopy of the catalpa tree, disappearing into the last flash of sunset's light.

Casey sags against the seats in Mr. Huddleston's van. Every bone in his body—every muscle, too—hurts with the kind of tired that comes when you push yourself beyond limits. That's what happened today. For eight long hours Casey and Mr. Huddleston and a team of strong-armed volunteers worked tirelessly to rescue dying sea turtles marooned on the seaweed-strewn sand of Everwood Beach.

Some of the turtles were fine, swimming away from shore the instant they were returned to the waterline. Some were listless and unmoving, barely breathing. These creatures were dragged to an ocean inlet next to the beach, where a temporary holding pool was created by constructing a barricade from wood left behind by the recent storm.

The pool, incapable of holding back the tide for long, was built in the hope it might contain the turtles long enough for them to recover—before they wash back into open sea.

Many of the turtles were injured by tangled fishing lines and nets. Some were partly suffocated by toxic trash pushed inland by the storm. Everyone did their best to free the tortured creatures. At the end of the evening, the strongest and gentlest of the volunteers carefully lifted the injured turtles into storage tanks filled with seawater and put the tanks in Mr. Huddleston's van.

It is dark now. The tanks are loaded, and Casey and Mr. Huddleston call goodbye to the volunteers. Flashing hazard lights, the van starts up the steep hill leading to the coastal highway. Casey winces at the sound of the tanks in the back sloshing, injured turtles bumping and flailing. It will be a long, precarious drive back to the marine sanctuary.

"Got to drive slowly," Mr. Huddleston says. "The turtles are badly hurt. Don't want to make it worse." With a grimy hand, he switches into low gear. "With all the hills and curves in this road, the trip will take three or four hours. Let your parents know we'll be late."

Casey fires off a text to his mom and dad. "One of the turtles has a rear flipper almost torn off," he says worriedly.

"Without that flipper, the turtle can never be returned to the sea." Mr. Huddleston sighs. "Rear flippers act like rudders. Without one, steering while swimming is almost impossible."

Casey knows this, but he refrains from saying so, thinking of Lorelei. When people are tired, it's better to listen. Mr. Huddleston is exhausted.

The oceanographer blows out a breath between his teeth. "Before we transfer the Everwood turtles into the big aquarium, we've got to make room. We'll release the turtles currently in the tank. They're ready to be returned to open sea."

Casey nods, trying not to groan aloud at the thought of how hard it will be to get the big turtle down to the dock when they return to the marine sanctuary. "Uh, okay," he says. "Will that be enough space?"

"I don't know." Mr. Huddleston sighs. "With the oxygen system of the big aquarium acting up, I'm worried about overloading the tank. There's another option."

"What's that, sir?"

"We can move the rare octopus out of the cephalopod house and put a few of the smaller turtles in the octopus tank."

Rare octopus?

Before Casey can digest the offhand remark, a car barrels around a sharp turn in the road, white headlights blinding. It whizzes past the van, almost striking it and causing Mr. Huddleston to swerve off onto the shoulder.

"Psycho." Muttering under his breath, Mr. Huddleston cautiously maneuvers the van back onto the highway.

By now Casey's collected his wits. With a gulp, he screws up his nerve. "Excuse me, sir, but did you say there's a rare octopus in the cephalopod house?"

"Didn't Lorelei tell you?" Surprised, Mr. Huddleston glances over, then moves his eyes back to the road. "She and that cute little brother of hers came to see me after she fell off her surfboard. The octopus showed up on the dock that very morning. It's a rare one, for sure. I haven't been able to identify it yet."

Casey is speechless, and he feels like he took a gut punch to the heart. Another thing Lorelei didn't tell him. Why should she? He didn't believe her when she told him about the octopus she saw under the sea. And now a rare breed of octopus has showed up on the dock of the marine sanctuary. No wonder she doesn't want to talk to him. He cradles his head in his hands. *Humiliation complete.*

"Er, Casey?" Mr. Huddleston clears his throat. "Sorry, buddy. Figured she told you about it."

"She's mad at me," he confesses.

Mr. Huddleston clicks his tongue in sympathy. "This morning Heath told me he is planning to experiment on the poor creature by drawing its blood—which is gold, by the way, instead of the usual blue." Mr. Huddleston shakes his head. "I hate to return a new discovery to the sea without classifying it, but I can't stand by and watch Heath torture innocent sea creatures." He hits an open palm soundly on the dashboard. "There, made my decision. When we get back to the sanctuary, we'll release the octopus, protecting him from Heath's ghoulish experiments and making room for the turtles."

Miserable, Casey nods. At least he'll get a quick look at the unusual octopus. He has no doubt now that what Lorelei told him might be possible. If the octopus has gold blood, an unheard-of condition, then it might also have different colored brain lights, too.

He reaches for his phone to text her, but then thinks better of it. After he releases the octopus and takes care of the turtles, he'll text.

And beg her to forgive him.

#

Squinting through smoke, Lorelei crawls under the gray haze, carrying Mrs. Hardy. In the garden, she found the old lady's frail body hanging out of the exploded glass of the downstairs bedroom window, still clutching her cane. Somehow, she eased the old lady over the shards of glass and put the old woman on her back, heading toward the sound of gurgling water.

"Lorelei!" Kait's panicked voice emerges from the smoke. Through the haze, Lorelei sees Kait dragging a wet quilt out of the fountain. She stumbles to her feet, picks up Mrs. Hardy and runs toward Kait.

"Wrap her up," Kait orders. "Hurry."

When they get the old woman wrapped in the wet quilt, Mrs. Hardy's cane clatters to the cobblestones. Coughing violently, her eyes roll back in her head, and she goes limp in Lorelei's arms.

Fire leaps out of the pitched eave above the mansion's entrance, roaring like a savage beast. Cauldron-black smoke billows from the rafters like a pot bubbling over. The roof folds in and collapses, sliding down over the front door. Flames engulf Mrs. Hardy's bedroom. The upstairs windows implode with the terrible sound of gunshots.

"Run for the road," Kait cries.

Tossing another wet blanket around their own shoulders, they lift Mrs. Hardy between them. Sparks fly around their heads, sizzling into the mist of the fountain's spray. Dodging flying glass and the fierce, raw heat of the blaze, they run to the front gate, where Lorelei keys in the security code. The gates roll back. Dashing up to the high beach road, they hurry away from the smoke.

"I don't think she's breathing," Lorelei tells Kait as they move Mrs. Hardy upwind from the flames. "I'll try CPR."

Kneeling, she uses the technique Mr. Marshall teaches his surfers in surfing school. Stacking the heels of her hands on the old woman's chest, she starts compressions. After three compressions, she pinches the old woman's nostrils, tips back her head, and exhales into Mrs. Hardy's mouth and lungs.

Compression, compression, compression...breathe.

Screams of sirens fill the air. A fire truck roars around the corner and tears down the hill toward the mansion. An ambulance pulls up beside them. Two EMTs hop out.

"You kids okay?"

"Fine," Kait answers.

Lorelei nods and sits back on her heels, catching her breath.

"Great job with CPR," the EMT tells them, slipping an oxygen mask on Mrs. Hardy. "She's breathing on her own, but we need to get her to the hospital. A ride is on the way for you. They'll be here any minute."

As the ambulance speeds away through the dark, Lorelei and Kait huddle in the soggy blanket, watching firefighters battle the conflagration that is now the mansion. Most of the upper floor is now in flames.

"Sorry about your things," Lorelei says quietly, thinking of the photo of Paddy McClain in the frame beside Kait's bed.

"Things don't matter, as well I know," Kait answers, hugging Lorelei close. "It's that aggravating old parrot I'm sad for."

"I'm pretty sure he's okay," Lorelei tells her. "The casement window was open, and the door to his cage."

"Thank the Great Powers for that," Kait exclaims.

Blinding headlights flash at the crest of the hill. *Sweets and Stories* roars around the curve in the road and screeches to a stop. Andy Marshall jumps from the driver's seat and the passenger side of the bookmobile swings wide. Vinnie climbs down, while Andy rushes over to Lorelei, his long white hair whipped into a froth by the wind, glowing copper in the light of the fire dominating the night sky. "How's Mary?"

"Breathing when the ambulance took her," Lorelei tells him.

"Thanks to Lorelei's quick thinking and CPR," Kait adds.

"Good girl." The surf master claps a relieved hand over Lorelei's shoulder.

"Thank goodness you taught us CPR in surf school," Lorelei says. "You said real surfers need to know rescue techniques." She smiles into his worried eyes. "CPR worked, the way you said it would."

"I thought it would save kids from drowning." Andy shakes his head, "Never dreamed it might bring Mary Hardy through a fire."

"Frank's place," He murmurs, gazing at the burning bones of the mansion. "Vinnie and I saw the flames from the high parking lot. I can't believe it."

Vinnie has swallowed Kait up in a mammoth hug, wet blanket and all. In silence, the four of them huddle together, observing the dousing of the fire from the buckets of the fire trucks.

A soot-streaked fireman jogs over to them. "No pets left inside?"

"We don't think so," Lorelei says. "There's a parrot that flies free that lives in the upstairs library. The window was open. I hope—"

The fireman chuckles. "Giant blue and red parrot?"

Lorelei nods.

“No worries about the parrot, miss. The parrot alerted us to the fire. Came swooping right down into the firehouse garage squawking, ‘*Fire! Fire! Hardy Mansion*,’ clear as you please.”

Chapter Seventeen

HALOED MOON

Pacing through the night shadows falling across the path, Tad concentrates fiercely, counting his steps from his house to the marine sanctuary.

978

979

980...

The walk is several miles. He's proud of himself. Without even one ragged, anxious breath, he's made his way through the hilly pass and over the scary, steep dune that separates the Finch house from Craggy Point. At the top of the hill, he gets a first view of the star-studded sea.

Thank you.

He smiles up at the rising moon. The orange halo is the predictor of a harvest moon. Orange is the color of courage.

Tad feels bad about sneaking out without telling Papa, but he has an important job to do. Squaring his shoulders, he breathes in blue. He can't worry about Papa right now.

With Cara stealing his leftover time and attention, Papa won't even notice Tad is gone. At least not until after midnight. Tad will be back home in bed by then.

Everything's going to be okay.

This is a night for being brave.

The whisper of the night tide runs along the shore, laying a mantle of reassuring blue across his shoulders as he makes his way down the hill to the marine sanctuary.

Almost there.

Isaac spent a long time hanging out with the turtles tonight. When he got home from the beach, there was a note with the security code to the aquarium on the kitchen counter. His dad left him in charge of feeding the turtles. He's working a stranding up the coast. Heath's out in *Limelight* again. Strange...it's well after dark.

Grabbing his guitar, Isaac wanders down to the dock to sit out under the stars. Being around the big turtle in the tank was relaxing. He lost track of time. The slow, graceful movements of the turtle reminded him of his mother's hands, playing amber tones on her cello to lull him back to sleep after he had a nightmare. A long time ago...when he was small and safe.

The moon, a luscious orange halo, scatters amber across the water. Strands of a mysterious melody rise and play in his mind.

A lullaby...

Maybe this time he can find the chords.

When he reaches the entrance to the cephalopod house, Tad is breathing hard. It is 5,446 steps from his house to this spot. All the while, he kept his mind orange, though red kept sneaking around, taunting him with scary thoughts.

I am here to rescue my friend.

One more step.

5,447.

He pushes open the door and moves inside. A friendly, salt-laden breeze greets him. The big window in the small hive-shaped room is open, letting in plenty of air and enough moonlight to see by. His fingers itch to turn on a light, but it is not a good idea. It will scare his friend. Octopuses like the dark.

"Hello," he whispers as he goes to stand beside the metal tank. Reaching through shadow, he fumbles for the rod which locks the latch on the lid. To his surprise, the security rod is not in place.

The lid of the tank lifts. Two glowing eyes examine him, and a long, suckered arm reaches out of the tank. Unwinding slowly, it tentatively reaches out and touches Tad's hand, lighting up in pinpricks of twinkling orange light.

Tad is not afraid, even when the creature's arm snakes around his wrist. He lifts the heavy lid all the way up. In a shimmering cascade, the elegant body of the octopus slithers up and out of the water, flowing over the side of the tank to the floor.

"C'mon, little buddy," Tad says kindly. "I will help you get home. We've got to hurry." Since octopuses can survive only a short time out of water, getting down to the dock fast is important.

The octopus raises a shimmering gold arm and gestures toward the open window.

"Good thinking," Tad agrees. "That way is faster."

Moving fluidly across the floor, the octopus leaves behind a trail of slime that glitters in the moonlight. Tad marvels at how the creature's arms light up as it travels: red, pink, green, yellow, orange, blue, purple, and aquamarine—all the colors Lori said. At the window, the octopus slides up and over the windowsill. Confidently, Tad follows, clambering up and over, dropping easily onto the path leading down to the dock.

The octopus takes his hand with a purple arm. A thrill of belonging rushes through Tad. Purple means love. This creature loves him. They are truly friends.

"We've got to get you down to the water," Tad says urgently, tugging on the arm.

The octopus resists. Raising a green arm, it points toward the aquarium.

"No!" says Tad. "The bad doctor will find you if you go to the aquarium. You must go back home to the sea."

The purple arm releases Tad's hand. With the green arm held high, the octopus slithers toward the aquarium at an amazing speed. Tad struggles to keep up. When the creature arrives at the front door of the aquarium, the bright arm lights go out. The creature spreads out flat over the cement floor of the entry, camouflaging to match the dull stone, disappearing before Tad's eyes.

The hairs on the back of Tad's neck prickle. Something is wrong.

"Hey, what's going on there?" a voice calls out of the dark.

Oh, no! The bad doctor!

Tad panics and whirls around, blinded by the violent beam of a flashlight.

The world goes red.

Flinging his arms wide, he starts to spin.

Hugging her knees to her chest on the outdoor couch of the high terrace of the yellow cottage, Condi pretends to study the moon, but she isn't seeing a single beautiful thing tonight. Not the spill of starlight over Windy Hollow, not the crashing of waves against the shimmering tower, not the sparkling grapes of sapphire kelp flung over the jagged rocks. No. Her mind is far away...stretching through time, plunging into the fathomless depths of the sea. She can't comprehend what Isaac might have meant with his comment today in the cove. Is it possible, could it really be—did Isaac encounter Trustin when he nearly drowned the night of the storm?

Or is he playing another game?

A rogue wave crashes on the high shore, grabbing her attention.

Anything is possible, Condoleeza.

Papa's baritone rumbles out of the strong tide.

Never abandon hope....

Mama's soft contralto whispers in the breeze.

Comforted, Condi curls up into the cocoon of blankets on the couch on the terrace, listening to the rise and fall of voices coming from the kitchen of the cottage. Grand Ella and Sheriff Coodle are in deep conversation, discussing the lost children living with the Beachlings.

"I've done all I can, Ella," the sheriff is saying patiently. "I must report this to the state authorities. If I don't, we'll all be labeled as negligent, and that won't advance our case."

"Give it a few more days, Clive," Grand Ella pleads. "Francie doesn't have much longer. We cannot separate her from Firth and Cissy and Malcolm. Those four have forged a bond."

The sheriff lets out a sigh. "Despite my better judgment, I will wait until next week."

"Thank you, Clive." Grand Ella's voice is soft and low.

Condi sighs. The break in conversation no longer surprises her. Much as she hates it, she's pretty sure her grandmother is falling for the sheriff.

Screech!

A piercing tone echoes through the night. The sheriff's beeper. Condi's heart beats fast.

"What is it, Clive?" Grand Ella cries.

"I've got to go, Ella." The sheriff's heavy boots thump on the kitchen floor. "I forgot my phone was off. I missed the news. There's been a fire. At the Hardy mansion."

Barking grim commands into his phone, he leaves the cottage. Siren screaming into the night, his patrol car races up the high beach road.

"*Eeeeeee!*"

"Stop, please stop," Isaac begs the small boy, throwing his flashlight down in the grass. He doesn't know what to do. The kid is spinning, yelling at the top of his lungs.

"I didn't mean to scare you." He grabs for the boy's arm.

Slap! Something slick and slimy slaps Isaac's hand away.

Jumping back, he stares at the opalescent blob jiggling in the grass. Illuminated in the flashlight's glare, the blob emits an eerie interior glow, glistening in the moonlight like gelatin.

After a long moment, the blob lifts a golden arm, pointing it at Isaac like a warning. Isaac steps back, pressing himself up against a beach elm. Anxiously, he watches the creature through an overhanging curtain of leaves. The blob unfolds, revealing itself as an octopus.

Bowing its head, the creature gently wraps its many arms around the boy's body. Instantly, the spinning slows. An expression of peace appears on the boy's face. He relaxes and grows quiet.

"Who are you?" Isaac blurts from the cover of leaves.

The creature swivels its bell-shaped head toward the leafy shadows, staring into the dark with spooky, unwavering eyes. Raising the imperial golden arm, the creature waves at Isaac as if to silence him. Then, with a blue arm, the octopus gracefully beckons for Isaac to come forward.

Taking a deep breath, Isaac emerges from the leaves. "Who are you?" he repeats.

The boy lifts his chin with an odd, quaint dignity. "My name is Tad."

"You shouldn't be here." Isaac bends over to pick up the flashlight. "Go home."

The boy hugs the arms of the octopus as if wrapping himself in a blanket. "Not yet. I came to save my friend." He caresses the octopus. "His name is Figment."

Isaac snorts. "You've got to be kidding." He picks up the flashlight, shining it on the octopus. The creature waggles a friendly arm, then blasts a blinding white light into Isaac's eyes. Shrinking back, Isaac drops the flashlight again, putting his hands up in surrender.

"Figment does not like to be in the light," Tad tells him

solemnly. "You should know that. I know who you are. Your name is Isaac. Mr. Huddleston is your father."

"What if he is?" Isaac says wearily. "You shouldn't be here. You need to go home."

The boy studies Isaac. "If you are Mr. Huddleston's son, then you should care about sea creatures."

Isaac shakes his head. "Wrong."

The boy lays his cheek against the octopus' mantle, looking worriedly at Isaac. "Figment is drying out. I need to get him down to the dock."

The colors of the octopus fade, and the creature slips listlessly down to the grass. Tad falls to his knees, trying to scoop up all the arms. "Help me lift him. Please."

Something about the small boy's caring touches Isaac. Reluctantly, he falls to a knee and leans forward to lift the slimy creature. With surprising strength, the creature's cold arms slither over Isaac's shoulders, gripping him tightly.

"Ugh," Isaac moans in disgust.

Tad stands up. "Give him back to me." Gladly, Isaac transfers the creature to Tad's open arms. The arm suckers release in a sequence of powerful pops.

Tad takes off running, heading down to the dock. The creature clings to his body like a faintly shimmering vine, otherworldly and beautiful. At the dock's edge, Tad bends over, and the octopus slips silently into the ocean.

For a long time, Tad stares into the sea. The orange haloed moon silhouettes his bowed head. Even though Isaac's never thought much about angels, he thinks maybe Tad looks like one now, bent reverently over the waves, sparkling in starlight.

He joins Tad on the dock and peers into the shadowy

water. The creature is floating upside down, barely visible, unmoving.

"Is it dying?" Isaac asks.

"I don't think so," Tad answers. "I hope he's hydrating. Octopuses cannot be out of water for long." He looks at Isaac, concerned. "But you could be right. Figment might be dying. Octopuses only live a few years. I don't know how old he is." Crouching, he leans over the water and chants, "Please don't die. Please don't die. Please don't—"

Slowly, the octopus turns over in the water, morphing into a brilliant star of shimmering colors, rocking gently in the tide.

Tad claps his hands. "Isn't Figment beautiful?"

The boy's joy is contagious. "You saved him," Isaac says gruffly.

"I wish I could save all the creatures," Tad says forlornly. "The new doctor is mean. He is hurting them with experiments."

Isaac looks puzzled. "Dr. Heath is a real tool, but he's a scientist. It's his job to conduct experiments."

"The doctor is mean!" Tad raises his voice. "Mean people cannot be trusted to do good experiments."

"Okay, okay. Calm down."

"Sea creatures belong to the ocean," Tad goes on. "The ocean is their home. Not tanks and aquariums." He tugs on Isaac's arm. "Help me. Let's go to the aquarium and set the turtles free."

"Release the sea turtles? That's crazy. We'll get in a lot of trouble."

"Sometimes doing the right thing makes a lot of trouble," Tad says, sounding about a million years old.

The octopus slithers up on the dock, arm lights blazing.

"He's hydrated!" Tad says in satisfaction. Figment raises the golden arm in a victory salute. "Figment thinks it is a good idea to free the turtles." The orange arm reaches out and takes Tad's hand, tugging him toward the stairs up to the aquarium. "C'mon, Isaac."

With the octopus leading the way, Tad resolutely heads toward the stairs up to the big aquarium. Reluctantly, Isaac follows them.

"Listen kid, my dad is in charge of the marine sanctuary. He might lose his job if we do this."

"Your dad is a good man," Tad answers sadly. "I hope he doesn't lose his job. But your dad is not in charge of anything. The mean doctor from the CDC is in charge—and he is bad."

Isaac goes quiet. Kid's logic is sound. Dr. Heath does whatever he wants at the sanctuary and his dad is helpless to stop it. Heath is a nasty piece of work. Besides, his dad is bringing back injured turtles. Maybe it's a good idea to make room in the aquarium.

"Okay, but we've got to hurry," Isaac tells Tad at the entrance to the aquarium.

Tad touches the mantle of the octopus. "Yes. We should hurry. Before Figment dries out again."

Isaac punches in the security code.

The glass doors shudder, but don't roll back.

Isaac keys in the code again.

No luck.

"Sorry." Isaac hates the look on Tad's disappointed face. "Dr. Heath keeps changing the security codes. He must have changed it again before he took *Limelight* out." Isaac glances down at the empty dock. "No way we're getting into the aquarium tonight unless we break in."

Tad's lower lip starts to tremble. "Oh, no. This is bad. Everything is red."

"Red?" Isaac asks, confused.

"My feelings are colors." Grabbing Isaac's arm, Tad digs his fingers into the flesh.

Isaac flinches. Squirming out of Tad's panicked grasp, he turns to face him. "Hey, I get it. I see colors, too. Maybe I can help you, Tad. What color do you want to feel?"

Tad points to the haloed moon. "Orange. The color of courage."

Grinning, Isaac whistles three clear, strong notes.

Tad stops squeezing Isaac's arm. "How did you do that? I feel braver."

"The octave of C is in shades of orange."

"What about blue? Can you whistle blue?" Tad asks eagerly.

Isaac purses his lips, whistling a few soft tones in F.

Tad's shoulders relax. "It's working. I feel calm." He beams at Isaac. "Blue is calm."

Flash!

A blinding white light illuminates the metal security pad as Figment shines a light beam on the numbers. The creature slithers over to the pad, climbs up the wall, and camouflages itself to match the exact color and texture of the bricks.

"Figment is trying to tell us something," Tad whispers excitedly.

A slender arm reaches out, lighting up in a glittering green. The golden arm lights, then blue, then purple. The delicate tip of the green suckered arm points at the security keypad and hovers like a ghostly finger. Figment flashes its arm lights in a sequence of four colors: green, gold, blue, purple. As each color flashes, Isaac hears different tones in his head.

"Numbers! He's signaling the frequency tones for the numbers," Isaac tells Tad. "I can distinguish subtle differences between security pad tones. Watch." Quickly, Isaac keys in the four numbers that match the sounds of the color sequences that Figment is flashing with his arm lights.

The doors do not budge.

Disappointed, Isaac turns to Tad. "It isn't working. Figment must be guessing random numbers because he doesn't know the real code."

Figment's golden arm seizes Isaac's wrist. The white light in his head shines like a laser, hitting Isaac squarely between the eyes.

"Ow!" Isaac yanks his arm away.

"He doesn't like what you said," Tad says soberly. "Key in the number sequence two times. He flashed the colors twice."

"The code to the aquarium is only four numbers," Isaac grumbles.

Tad shakes his head. "You are stubborn, Isaac. If the mean doctor changed the code, maybe he made it eight numbers. You don't know what you don't know."

Gritting his teeth, Isaac gives in. Tad's words sound familiar. Quickly, he keys in eight numbers on the pad, repeating the four-color number sequence twice.

With a rumble and a shudder, the aquarium doors roll back.

Figment raises his golden arm and does a fist pump. Detaching from the bricks, he drops to the cement floor of the entrance, slithers across the threshold of the aquarium, and skates down the hall, leaving a slippery streak of slime. The boys follow, slip sliding across the floor to the huge glass tank, where the octopus is slinking up the ladder to the feeding platform. On the platform, Figment presses a red button. The old machinery rattles and creaks. The top of the tank lifts, suspended from cables. Figment presses a blue button. A broad metal ramp descends into the water, flattening the kelp curtain, settling on the bottom of the tank in a puff of sand. In a flash, the octopus slides down the ramp, disappearing into the cloudy water.

The water in the tank sloshes. The large, scarred sea turtle appears with the two small turtles and Figment clinging to its carapace. Slowly, the turtle climbs up the ramp to the feeding platform.

"How will they get down?" Isaac wonders.

The drop to the floor of the huge aquarium from the feeding platform is at least ten feet. Except for the narrow ladder to the top, there is no obvious way for the turtles to leave the platform.

"Don't worry," Tad says confidently. "Look."

Detaching from the back of the sea turtle, the octopus hurries to the control panel and punches a yellow button. A second ramp appears, this one curved at the edges like a slide, leading to the floor of the aquarium. Another button push...and a small gush of water wets the slide, flowing down into the drain in the middle of the cement floor. Awkwardly, the big turtle lumbers across the platform to the top of the water slide.

"Wait. Something's wrong," Isaac cries. "The big turtle is walking weird."

"One of his flippers is bent underneath him," Tad says. "He can't slide down like that. It will hurt him."

"I'm going up."

Quickly, Isaac climbs the ladder up to the feeding platform and gently dislodges the folded flipper. The turtle can't be injured again if he is to survive in the ocean. Holding the turtle steady, he positions the giant creature, small turtles aboard, in the center of the ramp.

"Watch out," he yells to Tad. In the next gush of pulsing water, the turtle flops on its belly and slides down the ramp, small turtles clinging to his back.

Triumphantly, Isaac scrambles back down the ladder. Figment slithers down the ramp and grabs Tad's hand.

"My first friend," Tad whispers to Isaac. "Isn't it wonderful?"

The sea creatures exit the aquarium and head down to the end of the dock with the haloed moon lighting the way. With a soft *plop*, the great turtle dives off the dock. The small turtles follow. Silently, they sink into the inky black water, leaving a trail of bubbles sparkling in the moonlight.

The octopus lets go of Tad's hand.

"I don't want to say goodbye to Figment," he says sadly.

Gently, the octopus caresses Tad's cheek with a purple arm.

"Love," Tad murmurs. "Purple is love."

As Figment slides into the water, Isaac takes Tad's hand. The night sky is velvet black, studded with diamond stars. Figment melts into the roll of the tide, floating on top of the calm water. Each arm light flashes...orange, red, pink, blue, purple, yellow, green, and aquamarine. A swell of music rises from the waves. The octopus shimmers and disappears...into the symphony of the deep.

"Figment is my first friend," Tad says, "but he belongs to the ocean." Trustingly, he looks up at Isaac. "Will you be my second friend?"

Something breaks apart inside Isaac. This brave little boy, with his wide eyes and funny way of talking, wants to be his friend.

"Yes," Isaac answers, feeling more certain than he's felt in a long time.

"Thank you," Tad says simply, releasing Isaac's hand. "I think I better go home now."

"Do you want me to walk you home?"

Tad shakes his head. "I can do it by myself. I am filled with good colors."

Isaac whistles notes the octave of C, nodding at the haloed moon. "Courage, little buddy."

"Orange is for courage." Tad smiles. "I will count my steps all the way home."

Chapter Eighteen

LIMELIGHT

Casey is going out of his mind on the long, slow journey back to Dipitous Beach. With a line of emergency vehicles racing past them, the trip is extra slow. For hours, news of the fire at the Hardy mansion blared over the radio. He's heartsick, no one seems to know what may have happened to Lorelei.

At last, when they roll through the front gate of the sanctuary well past midnight, Mr. Huddleston gets the call that Lorelei and Kait are safe and well. Old Mrs. Hardy was rushed to the hospital in an ambulance.

Relief surges through Casey like a riptide. When the van rolls up to the aquarium, he hops out and hustles around to the back, eager to unload the tanks.

"Hold up," Mr. Huddleston says. "First, we need to free up space in the aquarium and the cephalopod house. Going to be an all-nighter. Call your parents."

To Casey's surprise, Isaac wanders out of the dark, holding a flashlight.

"I released the turtles, Dad." Warily, he looks at his father.

Despite his exhaustion, Mr. Huddleston looks as happy as Casey's ever seen him. "Excellent idea to clear the aquarium to make room, son. I didn't know you knew how to operate the control panel and lower the ramps."

Isaac shrugs. "The octopus got away. I went into check and the tank lid was open."

Mr. Huddleston throws an arm around Isaac's shoulders. "Good. We need the space."

Isaac hesitates. "The security system is messed up. I propped the door open with a brick."

Casey's eyes narrow as he looks at Isaac. Something's up. Sure, the kid did something useful, but there's got to be a catch.

Later, when the rescued turtles are safely transferred to the aquarium and cephalopod tank, the older man claps Isaac and Casey on the back. "Way to work together. Good job, boys."

Casey is too tired to reply. The least injured turtles are now in the tank in the cephalopod house. The sickest turtles and the one with the injured flipper are in the aquarium. Tomorrow Mr. Huddleston will assess them all and suture the injured turtle's flipper. With any luck, all the turtles will recover and live to swim free again.

"I'll run you home in a minute, Casey," Mr. Huddleston says, "but I've got to run down to the dock and check on *Limelight*. Sometimes Heath forgets to tighten the cables."

"Heath's gone," Isaac says flatly. "He took the sub out after sunset."

"What?" Mr. Huddleston's face blanches. Dashing out of the aquarium, he takes the stairs down to the dock two at a time. Reluctantly, the boys follow him.

"This is not good," Mr. Huddleston mutters, pacing and tugging on his beard on the empty dock, staring bleakly into the night. "Heath's been out too long. There's not enough oxygen in that sub for a long expedition."

Yanking out his cell phone, he calls the Coast Guard.

Chapter Nineteen

WHISPERS IN THE TIDE

At the breakfast table, Isaac blinks into the late morning light, yawning, willing himself to wake up.

"Any word on Heath?" he asks his dad, while pouring a mug of coffee.

His dad shakes his head. "No. I'm afraid something terrible has happened. The Guard is talking about organizing a shoreline search later today.

Isaac takes a long sip of coffee, welcoming the bracing taste. He isn't going to lie. Unless they learn that the doctor is dead or injured, he can't conjure up any sympathy.

"Were you nervous when you saw the octopus was out of the tank last night?" His dad passes Isaac a bowl of fruit. "They can be scary."

"Not really," Isaac mumbles. "The window was open. Thing was slinking over the sill, making a getaway."

His father chuckles. "Octopuses are escape artists."

"What kind of octopus was it?" Isaac tosses out the question, trying to sound offhand. His curiosity is killing him. Figment was amazing. Understanding musical tones and sequences—how is that even possible?

"Pretty sure it's something new. I haven't found a record of an octopus with golden blood anywhere." Digging into a plate of eggs, his father muses, "Tell you one thing. That was one clever rascal. Old boy was sneaking out of the tank all along. Found the lid unlatched a few times. No telling what he was up to. Octopuses can solve puzzles and morph into complex shapes and colors. They have a nine-brain nervous system."

"I followed him down to the dock," Isaac says casually. "All eight arms lit up like a Christmas tree when it hit the water. Different colors, and flashing lights."

His dad stares at him. "That's crazy."

If you only knew the half of it.

Isaac will never tell his dad about Tad's visit. They'd both be in big trouble, and he's not sure his dad would understand. He misses Tad. The odd, sweet boy who loves sea creatures is special.

Thoughtfully, Isaac spoons sugar into his coffee. "Need help with the turtles today?"

His dad stands up and clears the table. "Well, sure," he says, keeping his voice neutral. "I can use a hand. Suturing a torn flipper today. Want to assist?"

Isaac's stomach rolls. Blood and guts weren't exactly what he had in mind. Then he remembers Tad, walking bravely through the night, conquering his terrible anxiety. "Yeah," he says lamely. "I'll help."

At the aquarium, Isaac pays attention to everything his father does to oxygenate the tank and test for salinity. After his dad climbs up the ladder to the feeding platform, he slides into the water and disappears behind the kelp curtain. Nervously, Isaac holds his breath until his dad re-emerges with the injured turtle. Carefully, he hoists it up to the feeding platform. With Isaac helping, they manage to safely lower the injured turtle to the cement floor next to the drain.

"Turn on the hose," his father says.

Once the water is running in a comforting trickle, Isaac squats beside the turtle, captivated by its watchful, patient eyes. He feels a bond with sea turtles. Silent creatures, they protect their hearts, wisely keeping their vulnerable flesh tucked in tough shells.

"Stabilize the flipper. Relax as much as you can. He can feel your energy."

Holding the flipper in place, Isaac watches his dad's expert surgical skills in action as he trims away injured flesh and begins the long process of stitching up the severed flipper.

Isaac keeps his gaze fixed on the turtle's eyes. The turtle trusts him. Holding the flipper feels right, like it did last night when he held Tad's trusting hand. A quirky little tune pops into Isaac's head, making him smile. It reminds him of Tad. The tune is whimsical and light, the anchor melody true and clear as a bell. He whistles the tune softly under his breath.

His dad sits back on his heels and studies Isaac. "You're like your mother," he says quietly. "Bringing music into everything you do."

Isaac tenses at the mention of his mom. Then, slowly, he nods. After everything he witnessed last night—the octopus, the lights, the bravery and faith of one small boy—well, things are different now. Staying mad at his dad seems stupid and unimportant.

A little while later, after the turtle is safely back in the tank, his dad goes up to the house to shower and Isaac wanders over to the cephalopod house. It's hard to believe that everything that happened last night was real. The window is open, letting in a sea breeze. Isaac peers into the open tank, where three small, rescued turtles are swimming among a pile of rocks. They seem energetic, and he's glad to know he helped save them. Relaxed, he watches them for a long time.

"There you are," his dad says, breezing into the cephalopod house, his beard still wet from the shower. "Come on to the administrative offices with me. There's something I want to show you."

"All right." As Isaac turns away from the tank, a glint of something shiny between the rocks catches his eye. Leaning over the water, he probes the crevice between the rocks and extracts an oddly shaped piece of metal. Casually, he tosses it to his dad.

His dad snags the piece of metal and glances down at his palm. "Well, I'll be," he says under his breath. "No wonder the depth gauge on *Limelight* isn't working." He stares at Isaac. "This little baby is the most critical part of the measurement gauges in the submersible. Without it, the gauge isn't stable, resulting in unreliable depth readings." He inhales sharply. "Poor Heath."

Isaac stays quiet. After watching Figment crack the code to the security system and operate the aquarium's control panel, nothing surprises him. If the depth gauge in the sub isn't working, the doctor is likely dead.

His dad puts the piece of equipment in his pocket. "C'mon. Nothing we can do for Heath, except hope and pray that he got lucky somehow."

A few moments later, in his dad's office, Isaac taps his foot while his father rummages through a desk drawer. He only has a few hours before he meets Condi at the tide pool, and he wants to play his guitar. The threads to the song he's heard in his head are coming together.

"Here it is," his dad says triumphantly. He passes Isaac an old-school photo, curling at the edges.

Isaac's breath catches. The photo is of his mom; light years younger and heart-breakingly beautiful, holding a ruby-red surfboard. His dad is there, too, laughing into the camera, standing next to a cobalt-blue board.

"I loved your mother, Isaac," his dad says, a choke in his voice. "Correction: we loved *each other.*" Sadly, he looks at the photo. "We couldn't make it work—but it was real love just the same."

Isaac stares at the happy image of a time long past. A familiar voice floats back to him. "*Choose to remember what you've seen, and the good parts last forever.*"

The truth in the photograph shines through. Years ago, his mom and dad were young and beautiful. For a time, there was love and laughter and hope between them. Maybe—just maybe—he can remember it that way.

The afternoon light is dazzling as Condi hurries to meet Isaac at the tide pool. Her thoughts are stuck on his claim that he met Trustin under the sea. She needs to know the truth.

As she passes the stairs up to the decks of Craggy Point, she spies Triponica, ducking out of a tidal cave, carrying a basket of clams and mussels.

Condi slows down. Trippy is striding toward her across the sand. Patiently, she waits to say hello. The last person she can be rude to is Trippy.

"Hello, my dear." Trippy sets the basket of fresh catch down on the sand. Glancing up at the high dune beyond the tip of Craggy Point, she nods sagely. "Don't worry. I know you're meeting someone. I won't keep you long." A smile curls at the corner of her mouth. "You and Isaac Huddleston are alike, you know."

"Hardly," Condi says, flushing. As usual, she has no idea how Trippy knows what she knows.

Triponica clucks her tongue. "You will see. Look for the ways you and Isaac are the same, my dear. It will surprise you." She lifts her chin and squares her broad shoulders. Light fades from her amber eyes. "But that is not what I came to say. It is Francie. She will soon slip away from us."

Condi's breath catches. "Slip away...you mean..."

"Yes," Triponica answers somberly. "Please tell your grandmother that Francie's time is near. Come to the bunk-rooms to say goodbye. Tomorrow at sunset."

At the tide pool, Condi hears Isaac long before she sees him. She pauses, taking in the richness of the sounds floating over the circle of sea grass. His voice, low and mellow, rises above the beat of the waves. Softly, he strums a guitar.

When she steps through the thicket, he pauses. "Hey," he says quietly. "Thanks for coming."

"Don't stop playing," she tells him.

"Sure?"

"Yes."

With a dip of his chin, he turns away from her, facing a gap in the seagrass where he can look out at sea. A coarse wind bends back the grass, blowing through his hair. The riff he is playing is anguished, vibrating with jolts of love and yearning.

Condi recognizes the familiar chords. The realization shakes her. How could Isaac know this song? Or what it means to her? In shock, she sits down on the nearest rock. Pulling her knees up to her chest, she hugs herself tight, shielding her face with her hair.

He plays on, notes soaring on the wind. At last, she cannot fight it anymore. The music releases her, opening a long-locked space, allowing her to cry. The song he is playing is the one Mama and Papa were singing when they sailed away on that fateful day, when their boat was lost off the Hollow.

Lifting her face, she looks at him, tears streaming down her cheeks.

"My parents...they were musicians. That was their song." Awkwardly, she wipes her cheek with her hair.

Nodding, he lays the guitar across his knees.

They look at each other for a long moment.

Without taking her eyes from his face, Condi lifts her chin. "Tell me what happened under the sea."

Picking up his guitar, he cradles it gently in his hands. "It sounds crazy—"

He hesitates.

Vulnerability connects them. Suddenly, she understands what Trippy was trying to tell her. She knows how she and this strange boy are the same. The pain in him is deep and raw, like the scarred-over gash in her own heart. And Isaac, like Papa and Mama, lives and breathes music. If she wants him to talk, she must ask him to use his language, the language of music.

"Why don't you tell me in a song?" she asks.

Relieved, he cracks a smile. The breeze tugs at his unruly hair; the black leather jacket catches light in the sun; the tightness in his body releases. Bending over the guitar, he tunes it, plucking out a few sweet chords. At first, the notes barely vibrate. But then he finds the melody, putting words to a haunting ballad and singing her a story...about a journey under the sea.

The song enchants her. The protective sea turtle, the wisdom of Auramar, the Metamorphosis Pool, the musical octopus named Koan...and Isaac's encounter with her first love, Trustin, the boy with turquoise eyes. Of course, the song doesn't make sense. After all, it's Koan's world—it will never make sense until it does.

"Where have you gone?
Who are you now?
Are you the chord in the deep of mystery?
Or the beat in the heart of harmony?
Colored by light and clarity.
Where have you gone?
Who are you now?"

When the last verse fades away, Condi takes a white shell out of her pocket and hands it to Isaac. The shell is nearly identical to the one he found in his pocket after his time under the sea.

"You've been there, too."

She nods. "We can't ever tell."

"No one would believe us anyway," he answers.

Smiling, he hands the shell back to her and picks up his guitar.

She gets it. There's nothing more to say. All he wants to do is sing.

#

Later, on the high decks overlooking the cove, Triponica gazes up at the fullness of the haloed moon and sniffs the wind. The signs are there. A night swim to the underwater caves off the Point is favored. Firth will dive deep, accessing the tunnel leading to the Azure Grotto. There he will chip away crystals of the elusive ocean gem, Indigo Blue. Triponica will stay in shallower waters, floating through the sea strawberry forests, gathering what she needs for Francie's Last Goodbye.

"I am ready." Firth appears beside her. His sharp eyes sweep the horizon line, on the lookout for the subtle swell of a rogue wave, death to a free diver caught in an underwater cavern.

Together they walk calmly down the stairs from the high decks and cross the sand, controlling their breath cycles as they climb to the top of Craggy Point, to the lip of rock overhanging the sea.

"This dive is for Francie," Firth says.

"For Francie," Triponica echoes.

Inhaling, they rise on their toes, extending torsos and ribs. With inflated lungs, arms arcing skyward, they dive... piercing the gossamer veil of a star-studded sea.

Time passes as the moon moves across the sky. After a few hours, Firth hauls the heavy net filled with Indigo

Blue over the lip of Craggy Point. Collapsing on the broad rock, he breathes deeply, satisfied that his dive was strong tonight, powered by an energy he's never felt before.

Rolling over onto his back, he breathes in light and air, gazing up at the sleepy orange moon. Beside him, the bulging net glints silver as the stars cast shards of light over the sparkling dark blue gems, damp with sea water. Though Triponica has not yet returned from her dive to the sea strawberry forests, he is not concerned. In many ways the old woman's stamina is greater than his own.

As he waits, Firth worries about what is to become of Cissy and Malcolm. At sixteen, Firth is nearly a man. He can run away and survive. But what if the authorities put Cissy and Malcolm back in foster care?

Do not contemplate what-ifs...

Francie's voice.

The pain is like a punch in the gut.

How can he bear losing her?

A cold nose pokes him in the armpit. Rolling to his side, he cradles the old black dog in his arms, burying his face in the comforting ball of fur. Exhausted, he falls asleep on the rocks of the Point.

#

Trippy swims gracefully, stroking through starlight. When she reaches shore, a familiar black body of fur bounds down from the high ledge. Tugging on her net, glistening with crimson sea strawberries, the faithful old dog drags it up onto the sand.

"Thank you, old friend. You show up when you're needed, don't you?"

Smiling at Firth, asleep on Craggy Point beside a handsome harvest of Indigo Blue, Triponica climbs the stairs to the top deck of the Point and empties her net. There is no need to wake him. Let him sleep. Tonight, she will be busy, pounding sea strawberries and mixing the rosy mash with kava root. Then she will set her biggest pot to bubbling, brewing Francie's farewell tea.

Tomorrow...it will be time.

Francie will go home.

You are next, the tide whispers.

Triponica nods. The sea has spoken. She and Francie will not be parted for long. In an hour not yet appointed—but sometime soon—Trippy will be called to join her.

Chapter Twenty

THE LAST GOOD-BYE

The next evening, Condi and Grand Ella slowly climb the stairs to the high deck of the Beachling's bunk rooms with heavy hearts.

"It's hard to think of the Beachlings without Francie," Condi tells her grandmother.

Grand Ella slips an arm around Condi's waist. "I know."

At the top of the stairs, Condi stops abruptly. Firth is leaning into the deck rail, head low, muscular hands clutching at the wood. He nods curtly to acknowledge them, then moves back into the shadows.

"Best to leave him be," Grand Ella murmurs.

Outside Francie's bunkroom, Condi and Grand Ella pause, looking through the window. Lit with the warm glow of lantern light, the room shimmers with a sweet peace. Cissy and Malcolm are snuggled deep into the pillows beside Francie. Trippy and Charlene kneel on the floor beside the bed.

Slipping into the tiny room, Condi and Grand Ella close

the door and go to the bedside.

A book of poetry rests in Malcolm's small hands. Haltingly he reads from it, tremulous voice pitched high.

"*And hand in hand, on the edge of the sand,*

They danced by the light of the moon.

The moon,

The moon,

They danced by the light of the moon."

Slowly, Malcolm reads Edward Lear's *The Owl and the Pussy Cat*[2],—without a single stutter. When he finishes the poem, Triponica rises and takes the book from the little boy's hands.

"Remember me in the light of the moon." Gathering Cissy and Malcolm up in her arms, Francie holds them close in a hug. Then, releasing the children, she stretches out a hand to Grand Ella. Grand Ella takes the withered fingers, cradling them in the softness of the faded quilt. Condi lays her hand on top of Grand Ella's.

A knock comes from outside. Condi goes to the door and opens it. Firth steps inside, drawing in the crisp breeze of the autumn night.

At once, Triponica gets to her feet and gently guides Firth toward the bed. Charlene lifts a drowsy Cissy out of Francie's arms and Grand Ella does the same for Malcolm. The two women carry the children out to the deck.

"Condi," Triponica whispers. "Come along. We must go and leave Firth alone with Francie."

"But—" Condi stammers. "I didn't get—"

"Francie knows you love her." Firmly, Triponica guides Condi to the door. "Her energy is waning. Let Firth have this time. He is the least prepared to lose her."

Confused, Condi fights back tears, trying not to feel

hurt. Firth is taking the place she thought belonged to her.

When Grand Ella and Charlene carry Cissy and Malcolm to bed, Triponica lays a hand on Condi's shoulder. "Come, my dear. Let us go up to the high deck and look at the stars. I have something I wish to say to you."

Together they climb to the high deck. Condi moves to the high rail, glad for the brisk rush of air. Fighting for calm, she gazes at the shimmering sparkles in the indigo water. The tide is smooth and still as glass. In the heart of the deep, green and blue bioluminescent bands spin in swirls like hidden galaxies.

"Magnificent, is it not?" Trippy says. "Can you see all the worlds, my dear?"

"I do, Trippy," Condi answers miserably. "But I don't want to let Francie go...I wanted..."

"It is not about what we want, Condi," Trippy replies. "It never is." She wraps a strong arm around Condi's shoulders. "We must let Francie leave...so she can return to us in other ways."

Condi sighs. "I guess I'm just tired of losing people I love."

Triponica tilts Condi's chin and looks into her eyes. "Child, be honest. It is not only losing Francie that troubles your heart. You met Isaac yesterday at the tide pool."

"It's confusing." Condi buries her face in Trippy's rough sleeve. "I miss Trustin. I don't understand why Isaac is the one who got to see him..."

"Oh, my child." The old woman pulls her close. "You asked for connection. Now you've gotten it...but it did not appear in the way you expected. You prayed for signs—and signs were sent." She lifts Condi's face. "Come. Let us not dwell on things we cannot change. I have something you must do for me tomorrow." Pressing a bundle into Condi's hand, she wraps her fingers around it and squeezes. "Gabby Finch is awake. Take this medicine to Lorelei. It is a restorative powder made from a rare crystal called Indigo Blue. It will aid in Gabby's recovery."

"Lorelei's mom is better?" Condi exclaims.

"Yes." Triponica smiles. "Life holds surprises, my dear—and some of them are joys." She pulls a small packet from her pocket, glowing crimson in the moonlight. "I made this for you...Essence of Sea Strawberry, from the forest waters of the sea, harvested on nights like tonight, when bioluminescent bands are brightest. Sprinkle it on your pillow. It will give you peace."

Chapter Twenty-One

GUARDIAN

Leaning into the starfish mirror, Lorelei smiles at her reflection. Her healthy, shining face is framed within the living picture outside the window. Outside in the garden, Mama and Tad are sitting beneath the catalpa tree. Mama, thin and hollow-cheeked, is stroking Tad's hair, and they are laughing up at the red and turquoise parrot swaying on the lowest branch of the tree. After the fire at the Hardy mansion, Guardian has found a new home at the Finches'. Nobody is happier than Tad.

Everything is turning out better than Lorelei hoped. Day by day, Mama is getting stronger. In fact, the whole family is flourishing, ever since Condi brought them a restorative powder made by Triponica, something mysterious called Indigo Blue. Lorelei's hair is growing thicker, Tad's spinning is less frequent, and Papa looks like a much younger man. Even Cara is less moody (however temporary that may be).

The fire at the Hardy mansion was scary, but old Mrs.

Hardy is recovering well. Though most of the mansion was destroyed, an unusual thing happened—Mr. Hardy's upstairs library survived. Though the books and files are scorched, they can be cleaned and restored. Mama is relieved; she says the files contain the best of Mr. Hardy's research—especially the most critical data about melanin pools.

One of the biggest shifts within the Finch family is how much Tad has changed. Her shy little brother has found a new confidence. Tad is excited about going back to school next week, where he plans to make a lot of new friends—because now he knows he's brave.

Dreamily, Casey takes the last bite of ginger-honey pancake. Tonight, there will be a bonfire on the beach. He's hoping to get a chance to sneak off with Lorelei, snuggle under a beach blanket, and gaze up at the stars.

"Casey. Stop staring off into space." His mom's voice breaks into his fantasy. "After breakfast, please practice the piano. With the B&B reopening soon, I want you in prime form. Our hotel guests adore hearing you play show tunes in the evenings."

Casey groans. Even though he secretly likes playing the piano, he doesn't like being entertainment for his parents' guests. And he sure doesn't like show tunes. There were some good things about the Sickness. One of them was that he didn't have to perform for a bunch of boring old people.

"I'm making a special dessert for tonight's celebration at the beach." Impatiently, his mother rifles through the recipe drawer. "I never have any idea what to make when your father is away. He's the baker in the family." She sighs. "Your dad's been gone for hours. I hope it's not another false alarm." Since Dr. Heath disappeared in *Limelight*, search parties have combed the coast for days. This morning his father got a call from Mr. Huddleston. The submersible may have been found.

"Make brownie sheet cake with buttermilk-vanilla glaze," Casey suggests.

His mom laughs. "Easy enough. Why don't you help me grease the pans?"

Casey clears the table and gets out a large sheet cake pan and rubs it with butter. His mom melts bars of rich dark chocolate on the stove. He can't wait to see Lorelei. Tonight's bonfire at the beach will be the first time the whole town has gotten together since the Sickness struck. The Beachlings are hosting a celebration of life for Francie, the sweet, frail Beachling who died peacefully several nights ago.

"Casey? Amber? I'm home," his dad calls out. The double doors to the kitchen swing wide. "Umm, that smells good," he says, sniffing the chocolatey air in rapture.

"Did you find Dr. Heath?" she asks.

"Not exactly." His dad wrinkles his brow. "We found the submersible. In bad shape, wrecked on the rocks off Ghost Beach, close to Everwood. No sign of Heath." His dad glances nervously at Casey.

Slipping her arm around her husband's waist, she murmurs, "It's okay, honey. Whatever the news is, Casey can handle it."

"It's pretty ugly news." His dad grimaces. "The place where the sub ran aground is near Devil's Lair Canyon. At the top of the dune leading to the highway, there's a steep drop-off. If you're unaware, you're likely to fall into the canyon. If you survive the fall, the tide will suck you right out to sea."

"Oh, no." Casey's mom puts a hand over her heart. "Poor Dr. Heath."

Coolly, Casey turns back to the stove and stirs the buttermilk-vanilla glaze. He doesn't like Heath, and he doesn't like him any more now that he might be dead, though he seriously doubts the doctor stumbled into the canyon. Dude was a jerk...but he wasn't stupid.

"Sheriff Coodle is pretty sure Heath is dead," Casey's dad goes on. "To top it off, turns out the doctor was an imposter. He wasn't authorized by the CDC and his name wasn't Heath. The real Heath died of the Sickness. In all the chaos, Fake Dr. Heath stole the real guy's identity. He intercepted a confidential letter sent to the CDC. Nobody knows what the letter said, but apparently Fake Heath was looking for something at the marine sanctuary."

Casey sighs. If Fake Dr. Heath was smart enough to do all that, then logic says he survived the sub grounding, located the main highway, and somehow got away.

"Casey?" His mother steps to his side and lays a hand on his arm. "Are you okay, son? I know this terrible news is a shock."

"I'm fine, Mom," Casey answers, casually licking glaze off the spoon. He's not going to bother to convince his parents that the sheriff is wrong about Heath. Fake Doctor Heath is out there somewhere, alive, and well.

Tad is cuddling with Mama in the garden, watching Guardian sway in the top branches, a blaze of turquoise and red against a stellar sky.

"I'm proud of you, Tad," Mama says, hugging him close. "You were an amazing helper when I was sick."

"I was—but I did a few bad things." Pink anxiety is tickling him. Maybe he should confess to using Mama's computer without permission. It's not right to keep things from her.

"You know, Tad," Mama whispers into his hair, "I don't want to hear about bad things. At least, not right now. Nothing you did while I was sick was bad. It was a difficult time. All of you children did the best you could."

Tad squirms a little. The pink feeling recedes. He is relieved that Mama doesn't want to hear the bad things he did. He is glad not to tell. But she is wrong about Cara. While he and Lorelei did the best they could when Mama was sick, Cara did not try at all.

Cara's head appears in the door to the garden. "Mama! Andy Marshall is here to see you."

Mama smiles. "Ask him to come around to the garden. The gate is unlocked."

Cara winks at Tad. "Can I go to the beach?" she asks in her sweetest voice. "Inez and Lacy are waiting for me."

Mama hesitates. For a long moment, she studies Cara, pink-striped beach towel flung over her shoulder, floppy hat sliding over one eye. Hand on a hip, she looks respectful and innocent.

"Well, all right. Stay with the other girls. Be home by late afternoon. We're leaving for Francie's celebration around six. Promise me?"

"Promise." Blowing Mama a kiss, Cara disappears back into the house.

Tad's eyes narrow. Of course, Cara is lying. She is going

to meet boys. Lacy and Inez will not be at the beach.

"Tad?" Mama asks. "You look worried. What are you thinking?"

Tad opens his mouth, then shuts it. He is tempted to tell on Cara. But that is not fair. After all, he is keeping a secret from Mama and Papa. Papa never knew Tad sneaked out. When Papa came to tuck him in, Tad was safely back in bed.

No, Tad will not tell on Cara. Someday he will tell Mama and Papa he sneaked out. But not now. Right now, the adventure at the marine sanctuary is the special secret he shares with Isaac. He feels yellow and orange, happy and brave.

Andy waits nervously on the front porch of the Finch home. Small and snug, the bungalow is dappled in sunshine and draped in whimsical spirals of purple wisteria. Shifting his weight from foot to foot, he's surprised at the rapid beating of his heart. Holding the book Frank gave him in his hands, Andy recalls what Frank said the day before he died. *Give it to Gabby. She knows what to do with it.*

Now that time has come.

"Mama's out back in the garden." Cara Finch appears in the doorway, flashing him a wicked smile. "Go through the gate."

Andy follows the stone path around to the garden. *That one's going to be trouble*, he muses. He's seen Cara hanging out on the beach with an older boy named Dom Jacobs. Dom has a history of playing every girl in town.

When Andy ducks under the arbor of yellow roses leading into the garden, he's charmed by the sight of Gabby and Tad, resting in the sun under the catalpa tree.

"Andy!" Joyfully, Gabby points to a wicker rocker with a fraying cushion. "Please. Come and sit."

"Gabby," he says gruffly, swallowing hard. "How are you?"

"Better," she assures him, "though I still tire easily."

Tad grins. "Mama is getting well."

The small boy's contentment touches Andy. Gingerly, he sits down in the rocker, which creaks under his weight. Leaning forward, he hands Gabby the book. "I'll get right to it. The day before Frank died, he gave me this. Said you'd know what to do with it."

"Oh, Andy." Gabby cradles the leather book in her hands, staring at it in hushed awe. When she looks up, her soft blue-green eyes sparkle with tears. "This book is a record of Frank's most important research. During the Sickness we made a rare discovery...a discovery that may change the world." She clutches the book close to her heart. "I thought Frank's logbook was lost in the fire."

"The fire chief says it's a kind of miracle that most of Frank's library survived, "Andy says.

"A miracle, indeed," Gabby says, eyes shining. "This book contains everything we need to prove the greatness of Frank Hardy's last discovery. It may change the course of marine biomedical research."

"What do you mean?" Andy shakes his head. "I don't understand."

"Mama and Mr. Hardy discovered melanin pools under the sea," Tad interrupts excitedly. "Melanin is found in octopus ink."

"Melanin?" Andy asks. "Sorry, you're losing me."

"Melanin is an important component in medicines that strengthen the heart and lungs," Gabby explains. "Unfortunately, harvesting melanin has put the octopus population at risk."

"People who make medicine are hurting the octopuses!" Tad bursts out.

Gabby puts a hand on Tad's arm. "That's the bad news. The good news is that the discovery of melanin pools means that important medicines can be developed without damaging the ocean and its creatures as we've been doing."

Thoughtfully, Andy strokes his chin grizzle. He remembers how Frank used to stop by the Billabong after a long day, watching Andy polish surfboards. A dedicated scientist and conservationist, Frank was troubled about the shortsightedness of current bio marine research. *Marine life offers cures for horrendous diseases, Andy, but we are destroying the ocean...and our future.* "Frank worried about the harm that is being done to our oceans because marine research is dominated by pharmaceutical companies."

Gabby sighs. "Exactly. That's why we kept our research top secret. Frank wanted to be certain that the locations of the melanin pools are protected. With Frank gone, I must be very careful about who gets access to our mapping." She taps the logbook. "Our logbooks contain vital information about the pools. Many of them are close by, near the hydrothermal vents of the volcanic shelves of the Ring of Fire." She shivers. "After the scare at the marine sanctuary and that awful imposter who called himself Dr. Heath, I'm not sure who to trust."

Andy nods and lowers his eyes, hoping Gabby can't see his tears. Her story has shaken him to the core. If only Frank was here to celebrate the momentous discovery of melanin pools and continue his life's work. Mournfully, he stares down at his hands.

"Run inside, Tad," Gabby says quietly. "Ask Lorelei to help you mix a pitcher of Trippy's purple lemonade."

When the children disappear into the house, Gabby says in a low voice, "Please don't say a word about the melanin pools to anyone, Andy. I'm afraid. Something is going on at the marine sanctuary."

"I understand, Gabby," Andy answers. "We must protect Frank's legacy."

Gabby nods. "I'm sorry about Frank, Andy. You two were the best of friends." Her voice breaks. "I loved him, too. We will both miss him more than anyone can know." Opening the book in her lap, she pulls out a sheet of paper. "This letter is for you. Frank wanted me to give it to you upon his death." She smiles wistfully. "His most precious possession was this logbook." She pats it lovingly. "He kept the letter safe within its pages."

She hands Andy the letter and sits silently while he reads it.

"Why, this can't be true." Stunned, he looks over at her.

"It is," she says softly. "Frank left everything to you, Andy, his dearest and most trusted friend."

Andy stares at the letter. Frank has left all his property and research patents to him, with the single condition that Andy provide for the care of his wife, Mary Hardy, for the rest of her days. At the bottom of the page, next to Frank's signature and the notary seal, is a sketch of a double wave.

"I can't believe it." Andy flinches. "Why, I've got to go

get Mary out of that place. She's—"

"Slow down, Andy," Gabby says firmly. "Mary is doing quite well where she is. The assisted living facility in West Barrington is the perfect place for her. It's luxurious, and they are well known for the attention and pampering they give residents. Leave her there. I promise to visit once a month to see that she has everything she needs."

"I'll come along, of course," Andy says. "She's my responsibility now."

Gabby shakes her head. "No. You must leave the visits to me. You can pay the bills." She lays a gentle finger on Andy's arm. "Mary's always been jealous of you, you know."

"Me?" Andy raises a brow. "Why would she be jealous of me?" He tries not to sound bitter. "Frank chose her."

Gabby shakes her head. "Oh, Andy, you know that isn't completely true. After the wedding, Frank insisted on moving back to Dipitous Beach. Mary didn't want to move. She felt threatened by you—because you were his person—his best friend."

Andy lets out a long breath. The letter about Frank's will changes his perspective on his friend's marriage. Is it possible Frank was as filled with yearning as Andy was? Memories come flooding back. Frank dropping by the Billabong every chance he could, leaning against the counter, watching Andy work, all the while keeping up a steady stream of conversation. While Andy had cherished those times, Frank's relationship with Mary was a wedge between them. How strange...and sad...to think that Frank might have been missing him, too.

The back door swings wide. Tad walks slowly toward them, precariously balancing a plate piled high with cookies. Behind him, Lorelei carries a tray with glasses and a frosty pitcher filled with something icy and vibrant purple in color.

"I should be running along," Andy says, rising to his feet.

"You must stay for a snack," Gabby says firmly. "Tad is very proud of his snickerdoodles. And please take a glass of Triponica's purple lemonade. It's called Indigo Blue." She hands him a beaded glass. "Drink up. I don't know how or why it works, but it does. I'm not the only one recovering from something. You've had a shock."

Andy accepts the frosty glass and takes a cookie from Tad. The liquid slides down his throat. It tastes like nothing he's ever experienced before, lifting his spirits, filling him with hope.

"Drink up!" Guardian swoops down from the trees, stirring up a swirl of heart-shaped leaves.

The squawking makes them chuckle.

Raising his drink to the bird in a toast, Andy drains his glass.

"Funny that Frank's parrot is talking again," Gabby muses. "Did you know it was Guardian who alerted the fire department to the fire at the mansion?" She takes Lorelei's hand and squeezes it. "I couldn't be more grateful."

"Mrs. Hardy was obsessed with Guardian," Lorelei tells Andy. "She pestered me every day, asking whether Guardian ever said more than 'awk.' She believed Guardian was going to repeat Mr. Hardy's dying words."

The parrot perches next to Tad and cocks its head. Still and silent, Tad gazes into the bird's emerald eyes. Andy wonders what the small boy is thinking. With his serious expression and formal way of speaking, Tad appears wise beyond his years.

"Mrs. Hardy is right," Tad says at last. "Guardian knows Mr. Hardy's last words."

"Tad," Lorelei says quickly. "That was just Mrs. Hardy's silly idea."

A wrinkle appears between the small boy's brows. "No, Lori, it is not silly."

Drawing Tad close, Gabby whispers, "Why don't you go inside with Lori and offer Papa a glass of Trippy's lemonade and share your cookies?"

"Okay, Mama." Tad hops off the love seat. Guardian soars to the top of the catalpa, showering them with more heart-shaped leaves.

After the two children go inside, Gabby murmurs, "I'm sorry, Andy. Tad gets odd ideas sometimes."

"It's fine, Gabby." Picking up a catalpa leaf, he thoughtfully puts it in his shirt pocket. "I'll be getting along now. Lots of thinking to do. That purple lemonade was delicious."

Gabby laughs. "Trippy's medicines work better than any prescription. That woman is a marvel."

"Take care of yourself, Gabby." Whistling, Andy puts his hands in his pockets and ambles down the walk. As he leaves the garden, Guardian swoops down out of the treetops and flies alongside him. When he flings open the door to *Sweets and Stories*, Guardian hops to the top of the window frame.

"What's up with you?" Andy chuckles.

"Frank loves Andy."

Shocked, Andy stares into the parrot's eyes.

In the pupil, cresting twice, is a double wave of cerulean blue.

Chapter Twenty-Two

BONFIRES

Humming nervously under his breath, Isaac climbs the high dune, slipping and sliding on the steep slope of sand, keeping his eyes fixed on the stable, flat rock of Craggy Point. When he is safely over the dune and on the top of the rock, he is seriously out of breath. One of these days he's got to get in shape. Musicians need stamina, after all.

Sliding his guitar strap off his shoulder, he carefully lays down the guitar and balances on a driftwood log, shaking out the sand heaped in his electric blue tennis shoes. Though he misses his black rocker boots, it was a good call not to wear them tonight. Stashed in the back of his closet, the boots are retired until he makes it back to the city, a visit his dad promises will happen by the holidays.

Slipping the guitar strap over his shoulder, he gets to his feet, looking out over the cove. Moonlight twinkles capriciously over the waves, lighting up the sea. Below him, the wind-swept beach is drenched in buttery gold moonlight. Across the expanse of sand, glowing like a strand of orange-red pearls, are the flickering bonfires prepared by the Beachlings for Francie's celebration. Isaac draws in his breath. It is beautiful. Thousands of crackling embers fly upward, blending with the millennium of stars.

A sizable crowd is already arriving, gathering beneath the high deck where the Beachlings make their homes. People of all ages are trudging through sand, bundled in blankets, toddlers asleep on shoulders. Staying in family groups, they cluster around the small, individual bonfires.

Isaac takes a long gulp of air, trying to steady his nerves. He wasn't prepared for a big gathering. Even in the open air, it feels odd to see a crowd. It's been a long time since people have dared to come together like this. The multitude of people tells Isaac everything about the woman they've gathered to celebrate.

They loved Francie.

With a pang, he considers turning back. After all, he never got the chance to do this for his mother—and he didn't even know the sweet old woman. Except for Triponica, Isaac's never met any of the Beachlings. But Triponica asked him to come—and he owes Trippy his life.

The moon blinks.

Flushed in orange—

Courage.

Remembering Tad, he makes his way down the long stairs to the cove.

From the high deck, Triponica surveys the crowd clumped together in small groups, huddled around the small bonfires that she and Charlene wisely spaced across the beach.

Smatterings of starlight expose the hesitancy in many faces. The people are congregating in tiny familiar groups, showing up to celebrate the tiny woman with the broken body and wise, bold heart. Coming together after so much isolation is hard. It will be a long time before the wounds of the Sickness are healed and community is restored in Dipitous Beach.

Head held high, Trippy regally sweeps down the stairs from the high deck, a flowing caftan thrown over her dress, still damp from her evening swim. Her brine-crusted hair is pinned in pewter braids atop her head, sparkling like a crown. The caftan, borrowed from Charlene, is a soft pink. Like the interior of a shell, it moves in swirls, shimmering in the moonlight. Though the night is chill, she doesn't notice. It's been years since she's felt the cold.

Stepping onto the sand of the beach, she makes her way over to Isaac. Standing awkwardly beside Tad Finch, he is clutching his guitar. When Trippy approaches, Isaac flinches. Tad stares up at Isaac, then takes his hand.

Trippy chuckles. The gesture says everything about who Tad is, a thousand-year-old soul in a small boy's body. The two boys are friends, despite the difference in their years. After all, age never matters; these things are about bravery and heart.

"Hello, my dears." Stroking Tad's hair, Trippy smiles reassuringly at Isaac. "Thank you for coming, Isaac. I know you didn't know Francie, but you would have liked her." She points to his guitar. "After I say a few words, it would be a wonderful tribute if you would move among the crowd and play for us this evening."

"Oh, no." Isaac takes a step back. "I can't—"

"You can," Trippy tells him firmly. "People in this town

need to be brought together. Music is a great unifier." She lays a hand on his arm. "I rescued you for a reason, you know. Talents like yours are meant to be shared." Without another word, she goes back to the beach stairs and climbs until she is standing a few heads above the crowd.

The people on the beach fall silent.

"My friends, I offer no eulogy for Francie tonight." Triponica lifts her arms. In the misted moonlight, the pale caftan shivers like wings. "I shall simply share a few lines from her favorite children's books. Francie believed we are at our best in stories and poems. Children, if your parents are willing, please gather around."

After a stunned silence, the cautious energy of the crowd shifts. There is a soft murmuring of approval. Encouraged by their parents, children slowly move away from their family bonfires to gather at Trippy's feet, Malcolm and Cissy among them.

Trippy clears her throat, and winks at the children. "'Real isn't how you are made,' said the Skin Horse. 'It's a thing that happens to you. When a child loves you for a long, long time, not just to play with, but really loves you, then you become Real.'" [3]

"*The Velveteen Rabbit*!" Cissy cries, clapping her hands.

Trippy smiles. "And what about this? 'You're braver than you believe, stronger than you seem and smarter than you think.'" [4]

"*Winnie the Pooh*!" the children shout in unison.

For a thrilling hour, Triponica recites Francie's favorite poems and stories, covering the best of children's poetry and literature from times gone by. As the children dance and sing along, families relax and stand a bit closer to their neighbors. Everyone is drawn into the enchantment.

"Twas brillig, and the slithy toves
Did grye and gimble in the wabe
All mimsy were the borogroves—"

"*Jabberwocky*!" Jumping around and finally collapsing in a happy heap, the kids giggle and shout out the nonsense words of Lewis Carroll's timeless poem[5] into the starlit night.

At last, the embers from the bonfires fade.

Parents lift drowsy children into their arms.

The evening draws to a reverent close.

As the night mist deepens, Triponica makes her way over to Isaac. "Before the crowd leaves, please move among us and play, Isaac. No matter our differences, music brings us together."

#

"I don't know what to play," Isaac says miserably, looking at Tad. "I don't even know these people."

Tad tugs on Isaac's hand. "I'll help you. Feel the colors. Then you will know what to play." He points to the closest bonfire, where Kait and Vinnie are huddled together, wrapped in separate blankets. "Do you see the purple around them, Isaac? Purple is the color of love. Do you know a purple song?"

"Actually, I do," Isaac answers as a song pops into his head.

"C'mon, then. I'll go with you," says Tad. "Kait and Vinnie are nice."

#

After Isaac and Tad disappear into the shadows, heading toward another bonfire, Kait looks at Vinnie. "Are you even believing it?" she says to Vinnie. "That new boy, Isaac Huddleston, came out of nowhere and sang *Will Ye Go, Lassie, Go*. Never ever did I expect to hear that tune in America."

"I liked it," Vinnie says, whistling the refrain.

"Sure, and don't you know it, it's a grand love song," she agrees, tilting her face upward at the stars.

"Dude can play. I'll give him that at least," Casey agrees begrudgingly.

"Give him a chance," Lorelei replies. "You both like music. Maybe you two can get to be friends."

Casey doesn't comment. "Look!" Cautiously moving closer, he touches her chin with a tentative finger. "Is that a shooting star?"

Lorelei looks up. "I wonder how many wishes a shooting star can give?" she murmurs, quoting *Winnie the Pooh*.[6]

"Plenty," he answers, bravely catching hold of her hand.

Playing songs in the open air, accompanied by wind and sea, is easier than Isaac dreamed. With Tad helping him feel the colors, song selections come to him, flowing from a wellspring of musical memories he didn't know he had. Everything his mother knew about music is now a part of him.

After Isaac finishes making the rounds of the bonfires, the boys go over to the slowly-banking fire where the Finch family is hanging out.

Isaac throws himself down by the fire. Tad hands him a driftwood stick. Isaac grins and gives one good strong poke to the flames, releasing silver ash into the deepening mist. It's peaceful here. Lorelei and Casey are sitting on a blanket, looking up at the stars. Mr. and Mrs. Finch lean against a log, meditating on the sea. Only Tad's sister, Cara, looks unhappy, scraping at the sand with a broken piece of shell, drawing something in long, angry strokes.

"Cara is feeling red and making drama because she can't kiss boys," Tad explains in a loud whisper.

Isaac laughs. For an instant, he considers playing a moody boy band song for Cara. Then he thinks better of it. She looks like the scary type who might bite his head off.

The one person Isaac didn't see on the beach tonight is Condi. Probably for the best. With her straightforward ways and brave heart, she unsettles him, understanding things that are impossible.

"Impossible things can be true," Tad says matter-of-factly.

Isaac rolls onto his back, looking up into a canopy of endless stars. He has no idea how Tad knows the things he knows. But if Condi Bloom is in love with a boy who lives under the sea, he figures Tad is right. How much more impossible can things get than that?

Grand Ella slips her arm through Sheriff Coodle's. It's late. The crowd is gone, the beach nearly empty. Of course,

Clive, with his sense of responsibility, feels that he must stay until the final bonfire sputters out. The last thing the town needs is another catastrophe.

Together, they sit on the slant of a high dune, Grand Ella's long legs extended on a woven yoga blanket spread over the sand, the sheriff's legs, in stiff jeans, poking awkwardly over the edge of the blanket, weighted down by his worn work boots. Embers from the last of the dying bonfires fly skyward, spinning into the wind, melting into the night like snowflakes. Not far away is the shore, covered with a whispering tide. Cissy and Malcolm are standing together at the waterline, holding hands, gazing out to sea. Apart from them, though not far away, is Condi, a solitary figure, hair blowing in the wind, head tipped toward the old north shore of the cove.

"Do you suppose she'll ever stop feeling alone?" Grand Ella wonders.

Gruffly, the sheriff clears his throat. "She's not alone, Ella. She has you—and several good friends in the cove. Like Lorelei Finch."

"Never mind, Clive." Grand Ella gets gracefully to her feet. Brushing sand from her skirt, she lays a restraining hand on his shoulder. "Stay here, please. I'll be back in a moment."

Pulling her shawl more tightly around her shoulders, she moves toward her granddaughter. Though Clive has a constant heart, sometimes his certainty about matters he'll never understand tries her patience. He's a good man, but he lacks imagination.

The night is beautiful, starlit and clear, though a bit chillier than usual. Thankfully, the tide fell to a hush when Triponica was speaking tonight. Now the waves are speaking up, flinging up wings of foam.

Grand Ella comes alongside Condi and pauses, giving her space. Silently, she tracks her granddaughter's gaze, looking up at the top of the tall rock tower of Windy Hollow, drenched in shining spray and mist. Condi turns her head. Grand Ella slips an arm around her waist, wraps her in the shawl and points to shore. A tall shadow, framed in glittering moonlight, wades out of the shallows, squeezing water out of his long hair. Firth, despite the dropping temperatures, is returning from a swim.

"How glad I am to see that precious boy," Grand Ella murmurs. At the bonfires, she looked everywhere for him, but found no trace.

On the shore, Firth takes his place beside the two younger children. A moonbeam falls across his face, sprinkling his hair with starlight. Squaring his small shoulders, Malcolm imitates Firth's strong stance. Trustingly, Cissy looks up, and reaches for his hand.

Chapter Twenty-Three

SOMETHING NEW

At the tide pool, Casey sits atop the high rock, looking out through the rim of seagrass, willing himself to breathe easier. He's got to calm down. More than a little bit nervous, he's arrived at the tide pool early, hoping the beating of the surf will pound sense into him. He needs time to think. Last night at the bonfire, Lorelei was happy to see him, and she let him hold her hand, but they didn't get a chance to really talk.

He can't mess up today. He's got to remember all the things he *isn't* going to do. He *isn't* going to talk too much, he *isn't* going to act like he knows a thing unless she says it's so, he *isn't* going to try to kiss her unless she makes the first move. Wiping his sweaty palms on his jeans, he says a prayer about the last one...impossibly hard.

When at last she pushes her way through the rustling seagrass, he stands up awkwardly, resisting the urge to rush over and scoop her up in a hug.

Pausing, she smiles up at him, searching his face, biting her lower lip.

Embarrassed, he drops his eyes. He must be blowing it already. Abruptly, he sits back down on the rock.

"Casey."

He looks at her.

Hopeful.

Her face breaks into a brilliant smile. Climbing up to the high rock, she sits down beside him, dangling her feet over the edge.

He grins like a fool. Below, the tide pool makes great sucking sounds, filling with whooshes of water as waves crash hard against the Point. The powerful sounds give him courage.

"Lorelei, I'm sorry." He blurts out the words he's been practicing all week. "I should have believed you."

"I'm sorry, too." She scoots a little closer, tucking herself under his shoulder like she used to do when everything was okay between them. "I should have understood why you didn't believe me. It did sound farfetched."

They turn to look at each other. He reaches for her hand, then draws it back. She laughs and grabs it again. Relieved, he leans forward. Closing her eyes, she tilts up her face. He bends his head. She makes the kiss happen, like he hoped and prayed she would.

What each of them said is true. They both need to be sorry. Not for what they did or didn't do—but for the long spell of suffering they caused one another. Not forgiving is what they should be sorry for—

He takes her hand. "I'm trying to not be so sure about things, Lorelei."

Snuggling up, she rests her head on his shoulder. "The one thing you can be sure of is me, Casey Arondale."

#

On the long walk home from the tide pool, Lorelei marvels at the change in Casey. He asked her lots of questions about the octopus at the marine sanctuary and listened to every word she said. While he's disappointed that he didn't get to see the rare creature with golden blood, he really is happy for her.

At the top of the hill, she pauses to look out over Craggy Point. Today the sea is a soothing blanket of aquamarine and amethyst. At the end of the long dock of the marine sanctuary sits Isaac Huddleston in his odd black jacket, playing his guitar.

Lorelei is not sure what to think about the strange new boy in town. Somehow, he and Tad have gotten close. Tad claims Isaac is his second friend. When Lorelei tries to explain that Isaac is way too old to be his friend, Tad gets indignant. He says Isaac does not care about stupid things like how old a person is; all Isaac cares about is feeling colors and making beautiful music.

Turning away from the Point, she makes her way home. While she's happy that she and Casey are together again, she hates that she's keeping a big secret from him. Mama has asked her not to discuss the discovery of the melanin pools until the mystery surrounding Dr. Heath is solved.

Maybe it's just as well. The truth is, she is struggling with how to make sense of it all. The video Mama and Mr. Hardy took on their expedition documents that a new kind of octopus exists, one with colored brain lights. Bioluminescence explains the lights, but what about the creature's melanin? Is it possible that there's something healing in the ink? She can't shake the hunch that the octopus helped her breathe. A memory drifts into her mind.

The day Marissa Davis gave her Amethyst, she pointed to the shaper's mark of the octopus on the nose of the board. "I hope you find a sea creature as miraculous as this some day, Lorelei Finch."

Smiling, Lorelei murmurs, "Maybe I did."

A high-pitched giggle trills out of the grove of olive trees at the base of the hill.

Stopping in the beach road, she stares in disbelief at the fence sporting two beach towels, one striped pink and white, one black and gold. Beyond the fence is the olive grove.

Not again.

For a second, Lorelei contemplates grabbing the pink and white towel, charging into the grove, and dragging Cara away from Dom Jacobs.

Or–

She can walk on by.

Averting her eyes, Lorelei ignores the beach towels and continues up the hill. The only reason she knows about the make-out spot in the olive grove is because she used to go there with Casey when she was about Cara's age–before they discovered the hidden tide pool.

Maybe, just maybe, Dom really likes her sister.

If he doesn't–Cara needs to find out for herself.

"Grommets," Vinnie Maretti moans, rolling his eyes at Kait. On the beach below the Billabong, a pack of little kids are roughhousing, waiting for Andy Marshall to blow his whistle and signal the start of the beginner's surfing class.

Kait laughs. "Stop grousing about the wee ones. We're

grommets, too." Playfully, she swipes a dash of sunscreen across his nose. "Cheer up. Condi says she'll pull us aside after the safety lesson. She's promised to work with us separately."

"Best news of the day." Longingly, he looks up at the high beach parking lot where *Cones and Cream* is idling. "I was ready to tell Dad I'll work the Saturday morning shift after all."

"One class and you'll be hooked," she promises. Pushing her sunglasses on top of her head, she admires a line of high rollers. "Surfing gets in your blood. Why, Paddy used to say—" Her voice wavers.

"Kait—"

Yanking the glasses down over her eyes, she says. "Never mind."

Glumly, Vinnie sticks his hands in his pockets.

Kait sighs, afraid she's misleading him again. "Hey," she says quietly. "You're my best friend. You know that, right?"

"Sure thing," he answers.

She hates the way he sounds, serious and resigned. Placing her finger on the shaper's mark of the sky-blue board, she traces the ring of faerie lights in the oak grove. *Light to dark, dark to light, the magic of the faeries binds us.*

"I know you miss Paddy," Vinnie says, forcing a smile. "He'd be proud you're learning to surf."

"It's where he'd want me to be," she agrees, shouldering the sky-blue board. "I promised him. C'mon. Let's grab a spot on the sand."

Together they trudge through the throng of kids and choose a place in the back of the class. She hopes she didn't make a mistake asking Vinnie to take surfing lessons with her. The last thing she wants is to hurt him again. It will be a long time before Vinnie, or anyone, can win her heart. In time, she hopes her feelings may change. Right now, they're growing their friendship and learning something new together—and that's a start.

"Gather 'round, kids." Andy Marshall toots the whistle hanging around his neck. "Listen up and get serious."

The kids ignore him. Rolling his eyes at Kait and Vinnie, he lets out one loud whistle blast until his face turns red.

Shocked, the kids look scared and stop talking.

He chuckles. "Not quite that serious."

The kids laugh nervously.

"Well, kids," the surf master says, dropping the whistle. "Welcome to Gregarious Grommets Surf School. We'll have a lot of fun here if you pay attention." Checking names off a clipboard, he calls the class to order, and introduces Condi as his junior teaching assistant. Pointing to a wide assortment of surfboards on the sand, he tells the kids, "If you didn't bring your own board, you can borrow one of mine. Find the right size, around your height."

The kids without boards rush forward, jostling each other.

Vinnie hangs back, looking pained.

"Hold up, Vinnie," Andy calls. "I've got a board for you. Wait here."

Twirling his lanyard, the old surf master nimbly jogs up to the porch of the Billabong and retrieves a jade-green surfboard leaning against the doorjamb. Tucking the board under his arm, he jogs back to Kait and Vinnie.

"This was Frank Hardy's when he was your age," he says, handing the board to Vinnie. "Frank was a great surfer and the best man I've ever known. I want his board to be yours."

"What?" Vinnie says, sucking in his breath. "Andy, I can't accept this. It's vintage."

"You've earned it," Andy answers. "Making all those grocery deliveries during the Sickness." The old surf master punches him playfully on the arm. "Vintage boards are meant to surf." He points a craggy finger at the shaper's mark, a double wave in cerulean blue. "You can do anything on this board. Soon you'll be riding the big ones."

"Thank you, Andy." Vinnie chokes up. "I won't let you down."

Condi's more than a little nervous. Giving Kait and Vinnie a surfing lesson on her own today is a big ask.

"While I play a few games with these rug rats to settle them down, run up to the storage room, Condi." Andy Marshall jerks his head toward the Billabong. "Grab my whiteboard and markers for the safety lesson."

Relieved to be busy, Condi jogs up to the surf shop and hurries into the storage room. Lost in thought, she goes straight to the whiteboard and storage cabinet in the corner, practicing in her mind all the points she needs to cover with Kait and Vinnie on their first day of surf school. After collapsing the easel of the whiteboard, she frantically searches through a drawer for a marker that works. The one stored with the board is dried up, another casualty of the long months of the Sickness.

"Is this Trustin's?"

Startled, she wheels around.

In the shadows beside the garage-style window, stands Isaac, slouched in his black leather jacket, staring at Trustin's molten black board.

"What are you doing here?" Concerned, she hurries to the window. "Please tell me you're not learning to surf."

"Nope, sticking to music, thanks." Crossing his arms, he leans against the window frame. "Yesterday my dad introduced me to Andy Marshall. He said a kid named Trustin Davis was a surfing champion—and a dead ringer for me." Isaac jerks his head toward a row of posters on the wall. "He invited me to come over and see for myself." Pointing to a poster from the Junior Surfing Championships, he jabs his finger at a photo. "That's him, isn't it? Your boyfriend. The dude I met under the sea."

Condi nods. It hurts her heart to look at the poster. In the photo, Trustin is looking straight into the camera, capturing the sparkles in his turquoise eyes. Slowly, she rubs her finger over the shaper's mark on Trustin's black surfboard. "Yes," she says. "That's him."

Isaac shakes his head. Taking a deep long breath, he lets it out in a long whistle. Before she can respond, he taps the poster again, pointing to the girl standing next to Trustin, a tall girl with sculpted shoulders and amber hair, holding an indigo surfboard. "That's her. Auramar. The girl who took me on a sea turtle ride to meet Koan in the cavern."

"Auramar?" Condi bursts out laughing.

Isaac's brow wrinkles. "What's so funny?"

Condi meets his eyes. "When I knew her, Auramar was Trustin's twin, Marissa Davis."

THE TOP OF THE HOLLOW

TWO WEEKS LATER

Drinking in the beauty of the teal waters of the cove, Condi dangles her legs over the high ledge of the top of Windy Hollow. Above her the sky is bright autumn blue. Beneath her, the tide drifts in calm, slow circles around the jagged stand of rocks. The sun warms her face, and the breeze plays with her hair. Beside her is the comforting shell of the orange-red kayak that was split apart by lightening—the two halves oddly resembling a broken heart.

A lot has happened in the past few weeks. Kids are back in school. People are moving around town almost as freely as they did before the Sickness. Lorelei and Casey are back together. Kait Dooley has moved in with the Finch family. The older girl is sharing a room with Cara, who isn't happy, since it prevents her from sneaking out to meet boys. Kait has a new job. She is working for Andy, cataloging and cleaning the books in Mr. Hardy's extensive library.

The biggest change is that Firth, Cissy, and Malcolm are living at the yellow cottage. Grand Ella's years of faithful volunteering at the Overlook Home made her eligible to be a foster parent. Since Firth is nearly seventeen, the storage shed is now a small, detached bedroom overlooking the herb garden and Grand Ella's study is a bedroom for Cissy and Malcolm. To Condi's relief, her loft bedroom is her own private space. All in all, things are working out.

The wind swirls, playfully tossing up a wing of spray.

Eagerly, she turns to face the north side of the shore, where the biggest waves are crashing.

If only...

In her mind's eye, she remembers him, skimming across shining water on the molten black board, laughter in his turquoise eyes, sun sparkles in his onyx hair.

Will she ever get over missing him?

Not a chance.

On the ragged shoreline under the steep wall of cliffs, a lone figure is picking through the scree on the loneliest tip of the cove. Accompanied by the old black dog that lives with the Beachlings on Craggy Point, Firth goes out free diving almost every day. Grand Ella tries not to worry. His dives are long—and it seems like forever before he surfaces.

On the south side of the cove, Condi spies two tiny specks in the distance. Isaac Huddleston and Tad Finch are walking the shoreline, coming toward the yellow cottage. Those two are a funny pair of friends. Today Isaac is bringing Tad to the Hollow to play with Cissy and Malcolm on the beach. Later, Condi will join them, sitting beside Isaac on the rocks, listening to him play guitar.

They won't talk much because there's no need.

They both know what they know.

And they can't ever tell.

Where did you go?

Who are you now?

Where did you go?

REFERENCES AND CREDITS

1 “Comfortably Numb,” Pink Floyd, 1979

2 *The Owl and the Pussycat*, Edward Lear, 1871

3 *The Velveteen Rabbit*, Margery Williams, 1922

4 *Winnie the Pooh*, A. A. Milne, 1926

5 “The Jabberwocky,” Lewis Carroll, 1871

6 *Winnie the Pooh*, A. A. Milne, 1926

ACKNOWLEDGMENTS

Amethyst, The Shallows is Book Two of the Yellow Cottage Stories, a companion novel to Book One, *The Aquamarine Surfboard*. In this series, I hope to create a world that celebrates the extraordinary power of the senses and the transformative magic of the sea.

Thank you to my amazing Mom and Dad, for encouraging a shy and imaginative little girl to be brave enough to follow her dreams.

To my inspiring writing critique group partners, Amy Kelly and Emily Roberson, who improved this book in countless ways. Insightful feedback, creative guidance, and unwavering support keeps the writing life fun and rewarding.

To all the friends and family who have inspired and encouraged me on my writing journey. I can't thank you enough. Please know that your love and support make all the difference.

I can't say enough good things about the incredible team at Atmosphere Press. Your commitment to excellence makes bringing books into the world an exciting adventure.

A huge thank you to "my people", the artists and creatives at Art House of Dallas, the DFW writing community, librarians, booksellers, book club members and fellow readers everywhere.

Where would we be without our stories?

ABOUT THE AUTHOR

KELLYE ABERNATHY is a former business executive, happily transformed into a yoga teacher and practical life skills advocate for trauma survivors. She believes in creatively building unique and supportive communities, one relationship at a time. A graduate of the University of Kansas, she holds a Bachelor of Science degree in Secondary English Education. Currently, she lives in land-locked Plano, Texas, dreaming of her next trip to the sea.

Find her at **kellyeabernathy.com**

Printed in the USA
CPSIA information can be obtained
at www.ICGtesting.com
LVHW091026180224
772146LV00032B/573